DIAMOND DON

DIAMOND DUET
BOOK 1

ANNA COLE

Copyright © 2024 by Anna Cole

All rights reserved.

No part of this publication may be reproduced, stored in, or introduced into a retrieval system, distributed, or transmitted in any form or by any means, including photocopying, recording, or other electronic or mechanical methods, without written permission from the author, except for the use of brief quotations in a book review and as permitted by U.S. copyright law.

This book is a work of fiction. The story, all names, characters, and incidents portrayed in this publication are fictitious. No identification with actual persons (living or deceased), places, buildings, and products is intended or should be inferred.

Cover: Maria @ Steamy Designs

CONTENT WARNING

Dear Reader,

Please be aware that this book contains graphic scenes meant for a mature audience.

Trigger Warnings: dubious consent, kidnapping, explicit scenes, and descriptions of violence.

MAILING LIST

Sign up to my newsletter for exclusive bonus content and updates on upcoming releases! **New subscribers get an exclusive epilogue.**

Scan the QR code to subscribe:

1

KAT

THE MAN in the corner won't stop looking at me.

Five minutes.

I take a long sip of *Dom Pérignon*. Five more minutes and I'm home free.

I admit this dress was a mistake. The form-fitting gown is too eye-catching for my purposes this evening. After all, above all else, I must blend in tonight, and the dark velvet piece makes it a little too hard not to attract the male gaze.

But I had to improvise when the *stronzo* surprised me with his latest demand only two days ago. At such short notice, this dress was my closet's only appropriate outfit. Its luxurious fabric is too thick and warm for a hot, humid night in June, but the concealed pocket below the cleavage line makes it my best choice for tonight. It will come in handy in the next five minutes.

The things I do for love...

I take a calming breath, glancing around the exquisitely decorated grand hall.

The Metropolitan Museum pulled all the stops for tonight's gala.

Fragrant floral arrangements in rich crimson and gold hues adorn the spacious room, while elaborate crystal chandeliers illuminate the space. The ornate fixtures, casting a soft, warm glow, set an intimate atmosphere for the party's illustrious guests.

Nothing is too opulent or lavish for the Flame of Mir—the museum's newest exhibition's *pièce de résistance*.

It's almost hard to believe that the entrancingly beautiful red diamond sits just a few feet away from me, carefully enshrined in its high-security glass display case.

My prize.

I mean, the *stronzo*'s prize.

I mentally run through my plan one last time as the museum director delivers the opening speech for the *Sparkling Splendor* exhibition, rambling on about the infamous gem's significance and rarity.

If everything goes as expected, soon, the man will finish addressing the crowd and invite the gala's esteemed guests to step outside and join him at the museum's gardens, where live entertainment and hors d'oeuvres await them.

Unfortunately, I have a prior commitment with a particular priceless bauble.

All work and no play makes me a dull, dull girl.

At last, the director seems to approach the end of his spiel, expressing his gratitude to the gem's mysterious owner —who wishes to remain anonymous—for lending it to the museum and sponsoring tonight's festivities.

I discreetly move towards the ladies' room, hidden in the darkest corner of the large hall.

After stepping inside, I check every stall, ensuring I am all alone. There is no attendant. No rich girls doing coke off the marble countertops, either. Maybe it's a sign that my recent bad luck is about to change.

I wait behind the door until the noise outside dies down as the illustrious guests empty the museum's exhibition room.

After a while, I can faintly but distinctively hear the orchestra playing tonight's first live song as the musicians perform for the guests filling the gardens.

A guard whistles a cheerful tune while locking the exhibit area a few yards away from my hiding spot.

This is it.

After steeling myself, I inch the door open, peeking through the small opening to verify no one else is lingering around the immense hall. I waste no time before exiting the restroom.

A common thief would have positively quaked upon learning they had no choice but to steal the world's most famous and valuable diamond with only two days' notice.

But then again, I am no common thief.

As a matter of principle, I generally do not tolerate blackmail or extortion. I value my freedom and independence above all things. Well, almost all things, I suppose.

I would certainly have appreciated having more time to prepare before tonight. A job as big and ambitious as this one should not be taken lightly.

Unfortunately, I had to rush beyond belief to prepare for this evening's gala.

The *stronzo* insisted this heist had to be executed at the opening night for the Flame of Mir's first public exhibition since its discovery a decade ago.

I'm not ashamed to say I pride myself on being the best in my field. I didn't attain my reputation in the criminal underworld's most prestigious circles by foolishly rushing into heists—especially not high-profile ones like tonight's event. But a girl's gotta do what a girl's gotta do.

So, I strived to do the best job I could under the circumstances and prepared to sneak into the gala as one of the guests. With such high stakes and A.J.'s life hanging in the balance, I could hardly afford to be picky about my labor conditions.

Luckily, tonight's party led to the prestigious downtown museum temporarily deactivating many of its state-of-the-art security devices. God forbid some self-important socialite drunkenly trips one of the alarms while looking for the powder room.

I'm thrilled that the museum's powers-that-be decided to turn off their very effective and hard-to-evade laser detection system around the Flame of Mir. It is a highly appreciated gesture, considering that, as a rule of thumb, I always try to avoid doing acrobatics in a long gown and four-inch heels.

I wish I could be a fly on the wall when the arrogant fools realize what their careless hubris cost them. By all accounts, the Flame of Mir is priceless.

As subtly as I can, I reach inside my bejeweled evening bag to flick on the switch of my Security Bypass Unit—or SBU, as A.J. and I fondly call it—wirelessly interfacing it with the museum's security systems control hub.

Courtesy of A.J.'s unrivaled genius, I have the most ingenious little device at my disposal. It is no giant red diamond, but it is priceless as well.

The SBU should take control of the pesky little cameras around the gemstone, shifting them into a looped playback while disrupting the motion sensors' signal.

Impatiently, I fight the urge to fidget or pace until the device vibrates twice, indicating that the little gadget has successfully connected to the museum's security network. The wonders of the modern age never cease to amaze me.

I'll be long gone by the time they even realize what happened.

Free to work my magic unnoticed, I waste no time picking the exhibition area's entrance lock. Child's play.

I hasten to slip through the doorway, barely contained anticipation coursing through my veins to the beat of my restless heart. A fluttery, empty feeling in the pit of my stomach distracts me for a moment, and I don't think I can blame it on the champagne.

Almost reverently, I dare to approach the secured pedestal that houses the Flame of Mir, quietly navigating the dimly lit room.

Up close, the precious stone is even more exquisite than I expected. And to think that all its fiery beauty will soon belong to the *stronzo*...He isn't worthy of such splendor. The blood-red jewel glows under the faint overhead light. The diamond's brilliance is almost irresistibly mesmerizing.

I like to think I have very few weaknesses. As it happens, incomprehensibly expensive glittering jewels are one of them. But I can't let myself lose focus. I have a job to do.

My heart races even faster while I meticulously pick the lock mechanism separating me from the diamond, each calculated movement bringing me closer to freeing the priceless piece from its confinement.

With a barely audible click, it yields.

While holding my breath, I lift the glass enclosure, my hands somehow steady.

I allow myself a moment to admire the Flame of Mir's unparalleled beauty, pausing to take in its incandescent carmine glow fully. If only we could be together forever, my love...

Unfortunately, time is one of the many luxuries I currently lack, so I carefully grab the stone.

The diamond's cool and hard feel in my hands is almost surreal. So many have gone to incredible lengths to possess it, but at this moment, the jewel is as good as mine.

The realization is exhilarating, reminding me of why I chose this line of work many years ago. There is nothing like this feeling—knowing the world is mine for the taking. It is almost intoxicating.

It is a very welcome sentiment in my current circumstances. I didn't embark on this unwise adventure of my own accord, but I am still not helpless or powerless. And I never will be again.

I secure my prize in the concealed pocket of my dress, and its weight against my chest reassures me. A wonderful surge of triumph courses through my body as I get closer and closer to succeeding in tonight's bold endeavor.

I make my way to the exit before quietly stepping out. Gently, I close the door behind me before inspecting the large room.

No one saw my daring escape.

Somewhat relieved, I relax a little. After taking another deep, calming breath, I move towards the garden doors and stroll outside, where the expensively clad men and women attending tonight's gala enjoy the party. I school my expression into a relaxed smile before forcing myself to stroll among them.

It is the home stretch now—I got this.

I pretend to mingle with the distinguished guests as I glance around the assembly, accepting a fresh glass of champagne from a passing server. I could never refuse some liquid courage, and the sparkling drink does wonders for my dry mouth.

In a perfect world, I would have loved to linger and

enjoy the luxurious soirée, people-watching while sipping cocktails. But tonight is about work, not play.

My smile deepens as I visually confirm my planned exit's location. The museum's gardens extend to a service alley at the back, just a hundred yards away from the main building, as A.J. and I discovered during our surveillance work yesterday.

While caterers and servers efficiently walk among the guests, I will sneak past all of them to the street right outside, where my getaway car awaits me. As far as planned escapes go, mine is simple and straightforward. Yet, in my professional experience, that's never a bad thing. All I have to do is get to the car without drawing unnecessary attention.

This is always my least favorite part of any job. It's always a thrill to snag a beautiful bauble from under an unsuspecting owner's nose, but it is pure torture to force myself to stroll out of a job site when all I want to do is get the hell out of Dodge.

I glance down at my chest and spot the slight bulge of the Flame of Mir enclosed by my gown's cloth. The stone's solid pressure between my breasts is hard to forget, but it's still comforting to have visual assurance of its whereabouts.

Now, I must get out of here and place this beauty in that horrible man's filthy hands. I hate the mere thought of parting from it, but I can't wait to regain my independence, even if it is a temporary respite. Not to mention, it means A.J. will live to see another day. At least until the *stronzo* can concoct another one of his schemes.

Unless we strike first.

The diamond should buy us enough time to uncover his rumored secret and plot out the best way to give him a taste of his own medicine. I have no qualms about blackmailing the bastard who is making my life a living hell.

With small steps, I discreetly shorten the distance to the alleyway, avoiding making eye contact with the women and men taking part in the festivities.

I do my best to look casually bored while I make my way around the dance floor, the last obstacle in my path. As I unhurriedly stroll past an empty table, I set down my champagne flute. The drink has served its use as a prop and a source of much-needed courage.

As inconspicuously as I can manage, I touch the diamond through my outfit's fabric. It's a bad idea to keep drawing attention to it, but I can't help reassuring myself one final time that it's still right where I placed it.

After taking a deep breath, I allow myself a sigh of relief as all the pent-up tension accumulated during the past few days finally begins to leave my shoulders. I feel slightly lightheaded as I head to the alley.

Paranoia compels me to scan the celebration one last time, but nobody is watching me too closely as I take the last steps toward the exit.

And that's when I walk right into the arms of Mr. Tall, Dark, and Handsome.

2

NIK

I can't stop staring at the woman in the dangerously distracting black velvet dress.

As I sip my whiskey, I do my best to refocus my attention on the museum director's speech, but it's pointless. My gaze drifts to her again and again, almost as if irresistibly drawn by gravity's pull.

That dress ought to be illegal.

And I know a thing or two about illegal things.

As she glances around the museum's grand hall admiring the decorations, I admire her.

Her dark hair, artfully piled atop her head, temptingly exposes her neck. I wonder what she smells like.

She turns around, looking around the room, and I almost choke on my drink.

Mercy. I struggle to suppress my cough—her dress is backless.

The overhead light fixtures bathe her in their soft glow, and I can't help but imagine what it would feel like to run my fingers over that beautiful, mesmerizing stretch of skin.

I try to catch her eye, but she is lost in thought. She doesn't notice me at all, which makes me smile.

Many of the country's most powerful men and women are present at tonight's gala. There isn't much they wouldn't say or do for a few moments of my time. And yet, this slip of a girl doesn't seem to know who I am. She certainly doesn't realize she has my undivided attention.

Her careless disregard doesn't concern me in the slightest. I know how to get what I want. One does not rise from the direst, most remote parts of Siberia to reach the highest rank of the Russian *bratva* by being timid.

Over the decades, I have been many things. Most of them are, frankly, not any good. I'm not ashamed to admit it. Unsure of myself, however, is not one of them.

I have never been afraid of a challenge, either. In fact, it would be a rather welcome change from the wide-eyed, yes-sir girls I meet too often nowadays.

Truthfully, ever since the Forbes 400 list was published a few months ago, I have grown increasingly bored with the women who approach me. It's been too long since I've come across one so refreshingly uninterested in me.

It doesn't hurt that her eyes seem to glitter more than the Flame of Mir under the dim luminescence of the crystal chandeliers. Are they dark brown or deep blue? I can't tell from this far away.

Before the night ends, this breathtaking woman will be in my arms.

Any other outcome is unthinkable.

I lean against the wall, enjoying my drink and relaxing for a moment. Soon, the director will end his monologue, and I will get to make my move.

I only half-listen as the man almost reverently describes

everything he believes makes my most prized possession, the Flame of Mir, so unique and precious.

The director has his facts right, at least. The Flame of Mir is indeed the largest red diamond ever found, and those are the rarest of all diamonds. But he doesn't know any of the things that make it truly special.

He doesn't know, for example, that I extricated it from the ground myself a long time ago.

The man also could never comprehend what the discovery meant for me back then or how it altered the course of my life.

He doesn't understand that I almost certainly wouldn't be a multibillionaire or the *pakhan* of the Russian *bratva* if I hadn't found the massive blood-red gem in the Siberian Mir mine.

Just like my identity as the owner of the Flame of Mir, these are secrets I only share with a selected few. It's how I like to handle my affairs. Many years ago, I learned that all information is worth its weight in gold and that very few people deserve my trust. I am as careful with it as I am with the safety of my diamond.

It occurs to me that I know nothing about this beautiful stranger who has thoroughly captivated me tonight. This is an unsettling realization, to say the least, since I personally vetted everyone in attendance this evening.

Well, not exactly personally. I have people for that, of course.

However, I inspected the guest list, reviewing dossiers on all guests of interest and on anyone whose name was unfamiliar. If it had included her name or face, I would remember.

I can't say I'm surprised to find party-crashers among us tonight. It is, after all, par for the course with such a highly anticipated, star-studded event. The Flame of Mir has always been the subject of great curiosity.

Of course, with a face befitting an angel—and a body made for sin—this woman had no trouble sweet-talking the security guards posted outside into letting her sneak in to enjoy the festivities.

I force myself to stop gazing at the object of my sudden fascination for a second to search the room for a specific someone.

A moment later, I spot Dmitri Ivashkov, my favorite *shestyorka*, leaning against an adorned Corinthian column in a darkened corner.

I tasked him with investigating tonight's guest list and bringing anything or anyone even remotely worthy of a second look to my attention.

As the leader of the Russian *bratva* and the somewhat anonymous owner of the world's most valuable diamond, I had to ensure that none of the guests were a threat to the gemstone or my organization.

Dmitri finally realizes I'm glancing his way. Aware of my silent command, he walks over to me.

With amusement, I watch as women, young and old, discreetly—or not so discreetly—notice the young man. As usual, Dmitri is unaware of the attention he effortlessly attracts from the fairer sex. Tall and athletic, he cuts a striking figure in his tuxedo, even when he won't stop fidgeting with his longish hair.

As misplaced as it might be, I'm often struck by how proud I am of the remarkable man he has become. For many unfortunate reasons, I am one of the few who have been around enough to see him grow up. His mother—God rest her soul—would be proud of him, too.

Once Dmitri reaches my side, he smirks at me, cockily raising an eyebrow as if asking, *you called?*

Such petulance would land anyone else in my *bratva* into considerable trouble, but I let him get away with a lot—perhaps too much.

Still, even within the *bratva*, a lot can be forgiven when it comes to someone with so much promise. As I learned once he became my employee, Dmitri has an almost unparalleled ability to get shit done. I have never met anyone so obsessively single-minded. You can't lose people like that. No matter the cost, you retain that kind of talent.

"Do you see the brunette in the black dress next to my diamond?" I ask.

"You bet I do. How could anyone miss her? And before you ask, Nik—I don't know who she is. She isn't on the guest list. I checked. One of the museum's security guards must've let her in here."

"I figured as much."

With a sigh, Dmitri runs his fingers through his dark blond hair. "Well, I wouldn't worry about her, Nik. We knew we were bound to attract party-crashers tonight. At least it isn't Erin McGuire, anyway. Now, that would be a problem."

I shoot him a warning glance. "The last thing I need in my life right now is another one of my associates stirring up trouble with the Irish. Don't bring up Erin McGuire. If I never hear that name again, it will still be too soon."

"Interesting words from the man who invited her father to tonight's event."

"Vladmir's right," I say with a sigh. "One of these days, I'll have to teach you what respect for authority means."

"I think I'll take a rain check on that, Nik. Indefinitely." He has the nerve to wink at me.

The museum's factotum ends his interminable speech, inviting the party's attendees to step outside for refreshments and music, and Dmitri walks away, chuckling to himself.

I search for the woman I have spent most of the night studying from afar, but I have no luck locating her. She must be out in the gardens. I can't blame her. With the sizable crowd gathered inside the exhibition hall, it's too warm in here.

Thankful for the chance to leave the stuffy room, I step outside, still searching for her. Instead, I find Maxim.

"Nikki," he says, offering me a fresh whiskey. "There you are. I was looking for you."

With a smile, I take the offered drink.

It's good to have Maxim back home. Strange, but good. Even weeks after his return from Russia, I'm still somewhat startled whenever I walk into a room and find him standing there. I do my best to hide it and not let him notice it, but having him back on this side of the Atlantic still feels surreal.

Maxim has been my best—and sometimes only—friend for most of my life. Even before the *bratva* and the Flame of Mir, there was Maxim. And not much else, truth be told.

Long ago, I learned trust is too rare a commodity to be carelessly shared. Yet, once upon a time, I freely shared it with Maxim. Before Erin McGuire. Before he made me regret it.

But none of that matters now—not anymore. The past is in the past—at last. It's time we put it behind us. I must make amends with Maxim if I can. Somehow. Ultimately, that's what tonight is all about for me. No matter what it may cost me or the *bratva*, I'll make it up to him for all he had to sacrifice in the last year.

"Are you enjoying yourself?" I ask.

"Sure. I can't complain, Nik. Beautiful night, beautiful women. What more could a man want? Besides not having to look at Patrick McGuire's unsightly face, of course. It's the damnedest thing—even after all this time, I can't shake the feeling it would look so much better if someone were to fire a few dozen shots at it."

The Irish family's boss must sense our gazes on him because he smirks at us, raising his glass in a mock toast. He doesn't break eye contact with Maxim. As a matter of fact, he doesn't even blink.

With his longtime rival a few yards away, it's easy to see Maxim as the rest of the world sees him instead of as my oldest friend. In this instant, he's every inch the *avtoritet*— the authority, the cold-blooded enforcer of the *bratva*. Even within our circles, Maxim's name is feared. No one is better than my friend at his gruesome line of work.

"Maxim," I say in warning. I barely manage to suppress a sigh.

"I know, Nik. Trust me. I'll play nice with the man. Don't even worry about it. I'll do it for you."

I study him with concern for a moment. A welcome, cool breeze blows his thick brown hair over his eyes, but he doesn't flinch as McGuire stares him down.

A particularly ominous feeling grows inside me, and I struggle to hide my frustration. "Listen, Maxim. It's not like I love him any more than you do. But going to war with the Irish family won't make my life or yours any easier."

"I know. You're right, Nik, as usual. That's why you are the *pakhan* while I'm...well, I guess I'm the man who got sent to fucking Siberia of all places for thinking with the wrong head."

He laughs humorlessly before taking a healthy swig of his drink.

"Maxim—"

"I don't mean to sound ungrateful. You did the best you could. I owe my life to you. And believe me, after my long exile, I can't wait to get back to living the rest of it. There's so much left to do. I sure have a lot to make up for, and I've already wasted so much time. So I'm glad to be back. Really, I am. And I missed you, Nikki."

"It's good to have you back, Maxim. It wasn't the same without you here."

"Well, I don't know about that, Nik. You seem to have managed pretty well in my absence. When I left, you were still making a name for yourself within the Seven Families. Now, none of them can touch you. You sure seem to have more money now. I'm sure there are more women, too."

Maxims's striking blue eyes shine with humor, and, for a brief moment, things between us are just as they have always been.

Before I can remind him he's in no position to give anyone a hard time about women, I spot *her* from the corner of my eye. Instantly, I lose my train of thought.

She is strolling about the garden, holding a glass of champagne. Her full lips are stretched into a pleasant, casual smile.

Maxim disrupts my reverie. "Who is that?" he asks.

I reluctantly tear my eyes from her to glance at him. To my utter dismay, Maxim is unabashedly studying her from head to toe. Like me, he seems to like what he sees—a lot.

"As far as you and any other men at this party are concerned, she is out of bounds."

Still shamelessly eyeing my attractive brunette, Maxim shoots me a look, not bothering to hide his shock.

I tried to sound as calm and unaffected as possible, but

maybe I came off as a little too possessive about someone who is, after all, a stranger.

I can understand why my childhood friend is surprised to see me act so territorial about a woman when I have never done so before tonight. Not in all our many years of friendship.

I can't pretend to fully understand this perplexing behavior of mine any better than he does. But somehow, I know without a shadow of a doubt that I couldn't handle seeing her in another man's arms.

Mine. For all intents and purposes, she's mine.

Luckily, few men on this earth would dare stand between me and what I want. Even fewer would have the audacity to try to take what is rightfully mine.

And she is mine. At least for the night. I won't tolerate anything else.

"Okay," Maxim says in a peculiar tone. He stares at me as if I have grown a second head. "If you want her so bad, what are you still doing here with me? Why don't you go get her?"

"That's the plan. I'm leaving with her tonight. It's as good as done."

Soon, I will inform her of the same.

"Is that right? Well, I guess we're drinking to your good health then, my friend. Godspeed and God bless you, Nik. *Vashe zdorov'ye!*" Winking at me, he cheerfully drains his glass at once.

I finish my drink, too, before setting the empty crystal tumbler down on a nearby table.

She walks among the guests, skirting around the edge of the dance floor. To everyone else, she most likely seems to be merely strolling around the party, but it's obvious to me she's gradually making her way to the back of the gardens.

Perhaps for an illicit encounter with a lucky bastard who

managed to get to her first? If so, I feel sorry for the man. He stands no chance. I will happily destroy him if that's what it will take to get this beauty all to myself.

A moment later, it becomes clear that she's moving towards the service alleyway.

Leaving so soon? I don't think so.

So I quickly shorten the distance between us, dodging politicians and movie stars who try to get my attention in vain. I almost have to jog to catch up to her.

She suddenly stops by an empty table a few feet away from me. I can't see her face as she turns her back to me.

Up close, I notice things that had escaped me earlier tonight. Her glossy dark hair, for example, has a distinct warm chocolate hue, and her long nails are blood-red.

Distracted by these details, I take too long to realize we are on a collision course. Before I can move out of her way, she runs into my chest. As a reflex, my arms shoot out to hold on to her, ensuring she won't fall.

Her skin is so incredibly soft. She glances up at me, looking right into my eyes.

Fuck me.

Finally, I have an answer to my question from earlier.

Blue. Deep, dark blue.

Fuck. Me.

I'm a goner.

3

KAT

I STRUGGLE to stifle a sigh as I attempt to untangle myself from the gorgeous hunk of a man holding me in his arms.

The universe has a perverse sense of humor. There is no other plausible explanation for why it would drop this tall drink of water in my lap right now at the worst possible time.

It's unfair, especially considering how often I find myself parched nowadays. To no one's surprise, being at the *stronzo*'s beck and call doesn't leave me much time for dating.

On any other day and at any other time, nothing would delight me more than spending the evening getting to know a man this handsome better. Sadly, the museum's gardens are not the right place to entertain this idea, and tonight most definitely isn't the right time.

Sooner or later, someone is bound to notice that a certain red diamond is missing. I have no intention of sticking around to see that unfold.

Still grasping my upper arms, the man in question looks into my eyes for a moment before allowing his gaze to examine the rest of me. He towers over me even though I'm wearing my favorite four-inch high heels.

As discreetly as possible in my current circumstances, I take in the rest of him. I find no faults—from his luscious dark hair to his prohibitively expensive Italian leather shoes.

Of course, I can't help letting my eyes linger here and there during my thorough examination of him. That's how I notice his eyes are a brown as deep and dark as his gorgeous hair. They sparkle with undisguised intelligence and with a hint of humor. His broad shoulders and powerful hands are truly the stuff of dreams.

Unable to stop myself, I stare at his mouth, mesmerized by the way his lips, framed by his dark facial hair, twitch with barely contained amusement before he smiles at me.

Sexy, sexy mouth.

He seems exceedingly pleased with himself, and I have no problem admitting that it is a good look on him.

All at once, I am aware of the delicious feel of the roughened calluses on his hands as they graze the skin of my arms, where he still touches me.

Life is so unfair.

"Forgive me," he says. His voice makes me want to moan with pleasure. It's deep and yet almost melodic. "I didn't mean to startle you."

"No harm, no foul. Thanks for catching me," I say. As soon as the words leave my lips, I have to resist the urge to groan. *No harm, no foul*? That's my witty comeback?

He smiles again, and heat pools low in my abdomen. It's the best and the worst feeling in the world. What I wouldn't give for the chance to stay and maybe kiss those lips...

Not the Flame of Mir. And definitely not A.J.'s life. Or my freedom, for that matter.

"Anytime," he says, that panty-dropper smirk still front-and-center on his gorgeous face. "I'm Nikolai, by the way."

Still unable to pry my eyes from his mesmerizing mouth, I sigh loudly.

"Well, Nik—you don't mind if I call you Nik, do you? It's truly my pleasure to meet you. No. Really. Trust me."

My reply seems to amuse him. His smirk melts into a full-on grin. Frankly, it's some breathtaking stuff.

Sweet baby Jesus. I'm doomed.

"Won't you tell me your name?" Nikolai asks. He blatantly ignores my attempts to remove myself from his arms.

I detect a slight accent. Slavic? Russian, maybe? Whatever it is, I can't get enough of it. It's as sweet as honey. I could spend the rest of the night listening to him talk about nothing at all. Of course, that's precisely why I have to leave —right now.

"Sorry, Nik. But no, I won't. Meeting you has been lovely, but I must go. I'd love to stay and get to know you better, but I'm afraid that won't be possible. Places to go, people to see, yada yada yada. You know how it is."

I try to extricate myself from him again, intending to show him I mean business. Nikolai lets go of my arms, and I simultaneously feel relief and disappointment. It's a short-lived rush of emotions since he almost immediately grabs my right hand with his left one. He caresses my knuckles with his thumb as the palm of his hand brushes against mine.

"Well, you must stay a little longer. I insist," he says. "The night's still young, after all. I hear there'll be fireworks later. You wouldn't want to miss the show."

Nikolai brings my hand to his lips, staring into my eyes.

I can hardly breathe as he, boldly maintaining eye

contact, brushes his lips against my fingers. The moment is almost hypnotic. Even with a slight shake of my head, I struggle to clear the sudden haze overtaking my brain, unable to suppress another sigh.

"I wish I could stay. But I happen to know my carriage will turn into a pumpkin at midnight. So, you see, I really have to get going. You understand, I'm sure."

"A pumpkin carriage, huh? Should I call you Cinderella, then? I'm a little rusty on my fairytales, but I'm pretty sure even she stayed long enough for a dance."

"Oh! Are you saying you are my Prince Charming, and we are to live happily ever after?" I breathlessly ask him, pressing my free hand to my chest. Maybe my mock eagerness will scare him off so I can finally depart.

"Stay with me tonight, *milaya*, and I'll be anything you want me to be."

His intensity and self-assuredness take me by surprise, giving me pause. "You're dangerous," I say. I don't even bother hiding how deeply affected I feel by our encounter.

Strangely enough, Nikolai seems to consider my words earnestly. "Not to you. Not tonight," he says a few heartbeats later. His tone is more serious than I expected. His statement once again catches me off guard.

I really look at him. The man is obviously blessed with devastating good looks. He's also too charming for his own good—or mine, I suppose. Clearly, he's very aware of his talents and won't hesitate to use them.

To make matters worse, his dogged determination not to let me leave shows me he feels as drawn to me as I do to him. Even now, his gaze scorchingly caresses my lips, neck, and body as he looks his fill.

Once again, I stifle a sigh. The only thing more irresistible than a distractingly attractive man is a distractingly attractive man who wants me badly.

Something outside of his compelling magnetic field makes me uneasy. After glancing around, I groan in frustration when I notice a few people nearby peeking at us and whispering. The last thing I want or need is to attract undue attention.

Nikolai must be someone important or famous to have earned an invitation to this glitzy event. His bespoke tuxedo alone must have cost him a small fortune. He also looks like he belongs in this star-studded gala, surrounded by people I often spot on magazine covers or television. Besides, I can't fathom why else these men and women now staring at us would feel moved to gossip in such an indiscreet fashion.

Nikolai realizes that our back-and-forth is making many of the guests quite curious. He raises an eyebrow and makes eye contact with a few of them. To my immense amusement and surprise, they quickly glance away.

Fascinating.

I look into Nikolai's eyes once again. He tightens his hold on my hand and an extraordinary amount of excitement bubbles up inside me.

"Very well," I say. "One dance, Charming. No more."

Or so I fervently hope for my sake.

Nikolai smiles at me, pulling me closer, and my legs threaten to turn into jelly.

No man should look this hot. It simply isn't fair to womenfolk everywhere.

Without another word, he wraps his arm around my waist, guiding me towards where the orchestra just finished a lively song I don't recognize.

I take a deep breath, steeling myself. If the mere weight of his arm on my back feels this intoxicating, I dread to imagine how it will feel if he holds me closer to his body during our dance. Or underneath it, in a different type of dance altogether.

Nikolai glances at me as he leads me to a darkened corner of the dance floor, secluded from the other couples enjoying the music.

The band shifts gears into the first notes of a slow melody I'm too preoccupied to identify, and he leans in closer to whisper in my ear. "What will it take to get you to tell me your name?"

As his sensual lips graze my ear lobe, I catch a whiff of his scent, and I'm in heaven. Like the man it belongs to, it's intensely masculine, sophisticated, and impossibly sexy. He smells of man, whiskey, and sin.

I rise on my toes, unable to resist the urge to allow my lips to flutter against his ear as I say, "Nothing you have."

Nikolai glances at me appreciatively. Too late, I realize he's not the kind of man to walk away from a challenge like the one I just brazenly offered to him.

"I don't know about that, *milaya*. I'm a pretty resourceful guy." He pulls me closer as we sway to the tune played by the orchestra.

"What does that word mean? *Milaya*?" I ask.

He leads us through a slow dance, and I savor the feel of his right hand enveloping mine while his left one rests dangerously low on my bare back. Helpless to stop myself, I touch the hair on the back of his neck. It's surprisingly soft. His eyes grow heavy-lidded. It shouldn't please me this much that my touch brings him great satisfaction, but it does.

"Give me your name, and I will tell you," he says with a small smile.

"My name isn't important. What's in a name, anyway?

You know what they say, Nik. A rose by any other name would smell as sweet."

"Cute, but I bet even Shakespeare's Juliet couldn't have smelled as sweet as you."

"Oh, you smooth talker, you. Flattery will get you everywhere."

"Funny you should say that. As it happens, I have a specific place in mind."

Smoothly, he brings my body flush against his. I can feel almost every inch of his deliciously masculine frame. It's a heady and inebriating feeling.

As a self-admittedly fun-loving, hedonistic creature at heart, the mere thought of being physically apart from him is unnecessarily unpleasant. He's my type—strong, powerful, and larger-than-life. There's this aura of invincibility about him that is particularly impossible to resist.

I smooth my hand down his muscular chest. "Really? Well, don't leave me hanging. It's rude not to share with the class."

"I'd rather show you," he says, his eyes ablaze. "After all, if all you will give me is one dance, then I have to insist we move it somewhere private."

Nikolai's hand moves to my hip without a trace of hesitation, and I love every second of it. It's no surprise. Even from a young age, I took pride in appreciating life's finest things. In my experience, few things are as fine as a gorgeous man who would like nothing better than to show me a good time.

I always make sure to enjoy a healthy, varied diet of vigorous, red-hot, no-strings-attached sex. Unfortunately, I haven't had the time or energy to pursue this hobby for the past few months. Predictably, managing the *stronzo*'s demands has been an all-consuming affair. My needy libido hasn't exactly been a priority when A.J.'s life is still at risk.

As the band plays on and Nik's firm body brushes against mine, my misgivings and concerns start to sound terribly inconsequential. The Flame of Mir is mine, which means I won. Yes, the *stronzo* will get his prize—for now. But after tonight, A.J. will get a reprieve. I deserve to catch a break, too.

Since the work is done, why shouldn't I allow myself to celebrate a little? To let off some steam? God knows I need it after the trying months I have had recently. I have certainly earned it.

Nikolai's idea to take me somewhere we can be alone works just fine with my plan to escape this party and its nosy guests as soon as possible. In the grand scheme of things, as long as I'm departing the premises, does it matter if I do it by my lonesome self or with the man who undresses me with his eyes whenever he glances at me? Isn't it in my best interest to have someone who would vouch for me if one of the museum's guards notices the diamond is missing?

What an alibi.

As I gaze into Nik's warm brown eyes, I struggle to remember why giving in to him is such a bad idea. In fact, running into him tonight seems very serendipitous, and I'm never one to go against fate.

"Let's say I let you whisk me away," I say. I study his expression as I run my fingernails over the back of his neck. "Once you have me all to yourself, what's your plan?"

Nikolai seems to struggle to suppress a groan, drawing my body even closer to his. His mouthwatering scent envelopes me, and my body almost vibrates with pleasure when I feel a distractingly large bulge press against my stomach.

"I can think of a thing or two. Come with me, and I'll gladly demonstrate," he rasps against my skin.

"I had a feeling you'd say something like that. I won't lie to you, Nik, I'm tempted. You drive a hard bargain." I punctuate my words by slowly shimmying my hips against his to the languid rhythm of the song we are dancing to. He inhales sharply, and I smile in response. "But I'm afraid I'm still unconvinced. You might have to sweeten the deal."

"All you have to do is tell me what you desire, *milaya*, and I'll happily give it to you."

"Anything I want?"

"Anything," he says without hesitation.

His confidence in his power to provide me with anything I desire is a powerful aphrodisiac. Of course, he doesn't know how demanding and imaginative I can be when it comes to what I want, but it doesn't matter.

In the end, nothing else matters because with the Flame of Mir secured against my body, there is only one other thing I am craving.

Incapable of denying myself any longer, I brush his lips with mine before whispering, "Kiss me, Nik. Kiss me, and I'm yours."

4

NIK

I'M NOT surprised in the slightest when the woman in front of me demands I kiss her.

This moment was inevitable from the second I saw her from across the room and decided she was mine.

One way or the other, tonight would always end with her in my arms. Everything else was just details.

I didn't, however, foresee just how badly the mere thought of kissing her would affect me.

I suppose I should've had an inkling of it when the first glimpse of her blue eyes rendered me momentarily speechless.

If not that, then the fact that touching her soft skin had utterly driven me to distraction should have given me pause.

Yet, somehow, even after all these signs, I didn't expect to notice my heart thundering in my chest in anticipation of the warmth of her lips against my own. Or to feel my member uncomfortably strain against the tight confinement of my trousers when she scratched the back of my neck with her fingernails.

It is disconcerting to acknowledge that she effortlessly

evokes these visceral responses from me. Above all, I pride myself on being a rational and level-headed man, even under duress—especially under duress.

It was by keeping my emotions in check and dispassionately planning my every step that I managed to become the Russian *bratva's pakhan* in my mid-twenties and still hold that envied position a decade later.

Like most men, I have a healthy appetite and appreciation for sex and beautiful women, but it's still perplexing that a mostly innocent and platonic interaction with a girl—even one as naturally sensual and attractive as the one before me—has me struggling to conceal an erection in a crowded party. I haven't needed to deal with such humiliating embarrassments since I was a teenager.

The only explanation for this astonishing behavior is that I have allowed myself to go too long without a woman.

In all honesty, managing my legitimate business enterprises and handling my *bratva* affairs is enough to keep my plate full. This ordeal involving Patrick McGuire and Maxim hasn't made my life any easier. Since my friend's return, I've been too distracted to make time for sex. With so much on my mind, finding the time and motivation to pursue women hasn't been a priority lately.

Until tonight—everything changed tonight. One look at the woman in the sexy black velvet dress, and suddenly, it's hard to fathom that anything could be more urgent than the need to peel off her gown and fuck her until she can't remember the name she refuses to give me.

She licks her bottom lip while gazing at my mouth with a look on her face I can only describe as longing. I don't know if it is a calculated move intended to drive me over the edge or if she can't help herself. I'm not even sure which option is worse. Or better, I suppose.

Regardless, it doesn't matter. The result is the same either way. I can no longer restrain myself. I wrap my right hand around the back of her bared neck to pull her closer as I lean forward and take her mouth with my own.

Fuck.

I assumed—or hoped—that my awareness of her unnerving effect on me would lessen or even counter my inexplicable reactions to her. Short of physically bracing myself, I did all I could to prepare for what I knew would be a shamefully intense response to the velvety touch of her lips.

She softly moans against my mouth, eagerly greeting my tongue with her own, and I understand how ridiculously foolish and futile my attempt was.

There was nothing—*absolutely nothing*—I could have ever done to prepare myself for the reality of what kissing this woman feels like. Not in the meager few moments I had since she urged me to kiss her. Not in the thirty-something years I've had on this planet.

Had I been granted a thousand years to wander the earth and prepare for this instant, it would likely not have been enough.

I might as well have been struck by lightning—every inch of my skin is alive and electrified by her touch.

She runs her hands down my chest in an excruciatingly slow way that has to be designed to drive me to sheer madness. Without warning, she grabs hold of my jacket, pulling me closer, hard and fast. All I can do is groan against her mouth.

Our flirtatious banter from earlier was light-hearted and charming, but our kiss is setting a different mood. It changes things—it changes everything, actually—at least as far as I'm concerned. But if the intense way she's clinging to me as her clever little tongue twists around mine is any indication, I would say the feeling is most certainly mutual.

My plan was to convince her to leave the gala with me tonight. I meant to take her to the presidential suite of my favorite hotel, conveniently located only a few blocks from here. There, I was going to take my time uncovering and discovering what her pretty dress conceals until she begged me to fuck her. Repeatedly.

Now, I don't think I can wait that long. I have a feeling I won't even last that long. This desperate need is entirely foreign to me. Yet, somehow, I recognize with perfect clarity that self-restraint and delayed gratification are beyond my capabilities at the moment.

This realization is a profound shock to a man as self-assured and disciplined as I like to think I am. I can only assume that the fastest way to disperse whatever spell she has cast on me is to satiate this visceral hunger she has awakened as swiftly as possible. I don't think it would be wise to let this feeling grow, festering and taking hold inside of me.

Even more importantly, I can't risk her changing her mind. It took me a good deal of cajoling to even get this far with her. I have to close the deal as soon as possible. I couldn't bear it if she got cold feet and backed out now.

In a feat of truly exceptional mental dexterity, I manage to divert enough brain power to the vital task of remembering the museum's layout while her breasts are pressed against my chest. An impressive feat, considering how much of my blood flow is currently diverted to the opposite direction of my brain.

There must be somewhere around here where I can get her by herself. If I'm not inside her in the next few minutes, I don't know what I will do.

Even through the too many layers of clothing we're unfortunately still wearing, I can tell her nipples are stiff. My train of thought is derailed by my awareness of her, and it takes me a few seconds to stop wondering what shade of pink the hardened peaks might be.

My cock inadvertently twitches against the warmth of her stomach and I recall that, across the gardens, a few dozen yards beyond where the orchestra still plays, there's a vacant room. The museum's staff will sometimes store extra chairs or other supplies in there during events such as tonight's party.

It's likely unlocked and unoccupied right now. Most importantly, it's close by and private. It isn't the Four Seasons, but it will have to do.

Right hand still clinging to the back of her neck, I drag my left one down the smooth skin of her back until it reaches her generous ass. I palm it without hesitation, holding her hips close to mine as I move towards where the backroom is located.

She doesn't protest. Instead, she wraps her arms tighter around my neck, deepening our embrace. I want to drown in her kiss and her scent. She smells fresh, of freesias and bitter oranges. It's addictive, sexy, and hypnotic, just like the woman in my arms. I can't get enough of it.

With my lips, I trace a path from her maddening mouth to her ear. I kiss it before nipping her earlobe. She barely stifles a moan, allowing a deep sigh to escape her lips instead. I brush mine against her neck, lingering, relishing her delicious perfume.

Still entangled with her, I open the door to the deserted room once we reach it. As we stumble inside, I swiftly kick the door closed.

The overhead lamps are off, but the floor-to-ceiling glass

wall next to the entrance allows enough light in the darkened room. It's obvious that someone recently used it as a makeshift office. Extra chairs were stacked against the far wall, and a filing cabinet and a bookshelf stand next to them. A sturdy-looking writing desk sits a couple of inches away from the glass panels with an armchair that has seen better days next to it.

I envisioned taking her atop silk sheets in a place with an atmosphere more conducive to romance. This room isn't ideal, but it will suffice. At least it's mercifully cooler in here than out there. I plan on making it up to her in different ways.

Thankfully, she doesn't seem to mind. She most certainly doesn't voice any complaints as I pull her into my arms once more and begin kissing her anew. I pet the bare skin of her back, allowing my hand to drift to her hip, then her thigh.

She presses her breasts against my chest while moving her hips against my erection, and I direct my caresses to her upper body. My hand smooths its way up from her leg—all the way to her rib cage.

As my lips descend upon her neck again, I brush her nipple with my thumb through the fabric of her dress. I pinch it, feeling a surge of satisfaction when she moans in response.

Torn between nipping or sucking the velvety expanse of her neck, I go on to shower her skin with open-mouthed kisses. I need to claim her, to mark her as my own. It's an unsettling realization. I don't understand where these unfamiliar urges are coming from, but I can't bring myself to care at this particular moment. All that matters is the feel of her.

All night, I've watched her from afar, wondering what she would feel like and what she would taste like. Even though I gave my imagination free rein, I couldn't have dreamed she would taste this sweet or that her scent would make me feel as if I had inhaled a fifth of vodka in the span of a couple of minutes. And now she's as docile as a kitten in my arms, truly mine for the taking.

I cup her breasts and massage her flesh, rolling her nipples between my finger and thumb. She groans against my skin and tangles her fingers in my hair, pulling me closer. She stretches out her other hand, rubbing my shaft over my pants, and I find myself growling like a madman against the softness of her skin.

Impatiently, I hook a finger over the edge of the neckline of her dress. I need to see her. Like a schoolboy, I shudder in anticipation, almost dying to suck on the delicate skin of her breasts.

"Nik," she says, panting.

My mouth vibrates against her collarbone. "Mmm..."

"I need to touch you..."

I press her hand that currently covers my erection against it, and she lightly squeezes it. A groan escapes my lips.

"Then touch me, *milaya*. I'm yours for the taking."

Anxious to see her, I tug her tight-fitting dress a couple of inches down her torso. I spot the hint of a pink nipple over the neckline. Unable to resist it, I lower my head to it, licking it.

She grasps my member as she cries out in pleasure. I suck on the peak, and her moans become louder.

"Nik, I need to touch you *now*."

A hand still against the front of my pants, she forcefully pushes against my chest until my body lands on the armchair I noticed earlier.

She stands before me, slightly breathless at first, until a

subtle, almost imperceptible change comes over her. If I had blinked, I would have missed it. She takes a deep breath, squaring her shoulders. Fascinatingly, she slowly runs her hands over her hips and her stomach. Without pausing, her hands brush against her breasts and climb up her neck to her dark hair.

She waits until my distracted gaze, busy taking in her body and movements, meets hers. Without breaking eye contact, she smirks at me before letting her hair down. It cascades down her neck, enveloping her shoulders.

I want to pull her to me at once, but she is so mesmerizing at this moment that I find myself enthralled by her. I worry that if I move a muscle, I will dispel the magic of the moment, so I eagerly wait for her next move instead.

She turns around, showing me her back again before glancing at me over her shoulder. With a wink, she pulls her dress down her body. At last, it pools at her feet.

My eyes devour every inch of skin she teasingly reveals. My cock twitches when I take in the sight of her black silk thong.

My fingers dig into the chair's upholstered arms and I fight the urge to drag her to my lap so I can immediately and swiftly take her. I wouldn't dare interrupt her right now.

She glances at me over her shoulder before turning to face me with her arms crossed over her chest. She steps closer to me, smiling.

After placing a high-heeled shoe between my legs, dangerously close to my aching shaft, she leans forward.

While biting her bottom lip, she lowers her arms.

A curse escapes my lips. So beautiful...

As riveted as I am by the show she is putting on just for me, the sight of her so close—clad in nothing but a few straps of silk and lace—destroys whatever self-restraint I still possess. I reach forward to bring her body flush against mine, desperate to feel the bare skin of her breasts for the first time.

"Ah-ah-ah," she says while retreating from me. "Slow your roll, big guy. It's my turn now." She pushes me back onto the chair, and I let her have her way. For now.

Sitting back, I watch her approach me once again. She sits astride my lap, nothing but the thin scrap of fabric covering her where I long to touch her. I raise my hand to feel her chest instead, but she grabs my wrists before I can do so, placing my arms back on the chair's armrest.

She smirks at me. "Not yet." I comply for the time being, curious to learn what the siren has in mind for me. "There's something about sitting almost completely naked on top of a fully clothed guy that really turns me on. I like this, Nik. A lot. I think you like it, too."

With a teasing smile, she rotates her hips, rubbing her warm sex against my aching cock. I groan, clutching the chair so tightly I'm worried for a second that its old frame will snap in two. Even through the thick wool of my pants and the softness of her panties, I can still feel her wet heat.

"Let me touch you, *milaya,* and I'll show you just how much I like it," I say, my accent growing thicker.

"Mmm. That mysterious word again, in that voice of yours." She shudders, a mischievous glint in her dark blue eyes. "A girl can only get so wet, you know."

She moves my hands from the chair's armrest to her hips, leaning forward to kiss me. I expect her kiss to be as hard and urgent as before, but she surprises me by lightly touching my mouth with her own. Her tongue slowly runs over the seam of my lips.

My fingertips dig into the firm flesh of her ass as I thrust my hips upwards, craving the friction against her warm center. Her measuredly restrained touch is simultaneously pure bliss and torture. I can't hold back a groan as her tongue gently touches mine.

Spurred on, she tangles her fingers in my hair and picks up the pace, kissing me with renewed enthusiasm. Moaning into my mouth, she spreads her legs wider over my lap. She begins moving her hips again, rubbing my length against the silk of her underwear. Her breasts bounce and brush against my chest as she does so, making my thoughts grow hazy.

So warm... I need to bury myself inside her.

I move against her, matching her pace. Grinding harder and faster against my enlarged cock, she breaks away from our kiss to lean back. Unable to stop myself, I cover her breasts with my mouth. I flick her nipple with my tongue before sucking it hard. She yells out, clasping my head against her chest.

Her breaths grow more and more ragged while her hips forcefully press against mine in a maddening rhythm as she desperately tries to push herself over the edge. The warm feel of her silk-covered lips along my erection is almost enough to make me spill inside my pants.

Our hips buckle almost uncontrollably, and she gets closer and closer to climax. The scent of her skin and her arousal—coupled with the sight of her beautiful body writhing over my cock—make the pressure that has been building up inside me all night come to a boiling point. My frustration reaches an unbearable degree. Suddenly, I can no longer tolerate the idea of any barriers between me and her sex. I need to see it, and I need to taste it. I must feel it against my tongue and lips as she comes for me.

So, I rise from the groaning chair and carry her to the desk facing the wall-sized windows. I sit her down on top of it, not wasting a second before kneeling between her legs until my face is level with her hips.

Finally, I spread her legs wide, taking a moment to watch her from this angle. Her black silk tongue is visibly wet, and her scent makes me bite back a growl.

I trace a finger along the edge of her panties, and all thoughts of slowly savoring the moment and making her linger on the cusp of climax for a while are discarded in an instant once I feel her wetness against my fingertip. I hook my finger around the fabric and tear it apart, revealing all of her.

She gasps at my unexpected move, but I'm too distracted by the sight of her to say anything. I almost sigh. Gorgeous girl...

Raptly, I take in the glistening folds of her sex for a moment, but the urge to learn what she tastes like is too strong for me to resist it any longer.

As I settle in between her thighs, I don't even consider starting slowly. Instead, I kiss her hungrily. At my first taste of her, my eyes close and another groan escapes my lips.

She cries out and weaves her fingers through my hair, pulling me closer before spreading her legs wider.

I stretch out my arms, touching the tips of her breasts as I trace her lips with my tongue. I flick it over the tiny nub of flesh in her center. Her breaths become even more erratic, and she unabashedly grinds her hips against my mouth.

I'm high on her taste, her scent and her reactions. I never knew that it was possible to experience this much ecstasy simply from pleasuring another. Slowly dragging my right hand down from her hypnotic breasts to where my mouth savors her, I use my thumb to circle her opening lightly.

"Please, Nik," she says between pants.

I'm more than eager to give her what she's begging for,

but I'm not quite ready to let go of her taste just yet. She's close, so I take my time savoring her as she grows wetter and wetter from my kiss.

My thumb enters her, and she cries out again. So warm...I can't wait to be inside her.

I thrust my thumb in and out of her core as she moans in rhythm with my movements.

She pulls my hair so hard it wouldn't surprise me if tufts of it fell off my head. Her moans become louder, and her hips urgently grind against my face in an almost painful way. She's on the brink of coming. As much as I'm craving the taste of her orgasm, I need to feel it on my cock even more.

No longer able to restrain myself, I stand up, looking at her.

She's a vision, absolutely breathtaking. Her beautiful hair fans around her face, and her blue eyes are even darker.

As I study her, she raises her hands to cup her breasts, spreading her legs wider while meeting my gaze with her mesmerizing eyes.

So, I grab her hips and flip her body over until she is bent at the waist over the desk before me, her feet barely grazing the floor. I position myself behind her, smoothing my hands over her backside before grabbing hold of her flesh to hold her in place. She is as soft and warm there as everywhere else.

I make quick work of the bulging zipper of my pants while she turns slightly to glance at me over her shoulder. Her eyes first connect with mine, then trail down my body until her gaze lands on my hand clutching my erection as I'm about to put it inside her. I stroke myself once, and she bites her bottom lip, pressing her hips back against mine.

Holding her still, I place the tip of my shaft against her

wet sex. The feel of her warmth is almost more than I can take, and it's almost impossible not to bury myself inside her in one deep thrust. Instead, I move my hand up and down her back, watching her arch it in response.

She pants, her breath fogging the glass wall before us. "Please."

Still clutching her hip, I begin working my cock head inside her. As her body tries to accommodate me, she hisses in a breath, twitching and trembling. Inch by inch, I slowly feed my length inside her, trying to make this moment last as much as I can.

Once I'm fully buried in her center, I grind my hips against hers, and she cries out in pleasure. With the last shreds of my self-control, I manage to stop myself from thrusting immediately, allowing her a moment to grow accustomed to my size.

The onslaught she is wreaking on my senses is almost too overwhelming. The moonlight and the bright lights from the party outside bathe her skin through the window's glass as her heat envelopes my shaft and her tight pussy welcomes me. I can smell the perfume of her skin mingled with the scent of our arousal. Her erratic pants and my thundering heartbeat break the silence inside the room.

It's enough to make me wonder for an instant if I could go mad from this unbearable pleasure.

Unable to contain myself any longer, I begin thrusting. I move my left hand up her back and grab the back of her neck. I wrap my right arm around her waist until I am cupping her breast and pinching her nipple between my thumb and forefinger.

"Oh, God..." She undulates her hips against mine as the sound of her moans echoes around us.

I hiss in a breath as she rocks against me, my cock

pulsating inside her as I drive harder and faster into her body. I buck my hips more forcefully, and her teeth audibly clatter.

"Ah, yes, Nik! Do that again, please..."

So I do, over and over again, until she reaches back between our legs to cup my sack. I groan at her touch before grabbing her wrist. As I hold her arm against her back, I repeatedly plunge into her sex in a punishing rhythm, while my other hand tortures the hard tips of her gorgeous breasts.

"No, *milaya*. I won't let you make me come before I'm done fucking you."

She grinds her hips against mine and spreads her legs wider apart, wordlessly urging me to drive into her deeper. I draw her body up until she is leaning against my chest, my cock still seated all the way inside her core.

The large glass windows show us our reflection, and I can't stifle a groan upon seeing her breasts tantalizingly bouncing up and down as she moves against me. I raise my hands to touch them, and our eyes connect through the makeshift mirror.

Beyond our reflection, the gala goes on a few yards away. Hundreds of elegantly dressed men and women carry on, unaware that I have this naked beauty writhing on my cock.

I'm so deep inside her I feel the exact moment she notices the people on the other side of the glass. The undulating of her hips slows down for a brief second before she gasps.

I pinch her nipples again and buck hard against her, forcing a moan out of her plump lips.

"Shh. It's okay, *milaya*. It's much darker in here than out there. You see them, but they don't see you..."

She takes a second to process my words, but soon enough, she increases her pace again.

As I lean down to kiss her neck, I study her via our reflections. The view of her sensual body fully uncovered and displayed for my enjoyment is utterly mesmerizing and hypnotic, but it doesn't escape me that her eyes are lingering on the gala's attendees as they merrily dance and talk.

Her pants become more erratic, and the cadence of her hips grows more urgent. Somehow, her little sheath gets more slick as she bounces up and down my shaft.

I nip her neck before moving my mouth to her ear. "My naughty, naughty girl. You like having an audience, don't you?"

Her only response is to bite her bottom lip, turning her head to catch my mouth with her own. Her kiss is frantic and sloppy, and it brings me closer to the edge.

I break our kiss, meeting her eyes through the glass windows again. As she watches, I cover her right hand with mine before bringing it to her chest. I make her cup her breast before sliding our joined palms down her stomach until we reach her wet sex.

As I mercilessly thrust inside her, I use our fingers to spread her lips open and search for her clitoris. We lightly touch it, and she throws her head back, moaning.

"No, no, *milaya*. Don't close your eyes. I want you to watch yourself come in front of all of them."

With a gasp, she raises her head, looking at our hands through the mirror. As our fingers rub—and my cock drives deep inside her—I almost yell in ecstasy. Her little sighs of pleasure punctuate my heartbeats, and it isn't long before my seed starts to climb inside my length.

While our fingers work her sex mercilessly, I discern the first contractions of her sheath around me. I'm desperate to draw it out as much as possible, but we are both past the point of no return.

She leans forward, resting her other hand on the desk and arching her back. She grinds her hips against me hard and fast, crying out. So, I run my other hand over her plump ass, her back, until I reach her head. Too far gone to bother with pleasantries, I grab a handful of her luscious brown hair as I forcefully thrust into her.

She moans as she spreads her knees wider, writhing her hips with increased urgency. "Nik..."

I never stop plunging between her legs as our fingers rub the little nub of flesh above her entrance.

My cock pulses inside her again, almost in anticipation, just before she gasps, her entire body tensing. She screams as her sheath squeezes me, begging for what my body yearns to give her. Hoarsely, I groan against her skin, immediately joining her. A violent orgasm burns through me like a searing iron, and I shudder with mindless pleasure as I pour into her.

Sheer ecstasy...

5

KAT

It's true what they say. Bad boys do it better. And there's no doubt about it—Nikolai's a bad, bad boy.

I won't deny it took me a moment to realize it. But to be fair, I don't exactly make a habit of picking up men during jobs. This whole situation is a little outside of my comfort zone. From the start, this heist has been particularly stressful for me—a rushed, high-profile operation orchestrated by someone who controls my best friend's fate.

Of course, my recent involuntary celibacy compromised my judgment, too. To make matters even worse, Nikolai's good looks and charm blindsided me. I have always been a sucker for tall, dark-haired guys who look absolutely devastating in bespoken tuxedos.

Nonetheless, I knew he was a bad boy—maybe not from the beginning, but certainly by the time I boldly undressed for him. If anything, his powerful effect on me was another clue to his nature. I can never find it in myself to resist handsome men who are clearly up to no good.

Even now, I know I won't regret tonight. Not even for a second.

Long gone are the days when I felt guilty about seizing the things or pleasures I crave. And I craved him badly.

I have no qualms about living my life my way, playing by my own rules, and answering to no one but myself. After years of feeling powerless and helpless, I learned there was another way, and I have never looked back.

In the past few months, the *stronzo* and his schemes have prevented me from living my best life and enjoying it to the fullest. In time, he will pay for it—and for endangering my friend's life.

A.J. and I are close to the last piece of the puzzle. Soon, we will have everything we need to strike back at the villain. The Flame of Mir should buy us enough time to chase our latest lead and uncover the mysterious secret the horrid man has been hiding.

That's why I can never see Nikolai again.

Under normal circumstances, I would have loved nothing more than to hide away with the delicious man somewhere warm and luxurious for a week or so. We would have sex whenever the mood struck me, and I would have taken my time exploring the strong, masculine body his clothes still fully cover—even now.

But that is not meant to be. Unfortunately, I can't afford the risk of a lasting connection with anyone or anything linked to tonight. Our encounter can never amount to anything more than a mind-blowing memory of a hot summer night.

With a discreet sigh I almost don't catch, he pulls out of me long moments after our shared climax.

Still bent over the desk, I hear the sound of his zipper as he rearranges his clothing before grabbing my waist and lowering my body until my feet once again touch the ground.

I turn around to face him. The staggering effect his eyes have on me takes me by surprise once again. Whenever his gaze finds mine, my core muscles tighten of their own accord. If I were a woman prone to fanciful fits and daydreaming, I might have admitted to feeling the strangest sensation in my chest—something akin to my heart skipping a beat.

As it is, I'm nothing if not a practical woman. More importantly, I'm a woman on a mission. Not a romantic, simpering fool of a girl. As pleasant as our stolen moment was, it's time to say goodbye.

Nikolai glances at me again, his expression both vulnerable and guarded. After clearing his throat, he reaches inside the pocket of his exquisitely tailored jacket to pull out a handkerchief. He places it in my hand, his fingers lingering on it before wrapping around my wrist. He smoothly slides his hands into his pants pockets, breaking our eye contact.

Oh, God. I'm completely naked in front of a fully dressed man—a man who is, for all intents and purposes, a complete stranger. His gaze trails down my body, and it's clear that despite his portrayed aloofness, he is very much aware of my state of undress, too.

Fighting the urge to clear my throat, I take a deep breath instead. Maybe it will clear my mind. "Well, then," I say, patting his chest a few times before sidestepping around him to reach our discarded clothes.

Earlier, when his attentions were so intently directed at my *décolleté*, I was forced to improvise. I couldn't risk being caught with tonight's *pièce de résistance* between my breasts. Instead, I decided that an impromptu striptease was the perfect way to distract him from my secret.

I expected him to be a little taken aback by my boldness. That didn't happen at all. My performance might have been a surprise to him—but a welcome one. The scorchingly hot look in his eyes as he raptly watched me teasingly reveal my body to him will forever be etched in my mind.

I bend at the waist to retrieve my dress, my back turned to him. He hisses in a breath, and I can't help smiling. Good. Our brief acquaintance will soon come to an end, but I will leave my mark on him—just as he will leave his on me.

I don my gown, a small sigh of relief escaping my lips when I feel the weight of the diamond against my chest again.

I spin on my heels to face him again and find him still standing there with his hands buried in his pockets. His expression remains politely aloof and guarded, but I don't mind it. My life will be much easier if he doesn't try to stop me from slipping away as he did earlier in the evening.

Our gazes link once more. His eyes still burn as hot as molten lava. The man is clearly very skilled at composing his facial features into any expression that pleases him, but his expressive eyes tell a different story.

That funny feeling tickles my chest again, but I ignore it. After all, I'm a practical woman with a purpose.

With a half-smile, I sigh. "Well, I'll give it to you, Nik. You *are* a man of your word. This was fun."

My flippant tone catches him off guard. He raises his eyebrows just before shaking his head and smirking at me.

The only thing more irresistible than the almost gravitational pull of his eyes when they lock with mine is the full force of his smile directed at me.

A practical woman with a purpose. It should be my new mantra.

"I guess I don't have to ask you if it was as good for you as it was for me," he says, sounding as glib as me.

I walk towards him, stopping just before our chests touch. Our breaths mingle for an instant, and the memory of how it feels to be kissed and touched by him rushes me, flooding my senses.

Woman. Purpose.

He carefully studies me, his gaze lingering on my face. He is trying to play it cool, but it's obvious he is eager to learn my next move. I stand on the tip of my toes, stretching until my lips graze his ear. He shivers, and I have to hide my responding smile.

"I think we both know I had a blast. And I happen to know you did, too. I still feel it inside me," I say, nipping his ear lobe. I pull it before turning away from him to make my grand exit. Unfortunately, there will be no encore.

Nikolai, as it happens, still has a thing or two to say in response to my teasing remarks. His arm shoots out, and he grabs me, pulling my body flush against his.

I grin—so much for his indifference.

He holds me tightly, but there's no need—I don't want to escape him just yet. Instead, I want to memorize the feel of his hard body pressed against my back, his breath touching the sensitive point skin of my neck.

I chuckle. "I guess you are not so cool and collected after all, are you?"

"Are you *toying* with me?" he asks through gritted teeth, as if the mere notion is extraordinary and unthinkable.

"Maybe I am. Something tells me you like it." I punctuate my words with a teasing sway of my hips against his, rubbing against his hard erection pressed against my backside.

He walks forward until I am stuck between his body and

the desk again. It doesn't take a genius to understand he wants me to remember what happened on top of it not long before I dared *toying with him.*

"I ought to teach you a lesson about messing with the wrong man. As a matter of fact, I have half a mind to bend you over this desk again and remind you of what happens to flirty brunettes who like to tease me."

I go completely soft in his arms. This man will be the death of me...

"Aw, Nik. Don't threaten me with a good time."

He spins me until we face each other once more. Playfully, I wrap my arms around his neck, giving him a peck on his lips. He shoots me an exasperated—and slightly dazed—look.

"You think I'm kidding," he says in disbelief.

"No, no. You're a very serious man. I see that," I say against his lips, letting one of my hands snake down his body until it reaches his erection. I give it a firm squeeze. "Very serious, indeed."

"That's it. I'm going to bend you over my knee and spank that plump ass of yours until you show me the respect that I'm owed."

"Sounds amazing. But I'm afraid I'll have to take a raincheck on that, Nik. It's almost twelve, and this Cinderella has to hit the road before her carriage turns into a pumpkin. You know the drill."

Nik laughs darkly, and the sound sends shivers down my spine in the most riveting way. "You're not going anywhere."

"Oh, yes, I am. I don't mean to dine and dash, but I really have to go."

His eyes widen. "*Dine and dash*? You're out of your mind if you think you're just walking out of here after saying that to my face."

"No need to be offended, Nik. This was some fine, three *Michelin* stars dining. Trust me—ten out of ten. Now, what do you say we part as friends?"

He stares at me as if what I said is something so nonsensical that he can't decide whether to feel outraged or shocked. "I don't know whether to throttle you or fuck you senseless."

I nod in commiseration. "I often have that effect on men. Or so I've been told."

His expression turns dark. Clearly, it was the wrong thing to say.

"Is that why you're in such a rush to leave? Do you have another man waiting for you at home? If you're hungry for more, I'm happy to oblige. No need to leave. As a matter of fact, I'll have to insist. I don't share. Ever. So, whatever plans you had with him are officially canceled. Indefinitely. You'll be spending the night with me."

Unfortunately for Nik, he doesn't know me well enough to know that is likely the worst thing he could say to me. After being at the *stronzo*'s beck and call for countless months, the last thing I need is another man who thinks he is entitled to me or who believes he can control me.

Nik was the lay of the century. Truly. He is good enough to eat, and the orgasm he gave me was just what I needed after the trials and tribulations I have been through this year. But I will be damned if that gives him the right to act possessive or controlling over me. Hell will freeze over before I allow another man to dictate what I do with my life.

If we had enough time, I would have let him bend me over and spank me. Or fuck me. Hopefully, spank me *and* fuck me. But just because I would allow a man to have his way with me sexually, it doesn't mean he gets to control me. On the contrary, I'm experienced enough to know that a sexually confident woman is often the one with all the power when it comes to men and sex.

Just because I play the part of a submissive between the sheets, it doesn't follow that I will submit to him—or to anyone else—in any true sense. I never will—not to him, not to anybody. I love being my own mistress. The entire purpose of tonight is to get the diamond and rectify things in my world so I can be my own woman again.

If Nik thinks he will bend me to his will, I can't get away from him fast enough.

In the end, it doesn't even matter, anyway. I need to untangle myself from him and cut all ties with anything and anyone even remotely related to this party. The risk is too great, and it certainly isn't worth the reward. Any lasting connections could land me in jail—or, even worse, dead.

That is why I physically push him away—forcefully. Until now, I have been as soft as a kitten, practically purring in his arms, so my sudden move catches him by surprise and I manage to extricate myself from him.

"Whether I have a man—or a hundred—waiting for me at home is none of your business," I say.

My change in demeanor catches him off guard, and he doesn't move to grab me again.

"Maybe not. But maybe you made it my business when you begged me to make you come earlier," he says in the same tone.

"I wouldn't worry about it if I were you. Like I said, why don't we part as friends?"

He studies me for a moment, searching for something. His almost irresistible pull works over me as our eyes connect again, but I manage to break away from his gaze for the first time tonight.

"Very well," he says, his tone distant again. "We'll part as *friends*. Will you at least tell me your name?"

For a second, I think I see his dark brown eyes glimmer with some unidentified emotion.

A practical woman with a purpose. I remember.

Without answering, I glance at Nikolai one final time before walking away.

6

NIK

She storms out of the room, leaving me more confused than I can ever remember.

The woman went from practically purring in my arms to cold and distant in a split second.

It is clear that she didn't appreciate my offhand remark about her hypothetical boyfriend.

I can't even pretend to understand how such an inconspicuous question provoked such a sudden and intense reaction from her. I may have been curious about whether there was a man in her life, but my intent was to charm her and convince her to spend the night with me.

Evidently, my flirting skills could use some work.

I wasn't even particularly worried about a potential rival for her affections. I don't concern myself with such things. It doesn't matter to me if another man wants what I desire. If I want something—or someone, I suppose—I take it. As I did tonight.

Maybe I didn't fully get my way as far as she was concerned. I won't deny I wish the night had ended differently. I hoped she would leave the party with me so we could enjoy each other's company for the rest of the evening. Instead, she quickly dismissed me as if I was nothing more than a schoolboy.

She didn't even deem me worthy of her name. I will have no choice but to think of her as *the woman* whenever she crosses my mind—and I know I will be thinking of her often.

I admit that any man in my position would be perfectly capable of independently learning her name and figuring out how to contact her. But it still stings that I even have to resort to such underhanded tactics. I can't recall the last time I had to ask a girl for her number, let alone her name. They are usually more than eager to volunteer that information.

Her initial unfazed and unimpressed reaction to my pursuit of her had appealed to me at first. But now my pride is a little wounded by how easily she wrote me off after the bout of mind-blowing sex we shared. I'm sure I pleased her in that regard, but it wasn't enough to get me even her first name.

Regardless, all is well when it ends well. Or, at least, well enough. Maybe it's for the best that I unwittingly upset her. She is, after all, a complication I don't have the time or energy to handle.

Even under normal circumstances, I lead a hectic life. Managing the *bratva* is an all-consuming endeavor. It's not unusual for me to work twelve or fourteen-hour days. Not that I mind it. My job isn't the kind of work that complies with a nine-to-five schedule. Frankly, it isn't just a job but a lifestyle. I am the *bratva*'s *pakhan* twenty-four-seven, and I like it like that just fine.

On top of that, there is also the matter of my legitimate business enterprises. Those also demand a lot of my time and attention. Of course, my companies are only as important as the use my *bratva* dealings require of them, but unsurprisingly, the running of a *Fortune 500* company isn't exactly light work.

Even on a good day, I don't have the time or the inclination to pursue a romantic relationship. And since Maxim had the misfortune of getting himself involved with Erin McGuire, I haven't had many good days.

During the past year, all my energy has been focused on mending fences with the Irish and avoiding an all-out war with them. I doubt things will dramatically improve soon, with Maxim back on this side of the Atlantic. I love him like the brother I have never had, but I know better than anyone else that he is impulsive and reckless to a fault.

Above all else, I need to stay sharp and alert through the next few months—at least until Patrick McGuire mellows out. A relationship would be a distraction and a weakness I can't afford right now, especially one involving someone as captivatingly disconcerting as she is.

I would hate to drag her into the dangerous mess that my life currently is, anyway. Being the *bratva's pakhan* is always an unsafe line of work, but things have reached a critical point recently. The situation with the Irish is more delicate than most realize. Patrick McGuire is a treacherous, vicious man. More than ever, I must keep my eyes on the ball.

As dramatic as it may sound, forgetting about her may very well be a matter of life-and-death. I can't afford to be obsessed with a mysterious woman capable of driving me to distraction—not when everything I want is within my reach.

At last, there is nothing stopping me from making amends with Maxim, my oldest and dearest friend.

Besides, as the minutes pass and the cloud of lust her presence summoned dissipates, it dawns on me that I know almost nothing about the woman.

For starters, she isn't on the guest list for tonight's gala. Her motives for crashing the party may have been innocent. The event is the talk of the town. Someone as beautiful and charming as she could easily sneak into the museum.

But I can't know for sure. I have as much reason to believe her innocence as I have to assume that she is an operative sent by my enemies to get close to me. McGuire is undoubtedly capable of that, and so much more.

There is just so very little I know about her. I may know that her skin is soft all over and what she sounds like when she comes around my dick, but I can't let our sexual encounter create a false sense of intimacy in me, blinding me to the many, many things I don't know.

Why be so secretive about something so inoffensive as a name, anyway? Was it because she feared I would recognize it? Or maybe because she is married?

The mere thought of her belonging in name and body to another man makes me want to break something or someone. Somehow, I force myself to get my emotions under control.

This entire night almost feels like a fever dream. It isn't like me to be this emotional. I never struggle to act rationally.

I don't think she faked her passion and enjoyment of our shared moment, but without knowing her, how can I be sure?

My awareness of her overwhelming effect on me makes

me wonder if my optimistic assumptions about her are simply wishful thinking on my part.

I wanted her so badly, needed her to desire me just as much. Even now, the idea of her enthusiasm being faked is almost more than I can bear.

I have never responded to a woman as I did to her. I quickly gave in to my attraction to her and thought nothing of it, presuming that meeting her tonight was nothing but a serendipitous turn of fate. Every little detail about her seemed designed to bewitch me.

I believe in coincidences as much as the next person, but there is so much I don't know about her and almost nothing I know for sure. I fear I can't even trust my judgment where she is involved.

A man in my position has to be very careful with his trust. It's a commodity I don't part with freely. With as many enemies as I have, I can't afford anything else.

The woman was beautiful and captivating, and I long to see her again, but there is no reason to trust her.

It will haunt me that I will only experience the indescribable pleasure of being inside her once, but perhaps it's for the best that she left me.

If one quick fuck with her over an old writing desk in a dusty room can reduce me to a simpering fool with no common sense, then I must get as far away from her as possible.

Ultimately, it's good that she didn't make it easy for me to find her again. Otherwise, I'm not sure I could resist chasing her, even against my better judgment.

If a few moments with her make me this irrational, I would hate to see what she would turn me into if I had her long-term.

All is well, in the end. I should thank my lucky stars that she left me. I'm free to return to my old self, to my rational ways. In fact, I will return to the party, find Dmitri and Maxim, and enjoy myself with people I actually know and trust.

I won't think about her at all.

7

NIK

I can't stop thinking about her.

It's the most aggravating thing.

As soon as I leave the vacant room and step out into the museum's gardens, I'm accosted by people who want to chat me up. I couldn't care less about the insipid conversations I'm forced to endure, mainly because every little thing reminds me of her.

I repeatedly catch myself drawing comparisons between all the women approaching me and her. All of them are lacking in one way or another.

If their eyes are blue, their color isn't as deep or vivid as hers.

Similarly, if they are brunettes, their hair is a mousy, unappealing brown instead of her rich chocolate hue.

Whenever a woman gets close enough that I can smell her perfume, I must suppress a sigh—their scent can't hold a candle to hers.

I even resent having to shake other people's hands. After feeling the smooth expanse of her skin, I don't want to touch anything else.

Time after time, whenever the endless chatting inevitably dies down, I can almost hear her breathy moans in my head.

Naturally, I drain drink after drink to clear my hazy mind, but the bitter liquor only reminds me of how sweet she tasted in comparison.

It's hopeless. I'm nothing but a pathetic, lovesick fool.

This new character flaw couldn't have come at a worse time. I must forget this woman at all costs. Daydreaming about her is a waste of my time and energy, which could be better used fixing things with Maxim.

As I suffer in silence at the museum's gardens, a man I couldn't name to save my life rattles on and on about some unidentified topic I don't even pretend to be interested in until I feel a tap on my shoulder.

Grateful for this interruption to my endless torture, I turn around and find one of my *bratva* associates, Vladmir Smirnov.

"Nikolai," Vlad says, leaning closer to me. "There's something you need to see."

The man tries to convey his urgency to me discreetly. Vladmir's demeanor would seem casual and relaxed to anyone observing our interaction, but I know him well enough to understand that something is seriously wrong.

"If you will excuse me," I say to the man speaking *at* me before Vladmir's welcome interruption.

I let Vlad escort me away. At this point, he has been with the *bratva* for more than half a decade. Many of the other associates question his short temper and impulsiveness, but I keep him around because of his quiet reliability. No matter how complex or unpleasant the job is, Vladmir will get it done without voicing any complaints.

I study him as we pass through the ongoing party. Vladmir is taller than most of the guests who surround us. Throughout all the years we've known each other, he has kept his hair cropped short in an efficient buzz cut. In contrast, he has always sported a full, neatly trimmed beard.

As I watch him, he runs his right hand over his mouth, then over his head. His light green eyes never meet mine as he guides me towards the museum's main building.

An ominous feeling washes over me. Vladmir is always quick to display his emotions—often in a rash, loud, and impetuous manner. And yet, in all the years we've worked together, I've never seen him act this apprehensive. His forehead glistens with sweat as he glances around the surrounding area.

We climb the marble steps leading to the museum's entrance. Once we cross the doorway, I'm shocked to find most of my men inside the building. I assumed they were enjoying the festivities in the gardens.

I can think of only a handful of reasons for them to gather like this, and almost none of them would be good news.

Very few of my men openly meet my eyes as I follow Vladmir through the museum's hall. Most of them avoid glancing in my direction, looking down or away, instead.

Vlad guides me through a long, dark hallway cordoned off for tonight's event.

I familiarized myself with the museum's layout before tonight's gala. I'm always overly cautious with the security of the Flame of Mir. Still, my due diligence served me well this evening when I desperately needed to find a private area.

The corridor is deserted. Mentally orienting myself, I recall it leads to a large room dedicated to one of the museum's ongoing exhibitions, *Italian Masters*. It houses a dozen paintings and sculptures from the Renaissance and Baroque periods.

We approach the exhibition's entryway. More of my men linger outside the door. Unlike the edgy *shestyorka* out front, these are higher-ranking members of the *bratva*. They don't avoid making eye contact with me. The *vori* stare at me instead, somber expressions all over their faces. My sense of dread grows.

Dmitri is by the door. Covering the distance between us in a couple of short strides, I reach to open the door when he stops me.

"Nik, wait," he says. "Hold on for just a second. You need to prepare yourself, Nik."

I don't wait for Dmitri to finish his sentence. Shoving his hand away, I push the door open and step into the exhibition room, eager to end this endless suspense.

The first thing I see is Caravaggio's famous painting, *The Taking of Christ*. It looms dark and magnificent on the wall directly in front of me across the large chamber. In the back of my mind, I'm taken aback to see it here. I thought it was supposed to be housed in the National Gallery of Ireland.

The dark brown hardwood floors and the scarlet wallpaper covering the windowless walls lend the room a gloomy ambience. Its poorly lit state only adds to the grim atmosphere.

This shadowy environment is likely why I take a while to notice the body in front of the notorious art piece.

I can't tell the dead man's identity straight away. Not from this far away—the chamber is too dismally illuminated to allow that.

I slowly approach the cadaver, seized by that unsettling

feeling of foreboding again as my heart trashes and thunders within my chest.

Finally, I reach the body. Looking down, I glance at his face, immediately feeling as if my heart has come to a sudden, screeching halt. Utterly shocked, I inhale sharply.

Maxim.

8

KAT

I RUSH to meet A.J. at our favorite coffee shop, weaving in and out of inconvenient traffic on my way downtown. I don't want to—and can't afford to—be late for our lunch appointment.

After the night of the gala, something clicked into place within me. Simply put, I'm done letting others take the lead in my life. No more passively reacting to things that happen to me. It's time I start deliberately acting on behalf of my interests again.

It has only been a week since that fateful evening, but I have been busy.

After leaving Nikolai, I called A.J. to let her know the heist was successful.

I still haven't told her about the passionate moment I enjoyed in Nikolai's arms. I want to tell her everything, badly needing to voice my thoughts out loud to process my feelings about him. But for some reason, the words just won't come to me.

Instead, I asked her to set up the drop for the Flame of Mir with the *stronzo*'s contact. It is in everyone's best interests if my interactions with the man are kept to a bare minimum.

The diamond was such a hot item that I didn't feel comfortable keeping it overnight. It hurt me to part with the exquisitely beautiful jewel—and, worst of all, hand it to the villain—but it was a good idea to get rid of it as soon as possible.

Thankfully, when the news broke that the Flame of Mir was missing, I had already handed it to the *stronzo*'s man.

In the following days, I stayed busy caring for myself and working with A.J. to pursue our lead on the *stronzo*'s secret.

A.J. and I have been forced to answer to the old man's every whim for the past few months, ever since my best friend landed herself into some serious trouble with him.

In an uncharacteristic display of carelessness, she was caught red-handed defrauding the man's accounts. To her credit, she managed to relocate a few million dollars before he even noticed the money was missing.

A.J. and I are usually very careful about the people and businesses we target in our jobs. We never aim for anyone with organized crime ties or a history of violence.

This time around, A.J. didn't adhere to our one golden rule. She's very good at what she does, and over the years, she may have become a little too cocky about her impressive track record.

In our field, self-assuredness is essential. Self-doubt is of no help when one needs to be bold. My friends and I hate the term *con woman*, but our line of work is described as a confidence game for a reason. A good thief knows it is in their best interest to always hope for the best, but a *great* thief knows it is just as important to prepare for the worst.

A.J. forgot the latter when she set out to steal from the

stronzo, assuming he was an easy mark. But he was a made man—a detail she ignored when she chose him as her target.

The Italian did not take A.J.'s offense lightly. He refused to accept her apology, even after she returned the stolen money and offered to help improve his meager electronic security measures free of charge.

For a dark moment, we feared the worst would happen to her. We know there are dire consequences to harming the mafia's interests, so we try to stay out of their path at all costs.

In the end, he agreed to spare A.J.'s life in return for her services. He was enticed to show her mercy once he learned about her identity, and he was even eager to do so once he realized her connection to me—one of the few occasions we regretted making a name for ourselves within our exclusive circles.

At first, A.J. and I agreed to do his bidding until her debt was repaid—with all due interest, of course. However, we quickly realized that this debt would never be satisfied, and the man clearly planned to keep us under his thumb indefinitely.

It is part of my nature to resent being controlled and manipulated. Still, my urgency in extinguishing the man's leverage over us doesn't stem just from my personal issues with our unfortunate situation.

I have lost countless nights of sleep, worrying myself sick about what will happen to A.J. and me once the old man's demands grow too outrageous for us to satisfy.

I fear he will force us into an impossible position that will land us either dead or in jail. Or that he will demand something so immoral and unthinkable from us that we will have no option but to refuse him.

Above all else, I dread the day when we will no longer have any use for him. It is only a matter of time before that time comes.

A.J. and I aren't precisely civilians and know a thing or two about self-preservation. Still, we are very aware of our shortcomings compared to many players in our slice of the criminal underworld.

At the end of the day, we are just two white-collar con artists. Our street smarts might be above average, but we aren't equipped with the skill set needed to take on a mob boss who has no qualms about killing us.

A.J. and I are running out of time. We must find a way out of our unfortunate situation soon or risk an unthinkable fate.

For this reason, we have been desperately pursuing even the slightest leads, hoping to gain any leverage over our blackmailer.

Coincidentally, around the time my sense of urgency reached new, unbearable heights, our friend Alana overheard one of her boyfriends—a soldier in the Irish mafia—joke about an old rumor about the *stronzo*.

At first, we thoroughly disregarded the tale because it was too good to be true. But the more we learned about it, the more we realized it couldn't be unfounded gossip. It became clear that this secret—often disguised as outlandish fiction—could be our way out of the terror the man has been wrecking in our lives.

When the old mobster ordered me to steal the Flame of Mir, the world's most famous diamond, from the Metropolitan Museum during a high-profile event with little notice, I was initially prepared to resist. I refused his outrageous demand until I realized this task's sheer recklessness and audacity could work in our favor.

If I delivered such a valuable prize to him after the entire world learned of its disappearance, he would have no choice but to lie low and give us some reprieve. It would be the heist of the century, but it could give us enough time to get the proof we need to uncover the secret.

I was highly successful in the first part of my plan. Now that it's time to close the deal, I must keep my head in the game and stay out of trouble.

Mainly of the tall, dark, and handsome variety.

During the past week, in the rare instances when I had a moment or two of free time, I did my best to focus on taking care of myself. God knows I haven't had the chance to do so in the past few months.

I took A.J. to the nicest spa in town. We enjoyed deep tissue massages that didn't even begin to dissipate the tension I have been carrying in my whole body. We treated ourselves to fresh haircuts and even got cute manicures and pedicures. Every inch of us was mercilessly waxed, plucked, exfoliated, and moisturized.

Maybe if I looked my best, I would also feel at my best.

Perhaps keeping busy would help keep a certain man off my mind.

Much to my chagrin, it's been utterly pointless—I can't stop thinking about Nik.

Infuriatingly, everything reminds me of him and of the mind-blowing pleasure I inconveniently found in his arms.

If I'm out and about and spot a tall guy with glossy, dark hair, the most aggravating flutter starts in my abdomen. It always begins in the pit of my stomach before climbing to the left side of my chest. That's when my heart threatens to burst out of my chest for a breathless instant until I realize the guy isn't Nikolai.

I have even found myself unfavorably comparing other

male voices to his. More than once, I will try to relax by listening to music or one of my favorite podcasts and end up woolgathering about how much deeper and raspier his voice sounded in comparison.

Even during my luxurious massage at the upscale spa, I had to refrain from groaning in frustration. There was just no comfort or relaxation in it for me, knowing I would never get to feel his skilled hands on my flesh again.

In a moment of weakness, I succumbed to sniffing the velvet fabric of the dress I wore to the gala. It was an embarrassing attempt to get a fix of the scent of his skin. Even a week after the party, I can't make myself take it to the dry cleaner.

The night after the heist, I opened a deliciously expensive bottle of Cheval Blank wine I lifted years ago from a vapid French businessman who fancied himself in love with me. I was saving the Bordeaux for a special occasion but needed the pick-me-up from drinking something prohibitively expensive. Unfortunately, the alcohol only made me crave the taste of Nikolai's lips more.

I have conceded my defeat. Nik may be out of sight, but keeping him out of my mind is virtually impossible. His hold over me remains irresistible.

With any luck, time and distance from him and our moment of passion will eventually allow me to think of that fateful night as just an exquisite memory of a lovely summer evening.

In the meantime, I must keep myself occupied until I overcome this struggle to move on from our one-night stand.

With the monumental task I have at hand, it shouldn't be too difficult. Any day now, we will receive word from our blackmailer. Once he securely hides or fences the diamond, he will contact us with a new, outrageous demand, coupled with a handful of threats about the endless suffering he will put A.J. through if I go against his wishes.

We are closer than ever to securing the final key to his downfall. If I make it to our appointment with our contact in the next ten minutes, the man's reign of terror will be over before I can tell him *vai a farti fottere, figlio di puttana!*

The woman we are supposed to meet at the coffee shop was extremely hard to track down. Once we managed to find her, it was almost impossible to convince her to talk to us. The poor lady was terrified, dreading doing anything that could anger the horrid man. After the ordeal he put us through the past few months, I understand how she feels.

After a lot of reassuring, cajoling, and begging, we convinced her to speak to us. Her name is Camilla, and she was the *stronzo*'s secretary for a period over two decades ago. I can only imagine the horrors she experienced during her time in his employ.

If anyone can help us with the last puzzle piece, it is Camilla. Her assistance will guarantee we get our hands on the almost fabled proof of the villain's sin. With it, we will have the leverage we need to turn the tables on him.

I pull up to the block of our meeting place and miraculously spot an empty parking spot. It can only be a sign from above that our luck is about to change.

Quickly, I park my car, grab my purse from the passenger's seat, and exit the vehicle, my hands shaking with anticipation.

The alluring scent of freshly brewed coffee beckons me to the shop around the corner, where A.J. awaits me, likely even more excited than me. As bad as I have it with the *stronzo*, she has it much worse.

I walk towards the cafe, glancing at my reflection in the

window of a boutique. I must ensure that I look like a normal, trustworthy person to Camilla. The last thing we need is to spook her.

For a split second, I glimpse the man of my daydreams inside a dark SUV parked across the street. My heart lurches in my chest, and I spin on my heels to stare at the vehicle. Its heavily tinted windows are impenetrable, raised to the top.

Here I go again—daydreaming. Now is not the time for silly distractions. I turn around and resume walking towards our agreed-upon meeting spot. I run my hands over my skirt, nervously smoothing away a nonexistent wrinkle. The soft feel of the lush silk soothes my frazzled nerves.

As I approach the corner of the street block, I'm suddenly overcome by a deep feeling of unease. Just nerves, I'm sure. This is a huge deal for A.J. and me. Everything we have been working towards for almost a year has led to today. Anyone would be nervous.

Behind me, two sets of footsteps hit the pavement in rhythm with my heels click-clacking down the sidewalk.

Alarm bells ring in my head. My first instinct is to dismiss this perceived threat as mere paranoia, but my sense of self-preservation and professional experience warn me against doing so. There's no harm in staying alert and making sure there's no cause for concern. God knows the *stronzo* is capable of anything.

Still, it would be silly to let it rattle me. It's probably nothing. I should keep a cool head and remain calm. This is a busy, public street, after all. Not even the *stronzo* would risk causing a scene by hurting me out in the open like this.

I plaster an aloof smile on my face before glancing at my reflection in the windows of the shops I am passing, pretending to fix my hair. My eyes immediately land on two freakishly tall, burly men, wholly clad in black.

Fuck. There's no question—they are following me. Closely.

The one on the left has a long, aquiline nose on his face, framed by longish, wavy black hair. He is at least eight inches taller than me and probably a hundred pounds heavier. As he marches down the sidewalk, the unmistakable bulge of a firearm under his suit jacket is hard to miss.

Somehow, his colleague on the right is even scarier. His hair is cropped short, military-style, and he sports a long, uneven scar that crosses his face from his left eye to the corner of his mouth. He is wearing a black earpiece that matches the color of his dark attire.

He is dressed to kill. Possibly literally.

I quickly look away from the hulking, scarred man, accidentally making eye contact with his raven-haired brother-in-arms. His eyes narrow as mine widen, and I gasp. I take off running, abandoning all pretense of obliviousness.

The two men shout something unintelligible in a language I don't recognize, chasing after me.

The physicality of my job ensures I'm very agile and quick on my feet. Under normal circumstances, I'm confident I could've lost two burly men dressed in restrictive suits in the crowd.

Regrettably, I didn't expect having to run for my life this morning when choosing what to wear. I was only concerned with looking my best and staying cool in this eighty-degree weather. As a result, they shorten the distance between their terrifying hands and me as I sprint down the pathway, wobbling in my six-inch tall strappy Louboutin sandals.

The two thugs will snatch me if I fall on my face. I wish I could kick off my impractical shoes and continue my dash barefoot, but the leather straps are tightly buckled around my ankles.

Diamond Don

So I calculate my options, yelling at people to move out of my way and shoving innocent bystanders and any loose objects I can get my hands on at my followers as I race down the sidewalk.

A little out of breath, I look over my shoulder again. My despair grows when I realize they are almost close enough to grab me.

As I round the street corner, my right ankle twists painfully, and I lose my balance for a second. I right myself immediately, but it's too late. The black-haired man grasps my hair, violently pulling me close to him.

"*Suchka*," he growls. His lip is bleeding, a crimson line running down his chin. One of the objects I sent flying his way must have damaged his scary face.

He holds me tight in his grasp, tugging my hair hard as I fight him as hard as I can. His colleague approaches me, holding a white handkerchief and aiming at my face.

Panicked, I catch the first whiffs of the recognizable scent. Chloroform.

With renewed enthusiasm powered by my terror, I kick and elbow the men as hard as possible, but it's useless. They hold me firmly in place, not even straining themselves to subdue my efforts.

The scarred one gets closer, and fear like I have never known before boils over inside me. My chances of escape or survival are drastically reduced if they render me unconscious or take me to a separate location, and my odds of evading them seem nonexistent at the moment.

Turning my head, I bite down hard on the dark-haired man's arm, detecting the disgusting, metallic taste of his blood. He yells in fury, yanking me away from his arm by my hair. His fist sharply connects against my temple, sending my head reeling back.

"What the fuck are you waiting for? Do it *now*," he says, scolding his scarred counterpart.

Still dazed by his blow, I barely have a second to try to resist them any further before the overpowering chemical smell invades my nostrils and burns my throat as they cover my face with the chloroform-soaked cloth.

I don't have a chance to do anything but despair as the unrelenting darkness overtakes me.

9

KAT

I wake up with a start.

Once my eyes flash open, I can't suppress a groan. My head hurts like hell, courtesy of my abductors' idea of a sleep aid. The sunlight coming from the windows across the room makes the pounding ache even worse, so I shut my eyes again.

The unbearable feeling in my head reminds me of the morning after A.J. and I went on a last-minute girls' trip to Mexico. There, she decided it would be a good idea to play a game she called Margarita Pong. We had a great time, but the price paid for it the following day wasn't worth it.

My current headache is just like that, except a thousand times worse.

Somehow, I open my eyes again. The natural light streaming from the large windows still bothers me, but I make myself bear it. I can't afford the sweet oblivion of darkness or sleep.

The room's air conditioner is a welcome change from the sweltering heat outside, at least.

I suppose I ought to count my small blessings. Honestly, I should feel grateful for the excruciating pain in my head because it means I'm still alive. Even better, I'm not even unconscious anymore.

I wonder how long I was out. It was early afternoon when the two burly men captured me. My current view of the windows shows the sun is just about to set, which means I was unconscious for hours.

The idea of being at the mercy of those two for so long—wholly vulnerable and under their control—makes me shiver in disgust. Right now, I don't have the strength to let myself think about all the horrifying things they might have done to me while I was knocked out.

I know I'm lucky even to wake up at all. They could have easily killed me and disposed of my body during the multiple hours I was helpless and unconscious. I must make the best of this so-called luck, which means staying focused instead of stupidly worrying about things outside my control. I'm not safe yet. If I want to survive my present situation, then I have to concentrate on finding a way out of here—wherever that is.

I look around the room as I try to recalibrate my senses and calm my mind. While I slept, I was brought to a large chamber. It is very sparsely furnished, containing only the immense bed I have been placed on. It is a stretch to call this room a bedroom, but I guess the term is technically correct since it is a room with a bed. The large piece of furniture is covered by clean, white cotton sheets that softly graze against my skin as I move atop them.

I attempt to sit up and realize right as I do that my ankles and wrists are securely tied to the bed frame.

Not great. Definitely not ideal. Still, I won't lose heart.

Contorting my body, I manage to shake off the sheets

and uncover just enough of my extremities to glimpse at my restraints. They seem to be made of soft, brown leather. I test their strength and resilience, pulling and twisting them as much and as far as they allow me. No matter how hard I tug or how wildly I contort myself, I cannot slip out of them or break free. I stretch my arms and legs as much as possible, but the cuffs' confinement doesn't grant me the range of movement I need to use my fingers or mouth to pry them off my body.

With a sigh, I concede defeat for the time being. I will have to concentrate my efforts on something else since escaping my confinement on my own seems unlikely.

I turn my attention to my surroundings. The almost empty bedroom is cavernously large. The cream color of its walls makes it seem even more spacious, as do the expansive windows that face the bed from the opposite side of the chamber. I spot only one exit, a wood-paneled door to my left. There are two other doors to my right, but they were left ajar, and I can tell they lead to a bathroom and a walk-in closet. I doubt there are any accessible exits in either.

Confined to the bed, I can't see much through the glass panels. All I have is a stunning view of the clear, cloudless sky, blanketed in the golden and orange hues of the setting sun. My limited field of vision must indicate that I am in one of the top floors of a high-rise building.

Unfortunately, I don't see anything else of value—such as a recognizable skyline or a known landmark—so I can't pinpoint my current location.

Nonetheless, small details around the room and my previous realization of the building and its location make it obvious that I may be in a luxurious penthouse. After all, it is an immense bedroom with *Carrara* marble floors and a view that has to be worth millions.

Whoever sent those two thugs after me is very wealthy, which doesn't bode well for me.

Clearly, my abduction wasn't a random act of violence, and my actual kidnapper must be a rich bastard if they can afford a room like this as my cell. They are also bold as hell, daring to take a woman in broad daylight in one of downtown's busiest neighborhoods.

Who am I kidding? There is no point in pretending I have any doubts regarding my abductor's identity. I am painfully aware there is only a man with the means and the motive to do such a thing.

For so long, I feared the day would come when the *stronzo* would decide A.J. and I had served our purposes. It makes sense that it's happening right after I delivered to him the Flame of Mir, one of the most precious prizes any man could ever possess. It's also possible he has learned of our plan to destroy him.

Regardless, in the end, his reasons for taking me don't matter at all. One way or the other, he has decided to escalate our already precarious situation to an alarming degree. It just sucks that it happens to be right when we are close to finally taking him down.

I pray A.J. hasn't been abducted as well. If she has escaped the man, then not all hope is lost. With any luck, she will follow through with our plan without me. Now more than ever, we are officially fresh out of options.

Maybe A.J. managed to get the information we needed from Camilla. I hope they are safe and sound. Not for just my sake. Whatever hell the Italian has planned for me, it won't be as terrible as the torture he will unleash on A.J. if he sets out to punish her. He never got over the insult of her daring to steal from him. I was merely a useful pawn in his hands, while A.J. was the sole focus of his contempt.

I have to believe A.J. is fine. Otherwise, I won't be able to deal with whatever the villain has in store for me. My only chance of escaping this room alive is to keep a cool head. I must hold on to the hope that A.J. will succeed in our quest and this nightmare will end soon.

I force myself to take a deep, calming breath. Everything will be just fine. This whole kidnapping situation is just a bump in our road to victory. A.J. and I will laugh about it one day as we brag to all our friends about our daring feat.

I can handle it—I *will* handle it. Under no circumstance will I give the *stronzo* the satisfaction of seeing me even break a sweat.

The skies turn a deeper shade of orange through the grand windows as I mentally run through multiple scenarios, wondering what will happen next.

A rattling sound startles me, and I almost jump out of my skin. It's coming from the door at my left. I turn to face it as much as my restraints allow me.

The unmistakable sound of a key being inserted into the lock makes my heart beat a mile per minute. The doorknob turns and I stop breathing.

I suppose I should be flattered that the horrid man thinks so highly of my skills that he felt the need to lock the room's only entrance point in addition to tying me down.

With a mix of both dread and anticipation, I don't move even a muscle as the door opens.

My kidnapper enters the room, and I feel as if my thundering heart halts to a sudden, brusque stop inside my chest.

I gasp, loudly. I might faint for the first time in my life.

Nik stands in front of me, as devastatingly handsome as I remembered him.

Shocked, I struggle to believe my own eyes. I can't move, can't speak, or even breath.

The man I have fantasized about for the past week gives me a cruel smirk. It doesn't reach his beautiful, dark eyes, staring at me with undisguised contempt.

"Miss me?"

10

NIK

I SHOULD BE HAVING a great time. And yet, I'm having a terrible time.

Seeing Kat again is pure bliss but also sheer torture.

I want to kill her. I need to kiss her.

Will her maddening hold over me ever end? Or at least lessen?

I'm incredibly disappointed with myself. The woman stole my most prized possession and maybe even played a hand in my best friend's murder. But somehow, I still want her just as much as before.

Last week was a blur for me. Moments after I learned of Maxim's death, my men and the Metropolitan Museum's security staff informed me that my priceless red diamond was missing.

My recollection of the aftermath—and the commotion that followed both events—is uncharacteristically dim. I suppose I was too numb and shocked then to do anything beyond go through the motions of doing what I had to do— as Maxim's next-of-kin, sole proprietor of the Flame of Mir, and the *bratva*'s *pakhan*.

The time to grieve and fully surrender to my rage will come. For the time being I must set my emotions aside and perform my duties to the best of my ability. Just like the theft of the Flame of Mir, Kat is a complication I just can't afford. Maxim is dead—now more than ever, the *bratva* and I must not appear weak or unfocused.

It's unfortunate for me that, from the first moment I saw Kat, my carefully cultivated command over my emotions left me high and dry. She makes it impossible for me to be my usual collected, rational self. Instead, she turns me into a reckless, tempestuous fool.

I was surprised—to say the least—when a day after that eventful night, my longtime friend, Lucien Wroth, approached me with the unexpected news of Kat's involvement in the theft of the jewel.

Lucien is a very well-connected man. Now and then, I wear him down and convince him to work for me as my counselor—my *sovietnik*—for a period. But he never holds the position for too long. Inevitably, time after time, he comes to the conclusion that being his own boss suits him best.

My friend Lucien is a consultant of sorts. Many refer to him as the kingmaker, but he hates the moniker and strongly discourages people from using it.

He works in a very peculiar field and I'm lucky that he shares his expertise and wealth of information with me whenever possible.

Upon learning of Maxim's demise and the diamond's disappearance, Lucien used his vast network to try to help me. His search hasn't yet yielded anything of value regarding Maxim's assassination, but he provided me with the identity of the diamond thief.

I was profoundly shocked to learn that the woman who

gave me the most mind-blowing sexual experience of my life was the culprit.

Unfortunately, I have no doubts about it. Lucien's investigation shows that the museum's security systems were tempered with by a very unique and specific—and, therefore, easily identifiable—electronic device.

His contacts named the apparatus's creator, who apparently has an infamous reputation in certain criminal circles. The woman, known as A.J. Michaels, is bosom buddies with Katherine Devereaux, con woman and thief extraordinaire —or Kat, as her friends call her.

That name, of course, didn't mean anything to me at first. But once I saw her picture in the dossier Lucien prepared for me, I knew she was one and the same with the irresistible girl fucked at the gala.

There are no words to describe the all-consuming rage and betrayal I felt when I learned her identity.

Lucien's investigation was extensive. He isn't a man to leave any stone unturned. Once he suspected Kat was behind the gemstone's disappearance, he deep-dived into her life, pinpointing her exact whereabouts before and after her appearance at the party.

That is why I now have piles and piles of compelling proof of Kat's role in the diamond's theft. Suffice it to say that Lucien's military contacts are unrivaled, and Big Brother is always watching.

In the days following this reveal, I tried to carry on as usual, attempting to fulfill my obligations as well as I ever have. Still, inside, I was thinking of Kat nonstop.

At first, my mind was assaulted by the pleasant memories of our heated encounter and my anger at her deceitfulness.

My rage won once Lucien admitted he didn't know for

sure whether Kat had played any role in Maxim's untimely death.

I was disgusted with myself. My oldest friend lay cold and dead somewhere, while I was busy fantasizing about the feel of her soft flesh, the wet heat of her sex, and the rich blue color of her eyes. But no more—I wouldn't allow myself to be blinded by the spell she cast on me any longer.

So, I set out to track her down. It was astonishingly easy, as I knew it would be once I learned her name.

I tasked my men with discreetly tailing her from a safe distance. Day after day, they turned in pictures, videos and reports of her activities. I studied her in the many photographs and was glad to realize I felt nothing for her but contempt. Since the party, she has been happily enjoying herself, living a life of vapid luxury and leisure, while her actions have turned my life upside down.

I gave the order for her capture then. Relieved that my feelings towards her were finally acceptably rational, I felt ready to deal with her at last. I was also eager to retrieve my diamond. The Flame of Mir might be nothing but a bauble to her, but it holds sentimental value to me.

I was even eager to show her the consequences of fucking with me as deliberately as she had. Besides, it was my responsibility to find out if she is connected to Maxim's murder. It would be incredibly dumb to set out to avenge his death without a clear picture of what really went down on the night of the party.

I now know I have been an idiot.

I am an even bigger fool than I first assumed. Because I should have known better. There are no acceptable excuses for my complete disregard of her effect on me.

All along, I was perfectly aware that she has the power to

bring me to my knees. All this time, I knew I can't think straight when her eyes lock with mine. Even now, I worry I won't be able to stop myself from joining her in bed.

She took from me my most precious possession. It is possible—perhaps even likely—that she is involved in the cold-blooded murder of my dearest friend. But when I walked into the room and saw her big, beautiful, deep blue eyes, I was a goner.

Again.

On the night of the party, I worried I couldn't trust her. I even acknowledged I have no room for a woman in my life, especially one who affects me as much as she does. I can't afford the weakness or the distraction.

All my misgivings and fears about her are now confirmed. Still, I struggle to care about any of that right now.

"Miss me?" I ask her, breaking the silence between us. Her expression displays a mix of horror and fear, and it pleases me.

I missed her. Until now, I thought I didn't, believing her deceit had soured the longing and attraction I felt for her. I assumed I had realized at last that I am better off without her.

But I was an idiot. After a week apart, merely seeing Kat in person brings me a lot of relief. It's almost as if I have been painfully holding in a breath the entire time we were apart. But now that we are in the same room, I can let it go, exhaling and allowing the tension I have been carrying on my shoulders to leave my body.

"Nikolai, what's going on? What are you doing here? What am *I* doing here?"

I'm not sure what I expected her to say, but I feel too

emotionally raw to deal with her games. If she thinks that playing dumb or a damsel in distress will save her, then I have overestimated her.

"Isn't it obvious? You took something of mine, so I took you."

11

NIK

Kat seems even more confused and hurt than when I first walked into the room. She must be a very skilled actress to manage the stunt she pulled on me successfully, but I am still impressed.

"What are you talking about? I took something from you? I have no idea what you mean—" she says, stopping mid-sentence. A small gasp escapes her lips, and her big blue eyes widen.

"*No.*" She shakes her head in horror.

"*Yes,*" I say with a grin.

"It can't be."

"And yet, here we are." I gesture to the bed where she is restrained.

She dramatically flops back on it, closing her eyes tightly shut.

"This can't be happening to me," she says, groaning.

"I assure you, it is."

Kat lies down on the bed for a moment, staring at the ceiling and shaking her head in what I assume is denial. She suddenly repositions herself, sitting up as much as she can within the constraints of her restraints, which isn't much at all. Narrowing her eyes, she studies me with suspicion.

"Just who *are* you, exactly?"

I can't hold back a smirk. "Come on now, Kat. The game is over. You can drop the charade now. We both know you know who I am. Why else would you have set out to con me?"

She gasps at my casual mention of her name.

"That's right, Ms. Devereaux. You no longer have me at a disadvantage. I'm now very familiar with who you are and what you do. It was a little silly to deny me your name when you allowed me to get to know you so thoroughly, don't you think?"

The maddening woman has the nerve to shoot me an aggravated look.

"Look, Nikolai—if that's even your real name—" she says, looking down her nose at me.

My amused grin grows bigger, and I cover the distance between us, stopping next to the enormous bed. I smile at her as she glares at me.

"That's fucking precious coming from you. *I* am not the one who conned you. *I* am not the who crashed a party to commit grand larceny. *I* did not steal from you the most valuable diamond in the world. *I* do not go out of my way to seduce unsuspecting men into helping me get away with the heist of the century and maybe even murder."

"Whoa, whoa, now wait just a minute," she says. "First of all, don't flatter yourself. I did not set out to seduce you. *You* came onto *me*. Very strongly, too, if I recall correctly. You approached me. You wouldn't let me leave, though God knows I tried. I'd even go as far as to say you just wouldn't be dissuaded."

"I don't remember you putting up too much of a fight. Or

any fight at all, actually," I say. "I *do* remember you begging me to kiss you, though. And, of course, how could I forget? I specifically recall you stripping your clothes for me and grinding on my lap moments before you couldn't stop yourself from coming around my—"

Kat grabs one of the pillows from the bed and attempts to hit me in the face with it. The leather cuffs make her actions awkward and considerably reduce her speed, so I see the move coming from a mile away. I sidestep and grab the offending pillow, throwing it far away where she can't reach it.

"*You*," she says, grunting with frustration as her face blushes deep with emotion. "I may not know all I should about who you are, but I do know you are the most insufferable, overly confident asshole I have ever met."

"I may be an asshole, I'll give you that. You won't get any argument from me on that one. But overly confident? Really, Kat. You and I both know that, if anything, I'm being too modest." I wink at her. "But we are getting off track. I brought you here today for a complete different reason, as you know very well."

"And where exactly is *here*, Nik?"

"This is my place."

"Is that supposed to mean anything to me?"

"I'd think that a world-class con woman like yourself would have done a better job researching her mark."

Temptingly rising and lowering, her chest expands when she sighs heavily. Against my better judgment, I stare at her low-cut blouse, entranced by the sight of her breasts moving with her forced intake of breath. I force myself to look away before it is too late.

"Again, I have no idea who you are. Besides a self-righteous, arrogant prick, of course," she says.

"Cute. But save your breath, Kat. I'm not buying it at all. You know all about me."

"I gather you are very impressed with your likely underserved sense of self-importance, but I promise you I am not. I have no idea who you are. Only that you are an entitled prick, of course."

It's my turn to sigh, shaking my head.

"Honestly, Kat. Why even bother with this little game of yours at this point? I'd be more impressed if you admitted to the truth. Knowing who I am and what I do, you still set out to steal from me. True, in the end, I did catch you red-handed. But still, that took some nerve."

She rolls her eyes. "Look, I get it—you think I'm messing with you. But I have no idea who you are besides knowing your alleged first name and that you must be extremely rich to own something like the Flame of Mir. As far as anyone knows, the diamond was owned by an anonymous billionaire. All I was told when I took the job was that I had to take the jewel from The Metropolitan Museum during the opening gala for its newest exhibition. That's it."

"Do you honestly expect me to believe that you took a job so risky and high-profile as this one with that little information? And to think you called me overly confident." I scoff.

"Believe what you will. It's the truth." She shrugs.

I study her. Kat sports a deadpan expression with a hint of exhaustion. Before I can stop myself, something suspiciously similar to guilt grows in my chest. I had her drugged and abducted, and then I had her locked up and tied down.

Still, I must stay vigilant with this woman. I can't trust my instincts when she is involved, and she has proven to be untrustworthy. It doesn't matter that I can't shake the feeling that she might be telling the truth.

"Besides," she says, unprompted, "there were some special, extenuating circumstances."

I wait for Kat to continue, but she remains silent.

"Care to elaborate?" I ask.

"No, not really."

"I don't think you fully understand the seriousness of your situation, Kat."

"No, I do. I get it, trust me. The leather restraints kind of give away how seriously fucked I am. But that's all I'll say about it."

"If there is something—anything—that you can think of that would make you look better in this situation, why not tell me?"

"I have my reasons."

Brimming with frustration, I find myself sighing again. I don't know what to make of her. Or what to do with her, for that matter. I came into this room prepared to punish the woman for her crime against me, but now, looking at her, I can't imagine carrying out the tortures I planned for the little thief.

"Is your friend A.J. one of those reasons? Because I already know she had a hand in this whole thing."

She sharply turns to face me as far as the cuffs allow her. She gives me the darkest, most serious look I have ever seen on her face. That's how I know I have found her soft spot.

"Do *not* bring her into this, Nikolai. Whatever issues you have with me, you will leave her alone."

I could point out to her that there is nothing she can do in her current situation to stop me from going after A.J. Michaels. But somehow, I don't have the heart to threaten her beloved friend, even if emptily, while Kat stares up at me with the big, blue eyes that have completely captivated me.

"I hope I won't have cause to even think about A.J. ever

again, Kat, because I'm counting on the two of us coming to an understanding."

Kat slowly eyes the bed on which she has been placed and the leather cuffs that confine her to it. All at once, she seems to become intensely aware of the fact that she has been forcefully tied to a large bed by a man who has been sexually drawn to her from the start.

"What kind of understanding?" She sounds nervous, and a little guarded.

"Not *that* kind of understanding, Kat. Unless you ask me very, very nicely, of course."

Kat scoffs.

"I wouldn't hold my breath, Nikolai. Or whatever your real name is."

"My name *is* Nikolai. I had no reason to lie to you about it. I'm Nikolai Stefanovich, as I'm sure you already know."

Kat gasps loudly, staring at me wide-eyed. She even retreats from me slightly.

"I see that my reputation precedes me."

"Nikolai, you have to believe me. I had no idea. If I had known who you were, I would have never, ever—"

"Stolen my most valuable possession and assisted with my best friend's murder?"

"Wait, *what*? What the hell are you talking about? I may have taken the diamond, but I did not kill anyone. Ever. I don't even know what you are talking about."

I carefully study her reaction to my statement. She looks flushed and shocked as she refutes my accusation.

"On the night you took the diamond—the same night we first met—my oldest friend, Maxim, was murdered. You wouldn't happen to have anything to do with that, would you, Kat? It is one hell of a coincidence that you pulled your stunt on the same night he was assassinated."

"I would never—you must believe me. If you have looked me up, then you know I had nothing to do with it. I'm strictly white-collar. Everyone who knows me—or knows of me—will tell you that."

I gathered as much during the past week. She is incredibly notorious as a skilled con woman and thief, but her hands are clean of blood as far as anyone knows. It isn't much of a guarantee of anything, but it's at least more than my desire to believe her.

"Say I am willing to believe you weren't involved in my friend's murder," I say. "You still have stolen something invaluable from me. Surely you understand I can't just let that go."

"Nikolai, trust me—if I could take it back, I would. I'd have never taken your diamond if I had known it belonged to you. As a rule of thumb, I try my best to avoid incurring the wrath of the *bratva* if it can be avoided."

"And yet, you did, Kat. Which brings us back to why we are here. For starters, I must insist you give me back the diamond."

"I would if I could. I mean it. Unfortunately, I'm afraid that's impossible. It's out of my hands."

"Well, get it back, then. That's my first requirement for our little understanding, Kat."

"Like I said, I just can't. It's not going to happen. You're going to have to pick something else." She shrugs.

"*Pick something else*? There's nothing else! For someone who claims not to want to incur my wrath, you're doing a hell of a good job pissing me off. Do I need to remind you I decide what happens to you?"

"No need. The fact that I'm currently tied down to a bed really drives your point home. Trust me. But it doesn't change anything. I can't give you what I don't have, and I don't have your diamond. It's truly gone, and I can't get it back."

"Why the hell not?"

"I can't contact the person who tasked me with acquiring it. I don't even know if they still have it. For all I know, they might have fenced it by now. Even if I could get a hold of them and they still had it, I couldn't convince them to give it back."

Kat's tone is very matter-of-fact, as if I should just make my peace with the fact that my rare red diamond—worth over a quarter billion dollars—is gone forever. Simply because she says so. If anyone else told me such nonsense, I would kill them just out of spite.

"Don't play games with me, Katherine."

"I'm not. I'm just being honest with you. There's no way to get it back."

"Why don't you reach out to this mysterious person to set up a meeting and let me handle the rest?"

"You are not listening. There is no 'handling' anything. It's gone. I can't contact them, and you must accept that."

In a spurt of uncontrolled anger, I grab her by the neck with my left hand.

"Are you out of your goddamn mind? I'm not *accepting* anything. This isn't some trinket you shoplifted from Tiffany's, and I'm not your average fucking Joe. You *will* fix your mess, or I will make you regret the day you crossed my path."

Kat merely levels an unbothered look at me. "I already do. You can punish me however you see fit. It still won't change the facts. I can't get it back for you. I am sorry, but it's just not feasible."

Against my better judgment, I admire her bravery. She knows my reputation and what I am capable of, and she is entirely at my mercy. And yet, she doesn't even flinch at my sudden outburst.

Part of me can't help but wonder if that in itself isn't enough evidence that she is telling me the truth. Still, my rational side advises caution. She hasn't proven to me she can be trusted—just the opposite, actually—and I'm tragically prone to unforgivable bouts of wishful thinking when it comes to this woman.

I release her and step away, walking to the windows to collect myself. Whether it is rage or passion, I don't seem to control myself when I'm around her. I can't afford such emotional explosions right now. I must keep a cool head.

I stare blankly ahead through the glass panes as the sun slips behind the horizon. It takes me a while to feel ready to speak again. I turn to face her.

"We can revisit this issue at a later date. For now, we will move on to the next part of our understanding. You are going to help me catch Maxim's murderer."

12

KAT

I COULD NEVER HAVE GUESSED my day would end like this.

Over the past week, there were countless instances when I was too weak to stop fantasizing about Nik, but I never imagined I would end up tied to his bed, completely at his mercy.

Well, that's not true.

After all, I had longed for such an enticing scenario on more than one occasion. But the context and circumstances of my daydream were much, much different.

For starters, in my mind, my fantasy man was nothing but the sexy-as-hell, passionate lover I had assumed he was. He was just Nik.

No last name, no colorful background.

I didn't expect him to be my latest mark, the owner of the Flame of Mir.

I most certainly never thought he could be Nikolai Stefanovich, the Russian *bratva*'s *pakhan*.

I'm old enough to know that things are never so bad that they can't get worse. I thought my troubles with the *stronzo* were the worst thing that could ever happen to me. But my life has just become much more complicated.

There are now not one, but two mafia bosses who believe they own me.

And although I have always known that I'm fully capable of turning the tables on the Italian mobster if given half the chance, I'm not foolish enough to believe the same about Nikolai.

The Russian man inspires fear in the likes of men I've learned to dread. Even cutthroat evil-doers like the *stronzo* wouldn't dare get on the *pakhan*'s bad side.

And I've brazenly taken from him his most prized possession.

And, of course, as I know very well, when it rains, it pours. Not only is he aware of the crime I've committed against him, but he also thinks I'm involved with his best friend's murder for some reason.

Now I'm forced to sit before him, utterly helpless in the lion's own den. Whatever distress I've felt before concerning the *stronzo* pales in comparison to the wave of panic that shakes me when I think of the horrors Nikolai is capable of unleashing on me.

More than anything else in the world, I despise feeling helpless. Throughout my twenty-something years on this planet, I've been many things. An orphan. A petty thief. A juvenile delinquent. But throughout it all, I was never a victim.

True, eventually, I got out of the system and found a way to pursue a new, better life.

But I've never thought of myself as a victim. Even during the darkest periods of my younger years, I've always kept fighting and taking action. I've always strived to improve my circumstances, and I've succeeded magnificently.

As my skills grew, so did my power. I haven't felt genuinely helpless or hopeless in many, many years.

Until now.

Even during the worst days of our struggle against the *stronzo*, I've always known we were bound to catch a break eventually. And I've been confident in my ability to seize the opportunity when it presented itself. Maybe I haven't always been sure of the how or the when, but I've always felt I could defeat the Italian boss.

I even took care to account for the worst-case scenario of my untimely demise. If the man were to order my execution, then I'd have a plan in place to make sure he would be implicated in my assassination.

One way or the other, he was going down. I was just hoping it would be sooner rather than later and that A.J. and I would live long enough to see it come to fruition.

Now, with Nikolai, I feel truly at a loss. I hate even thinking about it, but I fear I might be as close to being helpless as I was back in my teenage years.

Still, I know I retain some of my power. I'll never be entirely helpless as long as I have ways to improve my circumstances and save myself. I know I have options. Unfortunately, not many, and not particularly good ones, either. But it's something.

Ultimately, that's what leads me to entertain this proposal of his—that I should help him catch the culprit behind his friend's mysterious murder.

Turning to face me from across the large room by the expansive windows, he decrees, "You are going to help me catch Maxim's murderer."

Normally, I would have laughed at any man who presumed to tell me what to do. But even I know that would be unwise right now. Men like Nikolai—if one can even say there are men like Nikolai—are not used to being laughed at. They are also not likely to appreciate it, and I realize that not antagonizing him can only improve my situation, giving me more power.

Besides, my current options are slim. I'm a practical woman. If Nikolai feels inclined to offer me an acceptable arrangement that will eventually lead to my debt to him being repaid, then I will gladly take it. It certainly isn't anything I'm not used to, and it most definitely beats being tortured or killed. I'll be glad if he doesn't choose to make an example out of me as a warning to anyone who dares to even think of crossing him.

So, instead of ridiculing him for having the nerve to issue me a command, I say, "What's in it for me?"

Nikolai shoots me a disbelieving look.

"For starters, I would let you remain in the world of the living. I might even be persuaded not to punish you too much. I'd hate to mark that beautiful skin of yours if I don't have to," he says in a measured tone, his gaze slowly roaming over my body. The knowing look in his eyes tells me he remembers every inch of me, making me feel almost naked, even while fully covered by his Egyptian cotton bed linen.

"You wouldn't punish me too much? Does that mean you would still punish me?"

I pull the sheets up to my chin, and his expression becomes amused.

"Well, you can't expect me to let you get away with the stunt you pulled on me completely unscathed. I have a reputation to protect, you know. At the very least, I owe you a good spanking. I don't know that I would call it a punishment. I have a feeling you would enjoy it."

God help me. I do, too. The mere mental image of

Nikolai bending me over his knee and slapping my bare ass with his large, calloused palm makes me start to grow wet.

I must remain in charge of myself. I can't let my emotions take control of me. My survival depends on my ability to stay focused.

"I thought you said this arrangement of yours wasn't of that kind, Nikolai. Sex is not on the table."

"Agreed," he says, too quickly for my taste. It's one thing for me to tell him sex is a no-go, but for him to so easily turn it down? I don't like that one bit. "We'll keep it strictly professional. It's better off this way."

I force myself to concentrate on the important stuff—like hashing out the details of our agreement—instead of licking the wounds to my ego.

"Glad we are on the same page," I say in my best aloof tone. "Just to be clear—do you give me your word that if I help you hunt down whoever is behind your friend's death, you will forget this whole thing with the diamond ever happened and let me go? No other repercussions or retributions."

"Forget is a strong word, Kat. And I'm not quite ready to accept that the Flame is truly out of reach forever, as you claim to believe. But I do agree with everything else you said in general terms. If you earnestly assist me to the best of your abilities, I'll forgive you for the theft."

"Very well. That's good enough for now, I guess. I have one more question, though. How the hell am I supposed to help you catch a murderer?"

"We can discuss the details later once you've given me your word that you'll work for me. For now, all I'll say is that I know who is behind Maxim's death. Unfortunately, I can't just accuse this man without some pretty damning evidence. Not without risking a truly regrettable amount of even more death and bloodshed, at least."

"I don't suppose you would tell me who this suspect of yours is? I can't imagine there are many men who would cause you to hesitate before striking. No offense, but from what I've heard about you and what I've experienced firsthand, you seem to be the kind of guy who will shoot first and ask questions later."

He grins.

"In due time, I'll fill you in. All you need to know right now is that I'm hoping you will be able to go certain places and ask certain questions that I can't. You are charming and famously good at what you do. Doors will open to you."

I roll my eyes. "Be still, my heart."

Nik smiles again, all charm.

"It makes you the perfect woman for the job."

"Lucky me," I say sarcastically. "And lucky you, I guess, that the 'perfect woman for the job' happened to be someone you could bully into doing your bidding."

"Lucky me?" Nikolai roars, marching over to me until he is so close I feel his warm breath on my face as he leans over to scold me. "My best friend was murdered in cold blood. A diamond worth over a quarter billion dollars with personal value to me was taken by a woman I naively thought was just as attracted to me as I was to her. You should be thanking your lucky stars that I'm showing you mercy. Any other man in my position would've made you wish you had never been born. Keep pushing me, and I might change my mind and do just that."

I stare up at him in awe of his passionate outburst. I'm in awe of my stupidity, too. Because even as he threatens to torture me in ways I can't even imagine, I can't stop thinking he is the most magnificent man I've ever met.

I suppose it was unavoidable that I would be attracted to him. He is, after all, a ridiculously powerful man, and I revere power above almost all else. I sensed it in him somehow, even when I didn't know his true identity.

I stretch out my hand to touch his chest over his shirt in an attempt to calm him down as he continues to stare at me angrily,

"If you kill me," I say in my most soothing tone, "then you'll have to content yourself with having only the *second*-best woman for the job helping you."

He seems shocked at my words for a second. I guess not many people talk back at him when he loses his temper like he just did. After a moment, I see his lips twitch in what I hope is amusement.

He straightens himself, running a hand through his luscious, dark hair. I'm pretty sure I see him shake his head, but the movement is so tiny I'm not confident I didn't just imagine it.

"Does that mean you will agree to my terms?"

"Well, I have one last question."

"You said that already, and then you asked me five more questions."

"Well, I mean it this time. I need to know one more thing. From what I gathered from the very little you told me, the man we are going after is very dangerous."

"Correct," Nikolai says, his gaze sharp and focused on me.

"It also sounds like I'll be risking my neck on the front line. And considering you are who you are, I'm going to take a wild guess and say this guy also has mafia ties. No offense, but my history with mafia men hasn't been the best, so I have to ask—should I be concerned for myself? Will he be able to hurt me in any way?"

Nikolai freezes for a second before frowning.

"Over my dead body," he says in a grave tone, sounding insulted I had even asked. "Here's something you should know about me, Kat. I take very good care of the people who work for me. You may have come to my service through unconventional ways, but that doesn't mean I won't take my responsibility towards you very seriously. I'm not in the business of having others—especially women—do my dirty work for me."

His eyes burn into mine, and I feel shaken to my core. He's the most delicious man I have ever encountered, but fate has a cruel sense of humor, so I can't have him.

"Okay," I say at last, once I realize I've been staring at him without uttering a word. "Thanks, I think. I'm glad we got that sorted out. I wouldn't agree to your terms if it meant I was just jumping from the frying pan and into the fire."

"Let me make something perfectly clear to you, Kat. That bastard is not taking anyone else from me. As long as you stick to our understanding, you're under my protection," Nikolai says almost solemnly.

His intensity and confidence in his ability to keep me safe are like a beacon to me. I know I am perfectly capable of taking care of myself, and I thoroughly prize my independence. I certainly don't need Nikolai to look out for me. But there is something positively irresistible about a man fiercely vowing to protect you, especially one who looks as devastating as he does, sounds as sexy as he does, and smells as delicious as he does.

I know this will be a dangerous game. I have to keep my wits about me at all costs, and it is impossible to do so when he stands so close to me. But I'm out of options. First and foremost, I have to look out for myself and seize my best chance of surviving to fight another day.

"Very well, Nikolai. You got yourself a deal. I accept your terms," I say almost ominously, sealing my fate—for better or worse.

13

NIK

I'm glad I have won our battle of wills, but I know the war between us is far from over.

Kat agreed to my demands, but it was far too easy. If I had to guess, I'd say she probably realized I have defeated her for the moment and decided to save her energy for a later fight—one she can win. I have a feeling we will have many, many more battles in the foreseeable future.

Even though I hold her life in my hands, there's no doubt in my mind she will challenge me every step of the way. A strange mix of exhaustion and excitement courses through me just thinking about it. I'm both dreading and looking forward to forcing her into submission over and over again.

Kat is a complication—an unavoidable one since I need her help with my plans for Maxim's murderer. Nonetheless, the woman and the uncontrollable emotional outbursts she provokes in me are an extra problem I must handle.

If only I could ignore the powerful, almost gravitational pull I feel towards her. After all, we are stuck together—for better or for worse.

As far as my plans are concerned, it's most definitely for the worse. There are important, life-and-death matters that demand my full attention. The future of the *bratva* is up in the air as long as the threat of war with a rival group looms ahead. I need my usual laser-focused single-mindedness more than ever.

Instead, even now when this need is fresh on my mind, I find myself standing before her, absorbed by senseless, foolish musings about the most meaningless concerns, such as whether she would still welcome my touch. Or if she's been thinking of me as much as I've been thinking of her since the night we first met.

I know so little about her, but this attraction is hard to resist. The mere sight of her mesmerizing eyes—or the echoes of her sensual voice—is enough to affect me, viscerally bombarding me with memories of that maddening scent of hers, her mouthwatering taste I can still savor in my mouth, and the soft feel of her lips against mine.

On the bright side, at least I'm no longer underestimating the woman and her power over me. Only by being fully aware of it will I be able to prepare myself. If I accept that this temptation will only grow as we work together, then maybe I can try to steel myself against it.

It's not like I have any other options. I didn't miss how secretive she was when I questioned her about her involvement in the Flame of Mir's theft. Kat didn't even bother hiding how unwilling she was to divulge anything that could be of value to me.

I caught the little thief red-handed. She seemed to have an appropriate amount of fear upon learning who I am and what I do for a living. One would think the woman would be eager to share anything that might make her look less guilty, or do anything to earn my favor. Instead, Kat has told me nothing.

Sure, she denied being involved in Maxim's murder. But it's not like I expected her to admit to it in the first place.

I can't ignore all these red flags. By all accounts, Kat is an extremely smart woman with a healthy sense of self-preservation. Surely, if she feels the need to keep the truth from me, it must be even worse than what I already know about her and her participation in this mess.

It would be reckless to trust her at this point. I can't afford the risk. There's too much I don't know, too much she won't tell me. Years of experience indicate that can only mean one thing—Kat must be kept at arm's length.

I learned a long time ago not to give my trust to people who don't deserve it. I know what happens when you let yourself care about those who only care about themselves They destroy you. They make you weak.

It's a lesson I learned thirty years ago. One I will never forget. It was, after all, the only one my parents bothered to teach me.

Now more than ever, I can't be vulnerable. I have to keep my guard up with her.

"Very well, Nikolai. You got yourself a deal. I accept your terms," she says, squaring her shoulders.

"Good girl. You're making the right call, Kat. Since we're on the same team now, let me get you out of these cuffs. They're probably chaffing you by now."

I pull the keys to the restraints out of my pocket and approach her. Kneeling next to the bed, I work on releasing her from the leather straps as efficiently and dispassionately as I can manage.

My fingertips graze the impossibly soft skin on the

inside of her wrists as I unlatch the cuffs. I fully intend to pretend that nothing happened until she inhales sharply.

I glance at her face, my fingers stilling where they rest on her arms.

Her eyes lock with mine, and I'm lost in their deep blue beauty, just like the first time I gazed into them.

I half expect Kat to glance away, breaking our unspoken connection. But she surprises me by inching closer to me. It's a slight, almost imperceptible movement, but I'm so hyper-focused on her that it's impossible for me to miss it. My senses are completely attuned to her—her sounds, her scent, the softness of her skin, the sight of her—desperately trying to make up for all the time lost since the moment we parted.

I should resist her pull. It's a bad idea to give in to this temptation and let this irresistible attraction defeat me. But I can't help it. I can't stop myself from wrapping my hands around her and bringing her even closer. The need to taste her is too overwhelming.

She will probably pull away from me. After all, I had her abducted and restrained against her wishes. Even now, I am bending her to my will. I'm likely her least favorite person in the world right now.

Yet again, she doesn't resist me. Her eyes widen as I inch closer to her, but her only other reaction is a small sigh when we are close enough that I can feel the heat of her body against mine.

She shouldn't want my touch, just like I shouldn't want to touch her. Still, like a couple of moths drawn to a flame, we can't seem to resist this need to be closer and closer to each other, inch by inch.

If she isn't pulling away from me, then she must want me as badly as I want her—even after everything I have put her through today. This realization only makes it harder to resist the urge to be inside her again.

I lean a little closer to her, our gazes still linked. Kat's erratic breaths hit my lips, making me even hungrier to taste her again, to feel her tongue tangle with mine once more.

I'm careful not to make any sudden moves. I don't want to spook her or dispel the magic feeling of this moment. Kat closes her eyes, and I choose to take it as a sign to end the distance between us. But just as I'm about to do so, her hand pushes my chest, stopping me.

The haze dissipates, and over the thundering beats of my heart, Kat clears her throat.

"Nik," she says, but I don't even need her to finish her sentence. I know where this is going, and, for once, I'm happy she had the presence of mind to stop me before things went any further. It shames me, but there's no point in pretending otherwise—I wouldn't have been strong enough to stop my emotions from taking control if she hadn't.

I move away from her to sit on the edge of the bed, my back to her, needing a moment to clear my head.

"Nik, we agreed it would be best to keep things professional between us."

"I know."

"I just think it's important that we keep that in mind. This situation is already complicated, and hot, passionate sex has a way of complicating things even further."

"I know, Kat," I say, harsher than I intended. But I can't have her going on and on about *hot, passionate sex* at this moment. My self-control is almost nonexistent as it is, and I must stop her before she says something that will push me over the edge.

"Well, excuse me for pointing out the obvious, but it

didn't seem like you were keeping that in mind a moment ago. You know, when you were staring at my mouth and leaning over me as I lay here, chained to your freaking bed."

"First of all, this isn't my bed. It's a bed I own, yes, but it isn't really my bed—"

She interrupts me. "Are you seriously going to argue semantics with me right now?"

"Second of all," I say as if she hasn't uttered a word, "if you don't want me coming on to you, how about you stop leading me on?"

"Leading you on?" she says, sputtering. "I did no such thing. I'll have you know I would never. Ever. And I didn't. And I won't—ever."

"You were making eyes at me, scooting closer to me, and sighing while longingly gazing at my mouth."

"You have a very vivid imagination, Nik. Not very gangster of you, I'll say."

I shoot her a pointed look, debating showing her how *gangster* I feel right now.

Ultimately, I decide against it. It would be unwise to do so. I need to be on her good side—so she will help me nail the bastard who killed Maxim. Not because I want her to like me and ask me to fuck her.

"This argument is pointless," I say, instead. "How about this? I'll make you a promise. If you can keep your hands to yourself, I'll do the same." Inwardly, I hope this is a promise I can actually keep.

"Deal," she says, too quickly for my liking.

"Great."

"It won't be a problem."

"Glad to hear it."

"Wonderful. How about you freaking unchain me now?

I'd like to go home." Kat regally crosses her arms while staring me down.

It's an impressive feat, considering that, standing next to the bed she is lying on, I tower over her.

I sigh. "First of all, stop being so dramatic. You're not chained to anything. You're making it sound like this is a fucking medieval dungeon. You're restrained by very soft cuffs in a very safe, very comfortable penthouse."

Kat scoffs. "Excuse me if I'm not particularly pleased with the luxurious cage I'm locked in."

"Also, I'll release you so you can move around freely, but you're not leaving this place."

"*What?*"

"As long as we are in business together, you'll be staying here with me."

She stares at me, seemingly at a loss for words. I expect her to scream at me in outrage, but, to my surprise, after blinking a few times, she speaks to me in a calm, measured tone. "You're delusional."

"Hardly. You, on the other hand, might very well be. You seem to have forgotten the delicate situation you are in and why you're even here. Maybe you're the one struggling to keep things professional. We may have fucked, Kat, but this is strictly business now. Please tell me you don't expect me to go easy on you because of our history."

The look Kat gives me tells me she believes it is beneath her to even acknowledge my accusation. "You may have leverage over me, Nikolai, but you don't own me."

"I thought you said you didn't want to argue semantics, Kat," I say, throwing her words from earlier back at her.

If looks could kill, I would be dead right now. Unfortunately for the little thief, I will live to fight her another day.

Regardless, I know I've made my point; more importantly, so does she.

I'm not stupid enough to think I actually own her, of course. That would be a fatal mistake—one I'm sure she would make me pay for dearly. But I have enough leverage over her to get away with making certain demands—at least as of right now.

"I've agreed to work with you, Nikolai. You have enough dirt on me to enforce it, and the means to chase me through the gates of hell if I'm dumb enough to go AWOL on you. Why the hell do you need me to stay in your home?"

Because I don't trust her. If I let Kat out of my sight, she might very well plot a way to escape me. I can't have her going back on her word to help me. I need to keep my eyes on her to make sure she isn't up to any shenanigans in my absence.

"Small correction, Kat: you work *for* me. So you will live under my roof while our arrangement is in place. I need to know where to find you when I need you. I don't have time to waste tracking you down."

"Uh, hello? Have you heard of cell phones? Or email?"

"Why bother with any of that when I can just have you right where I want you?"

"And where is that?"

"Under my thumb, of course." I wink, unable to resist provoking her further.

As I've learned today, Kat looks especially hot when mad. Unsurprisingly, of course. The woman can't do anything without driving me crazy with lust.

I study her as her temper flares up, deciding to cut her off before she explodes on me. I don't know if I can stop myself from kissing her senseless if she goes off on me again.

"Besides, the two of us living under the same roof will work well with your cover."

My statement triggers her curiosity, as I suspected it would.

"What do you mean by that? My cover? What cover?" she asks.

I smile in response. "All in due time, Kat. I'll explain everything you need to know tomorrow. You had a long, trying day. Let's get you out of these cuffs and put some food in your stomach."

"You're kidding me, right? Nikolai, you can't just tell me that and expect me to drop it. You can't just say I'll be virtually your prisoner for God knows how long and tell me it will all make sense eventually."

"I had no idea you had such a flair for the dramatic, Kat. You won't be my prisoner. You'll work for me. And as your boss, I get to make certain demands of you. I am, after all, compensating you very generously."

"Is that right?"

"Yes, Kat, it is. For starters, I'm sparing your and your friend's lives. I'd say that ordering you to live in my home is not too much to ask in exchange for that. You might even enjoy yourself. It's a pretty nice place if I do say so myself. And it's not like you are locked in here. Naturally, you can come and go as you wish. With an escort, of course. And as long as there's no conflict with my plans for you for the day, obviously."

"How generous of you, Nik," she says, sarcasm dripping from her every word.

"I'm glad you think so. Now, what do you say we finally get you out of these restraints and get you something to eat so you can get some rest? You have a big day tomorrow."

Wordlessly, she holds out her cuffed arms in my direction.

My smile grows bigger. "That's a good girl," I say, moving towards her to remove the leather straps around her wrists. Careful not to touch her more than necessary, I quickly unlock the cuffs, and the pieces fall to the bed.

Kat makes a scene out of stretching her arms and rubbing her wrists. I glance at the skin there and see no wounds. The area looks a little red, but she is milking it as much as possible.

I ignore her little show, moving on to her ankles. I grab one of them and yank her in my direction. Kat yelps as I drag her over the bed until she is close enough for me to work on the restraints' locks.

I kneel on the bed between her legs, and she gasps loudly.

"Everything okay there, Kat?" I ask, feigning innocence.

She narrows her eyes at me before trying to kick me with her right leg. Dodging her strike, I grab her leg before her foot connects with my face. Eyes locked with hers, I slide my hand down her thigh, past her knee, as she disapprovingly watches me.

Still maintaining eye contact, I wrap my hand around her ankle. Without warning, I yank it until her foot leans against my chest and her ass rests against my thighs.

Kat opens her mouth—surely to protest—but she seems to think better of it. After a second, she bites her bottom lip, our eyes still linked.

Hesitantly, Kat raises her arms, grazing her lips with her fingertips. She slides her foot down from my shoulder—down my chest, my stomach—until she reaches my cock, already straining against the fabric of my pants. A frustrated groan escapes me before I can stop it.

Transfixed, I stare at her hands as Kat slowly drags them down her body, caressing it along the way—past her neck, over her breasts, her stomach—before she cups herself between her legs, spreading them wide.

Crazed with lust, I sigh as a hazy, familiar feeling builds inside me. Just when I feel like it's about to take over me, she moans.

"Ah, Nik..."

My gaze searches her face, and there is an unmistakable teasing glint in her eyes.

Kat's toying with me.

A noise strangely similar to a growl echoes in the cavernous bedroom, and I realize after a moment that it came from me.

Grabbing her leg again, I flip her over before she can react. Kat ends up face down on the bed, her ass within my reach. Swiftly, I smack it.

She freezes in place for a moment. Then, she lets me have it.

"*You son of a bitch! How dare you!*" Kat screams at the top of her lungs.

Without hesitation, I raise my hand and spank her again. Harder this time.

"Nikolai!" she yells. "I'm going to kill you for this, I swear."

Every time she protests, I slap her ass. Over and over again, without uttering a word. Too soon, her cursing and screaming come to a stop.

After a while, over the sound of my blood rushing through my veins and the thundering beats of my heart, I realize she's panting.

I pause for a moment, wanting to make her wait for it. I

reach under her skirt, smoothing my hand over the soft skin of her hips.

She hisses in a breath at the same time I groan.

I drag my fingers over the curve of her behind until the palm of my hand rests against the bottom of her underwear. It takes all I have to stop myself from ripping the fabric to shreds once I feel how wet it is.

"Ah, Kat... you're a bad girl. You're so wet for me, *milaya*." I raise my hand again, slapping her almost bare ass—hard. Kat moans, spreading her legs further apart.

"Nik, please..."

"Which one is it, Kat? 'Nik, please stop' or 'Nik, please, *don't* stop'?"

"*More.* Don't stop, please, Nik," she says, panting. It's the stuff of my—wet—dreams, and not fucking her right now might be the hardest thing—no pun intended—I've ever done.

"Right. That's what I thought, Kat."

I caress her gorgeous, bouncy ass for long moments, before dragging my right hand up her leg all the way to the cuffs around her ankle. My other hand squeezes the plump flesh of her behind once more before my fingers slightly lift her underwear, tracing its edges.

"*Yes,* Nik. Yes. Please..."

I continue to tease her.

"Nik, please. Touch me..."

"I am, Kat. I am."

She is growing impatient, and I laugh under my breath. "If there is somewhere specific you have in mind, Kat, all you gotta do is ask..."

14

KAT

"Poor little Kat. Sounds like you could use my help right now," Nik says, his voice barely more than a whisper as his hand gently caresses the bare skin of my ass.

Panting, I don't move a muscle—I don't even blink.

"Maybe you should've thought of that before you played with me earlier," he says in a much louder tone, spanking me hard before dropping my now unrestrained legs and leaving the bed.

While I was distracted by his teasing, Nik unfastened the restraints around my ankles without my notice. Confused, I look around the bedroom, searching for him. He's standing across the room, looking smug as he smirks at me even as his erection tents his trousers.

One look at his face, and I understand everything.

He played me.

He spanked me until it drove me crazy with desire, all along planning to leave me wanting.

"Nikolai!" I yell, enraged. He laughs.

"You can't say I didn't warn you, Kat. Besides, it's been a long time coming, don't you think? I've never met anyone who needs to be spanked more than you. Some might even say you've been asking for it since the night we met."

"I'm going to make you pay for this," I mutter through gritted teeth.

"Can't wait. Bring it on. Do your worst. I can take it." The bastard has the nerve to wink at me.

In a fit of rage, I throw all the bed's pillows at him while grunting and screaming, too angry and sexually frustrated to form complete, coherent sentences. Nik chuckles, easily dodging the projectiles flying his way.

"Hey, you know what they say. If you can't take it, don't dish it out. Also, you really shouldn't start something you can't finish," he quips.

"You're going to regret this, Nik."

He pretends to consider my threat for a moment before shrugging one shoulder. "Nah. I don't think so, Kat."

I stomp to the bathroom, looking for something heavy I can use to cause some severe damage to him. Maybe a weapon I can use to maim him.

"I'll give you some personal space to, uh—how should I put this delicately? Alleviate yourself? Take care of business? Release the tension?—but come out and meet me in the kitchen when you're done making yourself come," he says over his shoulder.

There is a crystal pitcher on the marble sink. I hurl it in his direction without even glancing his way. A satisfying loud noise echoes through the chamber as the delicate object is smashed to pieces. His muffled, distant laugh reaches me through the closed door as he steps out into the hallway.

The sound of his footsteps grows faint as I stare at my reflection in the large mirror above the bathroom sink.

The woman in the mirror barely resembles the one I saw

early this morning as I finished getting ready for my meeting with A.J. and Camilla, the *stronzo*'s former secretary.

That woman was elegantly dressed and beautifully groomed. She looked like someone who had her shit together. Someone who was in control of herself and her life.

The reflection staring back at me looks like the complete opposite.

My clothing is in complete disarray. My silk slip skirt is twisted and wrinkled, and my button-down blouse is falling off my shoulders, revealing my bra straps.

I have no idea where my shoes ended up after my abduction or who removed them, for that matter. My purse is also MIA.

Most of my makeup has faded or is smeared all over my face. My hair is a mess, a far cry from the carefully combed style I strived for this morning. I look as if I've spent the entire day rolling around in bed with a delicious man, which I suppose is appropriate since that's precisely what has happened.

I assess the damage to my appearance for another second, taking a deep breath before working on fixing it. Then I turn the faucet on and wash my hands before splashing my face and neck with water.

There isn't much in the bathroom's vanity drawers. Certainly, nothing I can use to put myself together or maim Nik a little. I find a few scented soap bars, some tissue and nothing else. It figures. Typical bachelor pad.

Of course, it doesn't matter. Even if I found something I could use against him, it would be useless to me. Sure, technically, I could physically hurt him, maybe even render him powerless. But then what? There is nowhere I can go where

Nikolai Stefanovich won't find me if he wants to. I can't run or hide from the man.

Besides, the Russian *bratva*'s *pakhan* certainly has many bodyguards lurking around at all times. I doubt I'd get far before one of them caught me.

If my earlier encounter with Nikolai's henchmen is any indication of the kind of men I would have to deal with during my daring escape, then I will take my chances with the devil I know any day of the week and twice on Sunday. At least Nik is easy on the eyes. And I like how he touches me much, much better—even when he spanks me. If I'm being honest myself, *especially* when he does.

If I want to be free, my best bet is to try to give him what he wants as fast as I can. That's my only hope.

I still can't believe he spanked me—or that I let him. Even worse, I thoroughly enjoyed it.

The man kidnapped, drugged, and chained me to his bed so he could force me into working for him. But as soon as his hand slips under my skirt, I start positively purring for him in ten seconds flat.

Nikolai got me in such a state, so crazed for him, that I even stooped to begging him to touch me. Even when I wanted to resist him, to deny him, I was powerless to do so. It's obvious I can't resist my attraction to him. I'm completely unable to stop myself from giving in to him, to his magnetic pull over me.

Oh, how the mighty have fallen. I'm too weak to maintain any dignity or any sense of self-control when it comes to him. The overwhelming desire I feel for him takes over, and I forget all else.

If there were any hope of ever getting this maddening feeling under control, surely I'd have been able to do so earlier today when I learned his real, terrifying identity—after being abducted and practically violated by the man.

But none of it mattered once I felt his hands on me and the mouthwatering scent of his skin invaded me.

There might be no fighting or controlling this craving, which is not only unacceptable but also dangerous. I don't have the time or the energy to deal with this bullshit. A.J. needs me, and the *stronzo* and I have unfinished business.

Nik is a nuisance and a distraction I can't afford right now. The stakes are too high.

Truthfully, even if I had no other problems, I still wouldn't want Nikolai in my life. Sure, the man is fun as hell in bed, but he isn't worth the trouble. The very last thing I want or need is to become romantically involved with a freaking mafia boss. I've had enough interactions with the type to last me a lifetime.

Even if Nik's occupation had been something else entirely, he still wouldn't be someone I want in my life long-term. During the limited time we've spent together, he has repeatedly shown me how overbearing and controlling he can be. There's no doubt about it—with him, it's either his way or the highway. No questions allowed.

The mind-blowing sexual connection between us doesn't make up for his personal faults. I could never fall for a man as unbearably domineering as he is. Not now, not ever.

I learned a long time ago what happens when you let undeserving people have complete control and absolute power over you and your life. It's not a mistake I have let myself repeat since then—not in the last twenty years. I certainly don't plan on changing that now—or ever.

My best course of action is to treat this situation as just another job. I must avoid any distractions and focus on the task at hand. The sooner I give Nikolai what he needs from me, the sooner I will be rid of him.

I finish rearranging my clothes as best I can and tie my hair in a loose knot. When I walk out of this room and step further into the lion's den, I will look as professional as possible. With any luck, that should put Nik and me in the right frame of mind.

15

KAT

I walk toward the door that Nik exited through. I'm surprised to find it unlocked. It would be just like him to play infuriating mind games with me.

After a moment of hesitation, I step out onto the empty hallway. Just like the bedroom, its walls are a soft off-white color. The cold marble floors from my gilded prison cell also cover the corridor's length.

I follow the distant sounds coming from the opposite side of the penthouse. The hallway leads to an open sitting area. No one is around, so I keep walking, looking for Nik.

As I cross the sitting area, the smell of coffee and spices beckons me. I follow the scents, and the sounds grow louder. Finally, I walk through a doorway that leads to a kitchen. I expect to find a housekeeper or cook looming around, but instead, I spot Nik.

His back is turned to me, and I study him for a second as he moves around. He opens and closes cabinets, searching for something.

Nik doesn't notice me so I continue to watch him in silence. He's dressed in a black cashmere sweater that temptingly molds to the planes and ridges of his back as he reaches for a wine glass on a high shelf.

His matching black jeans hang low on his narrow hips, the fabric deliciously hugging his ass. Against my better judgment, I find myself staring.

I'm so uncharacteristically distracted by the sight of him in these jeans—trying to recall if I have ever grabbed his ass—that it startles me when he turns around and faces me.

"Oh, there you are. Finally," he says, a friendly expression on his face. "I hope you're hungry."

"Starving," I say, my mind still sidetracked by him. "What are we having?"

"Well, I wasn't sure what you wanted, so I warmed up everything we have—except for the sushi, of course." He shrugs, gesturing to a dozen dishes spread out over the kitchen island.

"Wow," I say. There's enough food here to feed a large family. Some dishes I can't identify but there are some classics, too, like fettuccine Alfredo.

"Did you make all of this?" I ask, incredulous. I walk up to the kitchen island for a closer look. Everything looks amazing.

He scoffs. "Hell, no. I can't fry an egg to save my life. But don't worry, Irina is an outstanding cook."

"Who's Irina?" I ask before I can stop myself, my voice ringing louder than I intended. Nikolai raises an eyebrow, but thankfully, he doesn't make any snide comments.

"Irina's my chef. She's been working for me for over ten years now." He places his hand on the small of my back before squeezing past me to reach the oven to my left. "Excuse me, I have to get the lasagna out of the oven."

A delicious shiver runs up my spine at the slight touch,

but I pretend I don't feel anything, and he doesn't seem to notice.

Nik pulls out the lasagna, and the scent is so good I want to moan. I didn't realize until now just how hungry I am. No wonder—I haven't eaten today. I planned to grab a bite with A.J. after our meeting with Camilla. I was hoping we would have cause for celebration.

After setting the dish down, Nik removes the oven mitts he's wearing. For some reason, I'm shocked to notice he is barefoot. He rolls up the sleeves of his sweater before grabbing a wine bottle from the refrigerator, and I realize I'm staring again.

The entire scene is so domestic that it's a struggle to reconcile the man before me with the sensual lover from the gala and the commanding, all-powerful mafia boss I encountered earlier today.

Not that he doesn't look sexy right now. The man couldn't stop oozing sex appeal even if he tried. But it's a different kind of allure. He looks approachable and inviting instead of forbidding and unattainable.

I kind of like it.

"Why are you doing all of this?" I ask, unable to hide my suspicion from my tone.

He pauses while removing the wine cork. His forearms look impossibly hot as he works the corkscrew, and I have a hard time focusing on anything else.

"Well, we have to eat, Kat," he says, shooting me a confused look.

"No, I mean, why are you doing this yourself?"

"Oh. You mean why not have someone else do this for me." He looks amused. "I gave the staff the day off today once I decided to have you over for dinner tonight." He winks at me.

"Once you decided to have me kidnapped, you mean."

"I thought we had agreed not to argue semantics, Kat."

Nik removes the cork from the bottle and pours out two glasses of red wine, not even bothering to hide his amused smile. Naturally, he doesn't ask me if I want a drink. Simon says I will have a glass of wine, and that's the end of it. I let it slide, as well as his remark.

"So we are all alone here, I guess." I sip my wine. It's rich, smooth and delicious.

"Why do you ask? Are you planning to have your way with me?"

"Ha-ha. Hilarious. You're the one trying to wine me and dine me, buddy."

"I'm just trying to feed you and myself. Everyone's more pleasant with a nice, warm meal in their stomach. And before you get any ideas, I should probably tell you we're not completely alone. A few of my men are still here. They're going to be hanging around the place until you and I are done with our little job. I'll introduce you later."

"Scared I will get the best of you?" My question amuses him, and his eyes glint with humor. It's a good look on him.

"They're not here for backup. So, if you were feeling good about your chances of subduing me with a butter knife, think again. I'm sure I can handle you, and I assume you're not eager to have me spank you again for misbehaving. Or are you?" He inches closer to me, a kitchen towel draped over his shoulder.

"In your dreams, maybe. And thanks for the reminder. It completely slipped my mind that I owe you payback for that."

"Aw, Kat. Don't threaten me with a good time," he says. I faintly recall telling him something similar the night we met.

Ignoring his attempt at levity, I press on. "If they're not here for backup—just in case I overtake you with my mad ninja skills—what are they here for? I thought you said I'd be safe with you, but if you need to keep security around..."

Nik grows a little serious at my concerned tone. "It's not that. You *are* safe here, Kat. They're here for the same reason you are. I don't want to waste my time looking for them if I need them."

"You know, Nik... They have these new gadgets nowadays that I think might interest you. You can use them to reach people anywhere whenever you want to. They call them cell phones. Maybe you should look into that."

"Cute," he says. Pulling a stool out, he gestures for me to sit down. "Sit. Eat. I saw you eyeing the lasagna."

After sitting down, I dish out a generous slice of lasagna. I don't appreciate his bossiness at all, but I don't have the energy to argue with him after the day I've had.

Besides, I really do want some lasagna.

He sits on another stool facing me, putting a bit of everything on his plate.

"Speaking of cellphones," he says, pulling something from his jeans pocket. He stretches his hand, palm facing up, offering me my phone back. "You probably have people worried about you."

I'm stunned for a second, but then I remember—Nikolai knows I can't escape him or his plans for me. It makes no difference to him if I have my phone or not.

Nonetheless, I take the device back, my fingers grazing his hand. Sparks fly at the slightest physical touch between us as if my life was a stupid teenager flick. I try to hide my response to the slight contact, but I look up and catch his eyes with mine, and it's obvious—the feeling is mutual.

"Thank you," I say. He nods.

I glance at my phone screen, and there are over two dozen missed calls from A.J. and many more unread texts. So I quickly type a message to her.

> Sorry for missing our meeting. Don't worry, I'm fine. But I can't talk now. I'll try to call you later tonight.

My best friend starts typing back immediately. A wall of text pops up, but I can't read it right now—not while Nik is paying attention to my every move. Instead, I send A.J. another message.

> I can't talk. I'll explain everything tonight. Promise.

She starts typing up a storm again before abruptly stopping. Her reply comes a second later.

> You better.

With a sigh, I set my phone down. Nik glances at it, before turning his gaze to me. He says nothing.

"So," I say. "Tell me about the job."

He studies me for a long moment, appearing to consider his answer carefully. At last, he says, "I think it would be better if we discussed this tomorrow, after you had a chance to rest from today."

"I feel fine. Thanks to your two friends, I had a lovely nap this afternoon."

Nik winces slightly. "Sorry about that. But it's not like you'd have come here given the choice. As a matter of fact, Boris told me you put up quite a fight."

His tone is a little too amused for my liking. I perk up in my seat, still furious at the brutes who abducted me for manhandling me. I'm even angrier at Nikolai for ordering them to do so in the first place.

"Which one of them is Boris?"

"Boris has a pretty noticeable scar on his face."

"Oh, *that* one. He'll get his comeuppance, I assure you."

"Easy, tiger. The man was just doing his job."

"And that's supposed to make it okay?"

"Well, Kat, I'd think you'd have some sympathy for Boris, since you got yourself in trouble for doing your job, too."

Another reason the *stronzo* must burn. It wasn't enough for him to endanger my life by making me steal from a freaking mobster. He had to add insult to injury and make me lose my moral high ground with Nik. Unforgivable.

"I didn't harm anyone," I say.

Nikolai scoffs. "Debatable."

"No, it isn't. I may be a thief—allegedly, of course—but my hands are clean of blood. Can you say the same for yourself?" It gives me great pleasure to lord this over him.

He pauses for a moment before speaking. "I won't apologize for doing what I have to do, Kat," he says. Another pause. "Like I said, I think we should wait until the morning to discuss businesses."

"What else would we talk about?"

He smirks at me, and I want to groan in frustration and hit myself. I can't believe I took his bait so easily.

"Well, we could talk about us, of course, Kat," he says—as I knew he would. His voice is as smooth as the wine he's been generously pouring for me.

"There's no us."

"Come on, Kat. You know that's not true."

"We had sex. Once. It was a one-night stand. Two ships

passing in the night. Nothing more. Our relationship is strictly professional now."

"So you do admit we have a relationship. Let me ask you this: do you consider what happened between us earlier today professional? Damn, I should've hired you a long time ago."

"That was a momentary lapse of judgment. Nothing else."

His smile grows wider. "Tell me, Kat. Did you touch yourself after I left you?"

The urge to throw the fine wine I've been drinking in his face is almost too strong to resist. But something gives me pause. As I look at Nik, I see the same smug, self-satisfied expression from earlier. He's toying with me again.

Of course, I can still splash him with my drink. But that would give him the satisfaction of thinking he's getting to me. It would also ruin his cashmere sweater, and I'd hate to destroy something so fine and beautiful.

More importantly, I'd like to get at least a little of my power and control back from him if I can. And I think I do. Two can play this game of his.

With a dramatic sigh, I set my wine glass down. "You know what, Nik? I didn't touch myself after you left me. I thought I'd save it for later tonight. You probably don't know this, but I'm really into delayed gratification."

He stares at me in silence with a playful but calculating look in his eyes. "You don't seem the type, Kat."

"I know, right? But I am. There's just something about bringing myself to the edge over and over again, feeling the climax build up as I tease my body repeatedly until I can't take it anymore. I just can't help myself." I say with a sigh. "So, I thought it would be best to wait until later tonight. Hey, if I'm lucky, you might even join me."

I bite my bottom lip before smiling at him. His eyes immediately fly to my mouth.

Still looking at his face, I raise my right foot, stretching my right leg as far as I can under the kitchen island until I reach his leg. Inch by inch, I run my foot up his calf before placing it on his stool seat, right between his thighs.

His eyes connect with mine, a dangerous glint in them. "I know what you're doing, Kat."

"I know." Raising my foot higher, I run it inside his thigh as slowly as possible. He firmly grabs it and stills it just as I'm about to touch his crotch with my toes.

"Kat..." he says in a warning tone. "You don't want to start down this path with me again."

"Oh, but I do."

He has no idea how much. Flirting with the Russian is never a hardship—the man is pure sex on a stick. But as it happens, seducing him just might be my salvation. If Nik is fond of me or of my body, maybe he will think twice before hurting me or A.J. Perhaps he will even come to see me as nothing but one of his lovers. It would be a vast improvement to his current opinions of me—a shameless thief and a possible co-conspirator in his friend's murder.

Besides, it occurs to me that Nikolai Stefanovich could end up being just what I needed all along—a powerful ally against the *stronzo*. A bit of sugar from me might be just the thing to get the big, bad *bratva* boss to claim the role of my protector.

Nik won't let go of my foot, so I reach for my blouse and run my index finger over the first button. I pause and look at him.

Shaking his head, he says, "Don't even think about it."

"Too late," I say as I free the first button, revealing the top of my breasts.

"Kat—"

I ignore him. An intoxicating, heady feeling of power inundates me—it's almost inebriating. I got him. He might be able to force me into working for him, bending me to his will in a hundred different ways, but it doesn't matter. I hold the cards.

Nik wants me—badly. I recognize the feeling in him because I feel the same way. It drives me crazy that I can't resist my attraction to him, but I can still use his desire for me.

"It's okay, Nik," I say, shushing him as I work down my blouse, one button at a time. Soon, my bra is revealed. He mutters a foreign word I don't recognize, and I stop.

"What does that mean?"

He stares at me, confused.

"What you just said. Is that Russian?"

"Yes," he says, transfixed by my breasts displayed by my lacy balconette bra.

"Won't you tell me what it means? It sounded like a curse word," I ask again. My fingers play with a button around my navel, teasing him.

"What if I refuse to tell you?" he asks, knowing the answer.

"Then, I will stop."

I start buttoning up my blouse again, smiling at him.

Nik rises from his stool in one fluid movement, unceremoniously releasing my foot. In the next heartbeat, he is by my side. He grabs me, lifting me from my seat. Wordlessly, he walks over to the kitchen counter and sets me down.

Brusquely, Nik spreads my legs wide so he can stand between them. Before I can react, he drags my hips forward until his erection presses against the bottom of my underwear. Next, he grabs me by the neck, pulling my head close to his. His forehead touches mine, and our breaths mingle. The Russian smells as manly and irresistible as I recall. His scent makes me crave his taste even more.

"I warned you not to toy with me, *milaya*. I'm starting to think you want me to punish you."

"Turnabout is fair play."

Nik shakes his head. "You started this. You teased me first, playing with me."

I don't back down. "I don't care who started it. You took it to another level. You *spanked* me."

He pulls me even closer. "And you loved it. There's no point in denying it. I felt how wet you were through the silk of your panties. I can still hear your breathy moans as you begged me to keep going."

"That's not the point. You meant to leave me hanging. I can't let you get away with that."

Nik smiles. He looks so handsome that I want to claw the clothes off his body until I can see all of him at last. "Is that what this is about? If you're sexually frustrated, *milaya*, then may I once again suggest you avoid starting something you can't finish?"

"Well, I am finishing this. We're done here. Let me down, Nik," I mutter through gritted teeth, pushing against his chest. It's pointless. He's relentless, and it's like trying to move a mountain.

"We are done when I say we are done. We can't carry on like this, with one upping the ante over the other repeatedly," he says in a pacifying tone, running a hand through his gorgeous black hair.

"Funny you should say that now that we both know I have the upper hand—great timing on your part. Well, guess what? You can't control me. I'll do whatever I please whenever it's convenient for me. And there's nothing you can do about it," I say, punctuating my words with my index finger against his chest.

Nik grabs my poking hand, before grabbing the other and holding both behind my back.

"Are you sure about that? Because I think you'll find out there's plenty I can do about it. You don't want to fight this battle of wills, Kat."

"I'm so freaking tired of you telling me what I want or don't want. You think I won't stand up to you? Try me, Nik. Just fucking try me."

He doesn't immediately respond, and we stare at each other for a while, both furious. Our breaths come out in pants, still mingling with each other. I smell the wine and him, and, even against my wishes, it makes my mouth water.

Nik's hand behind my back, still restraining both my hands, drags me closer to his body. I can't tell if he moves first or if I do, but his other hand grabs hold of my shirt, pulling me close before slipping underneath the fabric to touch my stomach.

My ankles lock behind his legs, and I pull his hips to mine, craving the friction of his erection between my legs.

We both groan in unison. We are so close that I can no longer tell my thundering heart apart from his. Our gazes connect, and I realize that things are about to slip out of my control. But an unexpected noise originating at the kitchen entrance startles me. I almost jump down from the counter, but Nik stops me, holding me tightly against his body.

A heartbeat later, it comes to me—it was somebody clearing their throat. *His man.* I completely forgot we weren't entirely alone.

"What is it?" Nikolai practically barks over his shoulder. I can't see the person who interrupted us with Nik blocking my vision.

"Nikolai," a male voice replies. "Lucien is here to see you."

Nik closes his eyes for a second. After taking a deep breath, he opens them again. As he studies me, his eyes harden.

"Tell him I'll be there in a moment," Nikolai says to the man behind him.

"Sir," the man replies. His footsteps echo in the kitchen as he leaves.

Nik closes his eyes again, pausing for a second. After a moment, he sighs. He picks me up from the counter and gently sets me down.

"I have to go," he says. "You should finish your meal. Then try to get some rest."

Before I can say anything, Nikolai departs.

16

KAT

My eyes snap open and I jolt awake, gasping for air.

As my heart races madly, I sit in bed, sheets falling to my waist. I take a second to realize I am not actually running for my life down a darkened street.

It was just a dream, but I'm safe now—or at least safe enough for the time being.

Unlike the faceless man chasing me in my nightmare, Nikolai has already caught me. For what it's worth, he seems uninterested in killing or torturing me at the moment. Maybe it's because he thinks he can use me to catch his own boogeyman. But something tells me it might be for another reason entirely.

My phone vibrates as I try to catch my breath, watching the sunrise through the windows in my new room. I check it right away and see it's a text from A.J.

> Sorry about last night. If you decide to tell the Russian to go to hell after all, I'm only one call away.

A sigh escapes me. After Nikolai left me in his kitchen

last night, I came back to the bedroom to call A.J. Her reaction to my news was explosive, to say the least.

At first, she was furious with Nik, worried out of her mind about my abduction and the identity of my kidnapper. Once I shared all the details of my predicament, her anger shifted to me. My best friend was livid that I had never told her about meeting Nik at the gala. It didn't matter to her that I didn't know then who he was or that the diamond belonged to him. A.J. was disappointed with me on behalf of our friendship but also of our plan to destroy the *stronzo*. We can't afford to keep secrets from each other when we're so close to defeating him.

I apologized because I knew she had a point. Still angry, A.J. told me all about her meeting with Camilla, the *stronzo*'s former secretary. The woman delivered more than we expected. She told my best friend that there is hard evidence of the man's secret. A.J. is working hard to track it down using the information Camilla shared.

After keeping Nik a secret from her, my friend's apology text is more than what I deserve. I hurry to type my response.

> Sorry again about keeping secrets. And I'm sorry I can't track Camilla's lead with you.

Her reply comes fast.

> Don't worry about it, boo. You have enough on your plate right now. And you've helped me too much already. It's my mess to clean up. You just worry about keeping your Russian happy. But not too happy.

Rolling my eyes, I start typing my reply, ready to defend my honor. But she has a point.

> Easier said than done, trust me.

After a second, I send her another quick text.

> Be careful, A.J. Please.

Her response is immediate.

> I will. And right back at you, Kitty Kat.

After promising to stay in touch and extracting the same promise from her, I set my phone down and prepare to face the day. I have no doubts it will be a tough one. Priority number one is to figure out how to get the upper hand with Nik—once and for all.

The alternative is unthinkable. To be helpless at the Russian's mercy? Subject to his every whim? That won't work for me.

Somehow, I must even the scales between us—sooner rather than later. The man has shown how mercurial he can be. I wouldn't be surprised to learn he is a Gemini. There is no time to waste. I must get him under control, even if it means seducing him.

So, I make quick work of getting ready since I don't have much at my disposal to do so. Although I showered last night, I didn't have any fresh clothes to wear. The closet I spotted yesterday is empty. All I could scavenge was basic toiletries—toothpaste, a fresh toothbrush, soap, shampoo and conditioner.

Less than fifteen minutes after waking up, I exit the room. It's early enough that I doubt I'll run into Nik. In my experience, handsome billionaires rarely wake up at the crack of dawn. I can't say I blame them.

I'm sure he will track me down eventually, but hopefully not before I can eat breakfast and inhale an ungodly amount of coffee. After last night, I won't be ready to face him until I get some food and caffeine.

I retrace my steps from the previous evening through the massive penthouse, and I find the kitchen. To my surprise, a tall stranger stands by the kitchen island, coffee mug in hand.

"Morning," the man says over his mug's rim before gulping some deliciously smelling coffee. "You must be Katherine Devereaux."

"I must be. And you are?"

"I'm Dmitri. I'm Nik's friend."

He smiles, all dimples, offering me his hand. Dumbfounded, I stare at it for a second before shaking it. His hand is big and warm, and the skin feels a little rough.

"And by friend, you mean henchman, of course," I say.

Dmitri laughs—a genuine, heartfelt laugh. His smile reaches his pale blue eyes, and dimples pop up on his cheek again. His dark blond hair bounces as he shakes his head. He's young, likely in his mid-twenties. He's also very tall, towering above me by more than a foot.

"You're funny," he says. "I can see why Nik likes you."

"He does? That's news to me."

He grins. Even though he's a few years my junior, I can't deny Dmitri is *hot*. His boyish good looks are cute and disarming, but his broad shoulders and lean muscular frame tell me he is all man. True, he doesn't make me all weak in the knees like Nik, but I still appreciate that he is a fine-looking man.

"Well, let me put it like this," Dmitri says. "Most people caught stealing from Nik aren't invited to hang out at his penthouse. I can tell you that much."

"You and I have a very different definition of the word 'invited', Dmitri."

"Fair enough." He shrugs. "But my point stands. You're getting off easy."

"Once again, our definitions of the word don't match."

"I guess we'll have to agree to disagree," he says. "Coffee?"

Sighing, I sit on one of the stools by the kitchen island. "I thought you'd never ask."

Dmitri fills a mug with coffee before handing it to me. I spot a pastry box on the kitchen counter, right next to where Nik set me down last night before shoving himself between my legs.

Before I even get a chance to ask, Dmitri picks up the box and places it in front of me on the kitchen island. I waste no time opening it, marveling at the different flavors of donuts and bagels. I grab one of each.

"So, how long have you and Nik been partners in crime? Excuse me—I mean friends, of course."

Dmitri chuckles. "I've known Nik almost my entire life."

"What's that? Sixteen years?"

He smirks at me, sitting on one of the stools across from me—right where Nik sat down last night before I started playing footsie with him.

"Cute. I definitely see why he likes you," Dmitri says.

"So you keep saying."

"For what it's worth, I can assure you I'm of age. I'm all grown up where it matters." He winks at me.

I can't help but laugh in response. He is delightful, especially for a made man. I lean forward over the kitchen island, ready to reply with an equally flirty comeback, when Dmitri glances over my shoulder. Wordlessly, he stands up.

"Thank you for letting us know, Dmitri," Nik says with sarcasm.

Dmitri smiles, not even the slightest bit remorseful. "Morning, Nik."

"I see you two have met," Nik says, sitting beside me. I try to scoot away, but he grabs my seat and pulls it back, keeping me at his side. He is so close I can smell his shampoo and feel the heat from his skin. I even detect the up and down of his chest as he breathes in and out.

"I've been keeping her busy for you," Dmitri says, winking at me again. I roll my eyes.

"Is that right?" Nik asks, his voice as dry as sandpaper.

"Yep. She's been bombarding me with all these questions about you."

"I have not," I protest with a scoff. Maybe a little too emphatically.

Nik glances at me, an eyebrow raised.

"Of course, we were also getting to know each other better. I figured that was a good idea since we'll be seeing so much of each other. You don't mind it, do you, Nik?" Dmitri asks the man at my side, a teasing glint in his eyes.

Nik shoots him a stern look. "Dmitri..." he says after a long pause. "Don't you have somewhere to be this morning? Last I checked, I don't pay you to stand around and drink my coffee, bothering my guests."

"I wasn't bothering her. Kat was enjoying herself. Weren't you, Kat?" Before I can answer, Dmitri asks, "You don't mind if I call you Kat, do you? You can call me by my nickname, too. It's Dima. Or you can call me D."

"Dmitri—" Nik says in warning.

Dmitri winks at me. "See you later, Kat."

I raptly watch him leave. I must know what he looks like

from behind, but most importantly, I want Nik to see me studying Dmitri from behind.

Nik remains silent.

"Wow," I say, breaking the silence once Dmitri is out of sight. "Just—Wow."

Nik sighs wearily. "Sorry about Dmitri. He can be a lot sometimes. I let him get away with way too much, and he knows it. I'll make sure he doesn't bother you from now on."

"No need for that," I say with a smile. If he can be civil after yesterday, then so can I. "At least not on my account. I haven't laughed this much in a while."

"Oh, is that right?" he asks, loudly setting his coffee mug down.

"Yeah, I think he's wonderful. Please don't punish him because of me. I'd love to chat with him again, so don't tell him to stay away from me or any nonsense like that."

"Wonderful, huh?"

"I thought so."

"Right. Well, I hate to disappoint you, Kat, but you and Dmitri are here to *work* for me, so I'm afraid you won't get a chance to—how did you put it?—*chat* again. I expect you both to do your jobs to the best of your ability, which won't leave you much time for *chatting*."

I shoot him a displeased look. The nerve of this man. He might be able to force me to work for him, but that doesn't give him the right to dictate how I spend my free time or who I socialize with. If he thinks I'll let him keep me on a short leash like that, he is in for a surprise.

I smile even more sweetly at him. "Sounds good to me, Nik. I wouldn't want to waste any time I could spend working, trust me. After all, the sooner this job is finished, the sooner we can go our separate ways."

"My thoughts exactly. Glad we're on the same page," he says in the same tone.

"You bet. It's not like there won't be plenty of time for Dmitri and me to *chat* after this job is done, right? I'll give him my number so he can reach me."

The look he gives me could burn through stone. Undoubtedly, Nik hasn't forgotten I refused to give him my number and name when we first met.

"I hope you aren't too preoccupied daydreaming about Dmitri to do your job properly, Kat. As his boss, I can tell you he'll be too busy to *chat* with you in the foreseeable future. As *your* boss, I can say you will be, too."

"That's okay, Nik. For someone as *wonderful* as Dmitri, I can wait."

"He'll be busy indefinitely."

"Forever?"

"If that's what it takes, sure."

Forcefully setting my cup down, I turn on my seat to face the infuriating man next to me fully. "What the hell is your problem today? Do you get off on antagonizing me or something like that?"

"I could ask you the same thing. And for your information, not everything is about you, Kat. You might be surprised to learn this, but my life doesn't revolve around your wants and wishes. I run a tight ship around here. Get used to it."

"Right. It's all about efficiency with you. That's all you care about, of course," I say, sarcasm dripping from my every word.

A small smile curves his mouth. "Right on. See? You're learning already."

"Uh-huh. So, this whole animosity vibe you're giving off has nothing to do with you being jealous of Dmitri, right?

You wouldn't care about him flirting with me, would you, Nik?"

"As I mentioned, all I care about is that you and Dmitri focus on this job. With that in mind, I'm afraid I must insist that you two avoid any distractions until the work is done."

Nik stands up, evidently considering the conversation finished.

"And I'm afraid I must insist you mind your own business."

Slowly, he turns to face me.

"Your business is my business, Kat. You work for me now. And as long as I'm your boss, I'll set the rules. Unfortunately for you, that means no dating anyone until your work for me is finished."

I can't possibly have heard him right. He doesn't intend to just forbid me from interacting with Dmitri, even if only platonically. The bastard means to tell me I can't see any men for God only knows how long.

"No dating anyone? Are you completely out of your mind? Who the hell do you think you are? You don't get to make demands like that. I'll be working for you, not signing my life away."

Nik leans against the kitchen counter, crossing his arms against his chest. His biceps bulge enticingly, and even while furious, I can't help staring at it.

"Well, that's because you already signed your life away when you stole from me, Kat. And you didn't steal just a trinket, but a diamond worth more than you could imagine. Don't act like you're doing me a favor out of the kindness of your heart by working for me. If anything, I'm the one cutting you some slack. Men have died for less."

"I'm starting to realize that there are some fates worse than death," I say under my breath. It's frustrating beyond belief to be reminded of his leverage over me. I'm sick and tired of being owned by men with no scruples about bending me to their will.

Nik laughs at my dramatic statement. "There sure are, Kat, but I assure you this isn't one of them. You're getting off easy, and it's about time you realize that."

I shoot him another venomous look before glancing away. I can't bear to see his smug expression. He's got me, and he knows it.

After a moment, Nik sighs. He pushes off the counter and walks over to me. After pulling the stool next to mine out, he sits down again. This time, he faces me.

"Come on, Kat," he says in a soft tone. "You know who I am and what I do for a living. You agreed to the terms of our deal. What did you think was going to happen? You knew what you were getting yourself into. You can't be surprised I'm demanding that you stay focused."

I stare at him wordlessly. To no one's surprise, it's not enough for Nik that he gets to have me at his beck and call. It doesn't satisfy him that I have no choice but to obey his every whim. He wants me to be happy about it, too.

The nerve of this man doesn't cease to amaze me. It wouldn't surprise me to learn he also expects me to thank him for his mercy.

"Look," he says, appeasingly. "There's no reason for us to be any more miserable than we have to be. Come with me. I think I have something that will cheer you up a little."

Nik stands up, holding out his hand for me. I glance at it and sniff, not moving from my seat.

"I really doubt that."

"Come on, Kat. Give it a chance."

I dislike the idea of making any concessions or giving him any chances. But really, what choice do I have? At the end of the day, he owns me for all intents and purposes. Do I want to tell him to shove it? Absolutely. Is that in my best interest? Probably not. Antagonizing him won't do me any favors. If there's any chance I can butter him up so he will go easy on me, I would be stupid not to take it.

So I stand up and take his hand as reluctantly as possible. Nik doesn't seem to care. He smiles at me, squeezing my hand before caressing it with his thumb.

"Good girl," he says. "Follow me."

17

KAT

Nik leads me down a darkened hallway without letting go of my hand.

We walk past closed doors to my left and right, and I hear muffled voices here and there—his men, I assume.

At the end of the long corridor, a door is slightly ajar. Nik pulls me towards it and pushes it open with his free hand.

We enter a large corner office. Nobody is in it but us. Nik lets go of my hand, quietly closing the door behind me. Curious, I glance around the room, surprised to realize it is quite cozy—or at least as cozy as an office big enough to fit half of my apartment inside can be.

The room is beautifully furnished with a massive mahogany desk and numerous built-in mahogany bookshelves. Countless leather-bound books and a few framed photographs populate the shelves.

A plush, oversized antique rug stretches over the floors. At the furthest corner from the door, there is a brown leather couch in front of a large, wall-mounted TV. Next to it sit two matching armchairs, with a large coffee table in the middle.

Intricate wall sconces invitingly illuminate Nik's office. Their warm glow makes up for the room's lack of natural light. Only a few rays of sunshine make it through the dark velvet blinds he has pulled down to cover the wall-to-wall, floor-to-ceiling windows.

I'm not sure what I pictured his office would look like, but this cozy, comfortable, lived-in room isn't it.

Besides the expensive furnishings, his office also sports little bits and pieces that shine a light on the man that occupies it. Multiple sheets of paper are haphazardly spread out over every flat surface available. I count at least five coffee mugs left around the room, plus a couple of half-empty whiskey glasses.

I'm surprised to see several personal objects as well. A soft-looking, slightly worn-out Kelly Green sweatshirt is crumpled on one of the armchairs. He has a framed sports jersey on the wall by his desk. I'm too far away to fully see the photographs all over the room, but he seems to be in many of them.

As a professional burglar, I'm used to making myself at home in the most unusual, unfamiliar places. But this room is so personal—so *Nik*—that I almost feel like I'm intruding. It's a strange thought, made even stranger by the realization that by being here I'm stepping into his mind in a way and getting a sense of what makes him who he is.

I'm not entirely sure how I feel about it—or about the fact that he invited me here himself.

It's the perfect spot to advance my plans for his seduction. Yet, something about being in here with him gives me pause. Just like last night at dinner, this setting makes him look almost human. It's almost easy to forget the man before me is one and the same with the Russian *bratva*'s *pakhan*—

and the tall, dark, and handsome god who ravished me at the gala.

Unthinkably, seeing Nik in his natural habitat makes me hesitate about working him. For once, he's not the larger-than-life man of my dirty dreams—he's just a man. A dangerously hot one, but a human male, nonetheless. I have no qualms about deceiving Nik's devilish *don* persona, but this mortal man before me is a different story altogether.

"Here," Nik says, handing me a manila envelope.

"What is it?" I ask as I open it.

"Some stuff I think you'll need. If there is anything I missed, let me know, and I'll make sure you get it."

The first thing I fish out of the package is a black American Express. With a loud gasp, I almost drop the entire thing.

I glance at Nik, but he has moved on already. He's distracted with the TV, fussing with the remote.

"This is a credit card," I state for mysterious reasons.

"Uh-huh," he says, paying me no mind, frowning at the screen.

"It's a black AmEx. With my name on it." I can't wrap my mind around the fact that this man has given me a no-limit credit card out of his own free will.

"I know. It's for any expenses you may have when I'm not with you. There should be more in there. I gave Dmitri a list."

More? What else could I possibly need?

I pull out the heaviest object inside the envelope. It's a car key with a beautiful, shiny three-point star. I gasp. "You're giving me a Mercedes?"

"Lending it. It's in the garage. I'll show you how to access it later," he says, almost as an afterthought. As if he's in the business of lending practical strangers luxury vehicles every day. For all I know, he might very well be.

I'm still daydreaming about all the places I'll drive it to so I can use my shiny new card when Nik starts speaking to me again.

"You will probably not have much use for it." He shrugs. "I'd rather you let me or one of my men take you wherever you need to go."

My first instinct is to protest against his remarkably controlling request, but thinking twice about it, I decide to let this one slide so he doesn't get any ideas about taking my new credit card away.

"I'll take that under advisement, *boss*," I say instead with a smile. He shoots me an unamused look before turning his attention back to the TV again.

The next object I take out of the envelope is a stack of papers. I leaf through it, skimming through the documents verbiage, curious about what other little treats Nik has in store for me.

"It's your account information." His voice sounds closer than I expect. I'm so distracted by the papers that I didn't notice he has closed the distance between us.

"My account?" I ask, dumbfounded.

He smirks at me. "You didn't think I wouldn't pay you for your services, did you?"

"Well, you did lord over me that you would be sparring my life for displacing your little bauble. Over and over again, if I may add. I assumed that was my compensation."

"Hey, if you don't want the money, I'm happy to take it off your hands," he quips, reaching for the papers.

I slap his hand away.

"Nope. No returns, refunds, or takesies-backsies. I'll gladly accept your humble offering. You said Dmitri put the package together? Remind me to thank him properly when I see him next." I wink at him.

Nik scoffs. "You should stop talking before I change my mind. Now come here. I want to show you something." He leads me back to the couch area where the TV he's been fussing about is located.

Folding the papers, I shove them back in the envelope before following him. I'm not taking any chances.

Nik motions for me to sit down on the leather couch. I oblige him, glancing at the screen with curiosity. What seems to be a paused surveillance feed is featured on it. He grabs the remote and sits down on the couch next to me.

"What am I looking at?" I ask.

"Can't you tell? This is the surviving footage from the night of the gala," he says, letting his weight sink on the soft leather of the sofa. We are close enough for me to feel the heat radiating from his body.

I study him as he props his feet up on the coffee table in front of us. He is so comfortable and in his element that I feel like I'm sitting in the lion's very own den. It's a sensation that should be alarming and troubling. Instead, I'm shockingly content, if not a little excited. For some reason, his relaxed state creates an atmosphere of comfort and—dare I say it—intimacy between us.

More puzzling still is the realization that seeing him so at ease makes me relax, too. I exhale a breath I didn't realize I had been holding this entire time. Somehow, Nik's belief that there is nothing worth worrying about right now is all the guarantee my body and mind need to relax.

It's not a thought I want to—or can afford to—dwell on and it's not a feeling I'm even sure he shares.

I focus on the task at hand, instead. I don't have the luxury of falling back under his spell.

"Oh, I see it now. Are those the gardens outside the museum? What about the footage from inside?" I ask, trying to shift my brain into work mode. This is a surveillance feed. This is my bread and butter. I'm in my element. I can do this.

"We haven't been able to recover any of it so far. Apparently, someone was messing with the feed that night, jamming the signal with this clever little electronic device. You wouldn't happen to know anything about it, would you, Kat?"

He glares at me, an eyebrow raised. I know he means to look menacing and forbidding, but his intended effect is ruined because he looks absolutely sexy. There's nothing I can do but resist the urge to climb on his lap to kiss that mean look off his beautiful face until he's nothing but smiles for me.

Instead, I say, "Oh, my bad. Oops, I guess."

"Oops, indeed," he says with a sigh.

"I could ask A.J. if there is anything she can do to salvage the feed. The SBU is her invention. She could try to work her magic."

Nik's expression reveals he didn't expect me to offer A.J.'s help.

"SBU?" he asks after a second.

"That's what she calls it. The Security Bypass Unit."

"Cute," he says, almost dryly. "Thanks for the offer. I'll keep it in mind."

I shrug. "You're welcome."

Nik and I watch the footage in silence. He's deep in thought. I try to think of something to say, but he speaks again before I can come up with anything.

"I meant to tell you something earlier, but you sidetracked me," he says, a teasing glint in his brown eyes. "I'm sorry you didn't have a clean change of clothes this morning. Or shoes. A personal shopper will be around later today to address that. She'll bring all you need to choose a new wardrobe. Also—"

I interrupt him. It's like he's speaking to my heart. "A new wardrobe?"

Nik smirks, glancing at me with amusement. "You'll need to look the part for what I have in mind."

18

KAT

"What's that supposed to mean?" I ask, suspicious.

"You'll see. In due time," Nik says cryptically, the corners of his mouth twisting in amusement.

"You can't just leave it at that."

He grins. "Watch me. As I was saying before you tried to sidetrack me—again—you may not have entered this agreement out of your own free will, but I hope we can manage to make the best of this situation for however long it lasts."

"Okay..." I say, unsure of where he is going with this and uncertain of where I want him to go with it.

"You might not have volunteered to work for me, but you are now working for me. And I take care of my people. So, as long as you and I are in this together, I want you to feel like this is your home. You're not my prisoner, Kat."

Is Nik kidding me? I scoff. This may be a gilded, limitless-AmEx-card-adorned cage, but it's still a cage. He had to kidnap me to have me in his home—quite literally. And now that I'm here, he won't let me leave, or interact with other men, for that matter.

"I understand you may disagree," he says, choosing to

ignore my reaction. "But, for what it's worth, I really do hope you can make the best out of a bad situation. I know you don't like the restrictions I put in place—"

"To put it mildly," I say, interjecting.

"But I believe you'll see that I'll compensate you fairly for my strict demands. On top of that, I want you to know that you're more than welcome to invite A.J. or any of your friends over at any time. Also, obviously, you're free to come and go as you please. As long as you give me proper notice, of course."

"Of course," I say sardonically.

Nik sighs.

"I don't mean to be overbearing, but the man we're up against is dangerous. I won't have you or anyone else under my protection harmed by him. I understand I might come across as a controlling jerk, but I'll do what I must—always. Especially when it comes to keeping my people safe."

His earnest concern for my safety makes me uncomfortable. It's a very novel and unfamiliar notion. I'm not used to people looking out for me. I'm the one who takes care of others. Hence my current predicament, of course.

"Right. So you've told me," I say. "But I'm not convinced you aren't just getting off on making me do whatever you damn well please."

Humor sparkles in his gorgeous eyes. "Maybe a little."

I smile. "That's what I thought."

Nik returns my smile before turning his attention back to the screen. I do the same—or at least, I act like I do. Deep inside, my mind is racing, trying to make sense of the avalanche of conflicting emotions rushing through me.

On one hand, Nikolai's still the enemy. The Russian's the huge, insurmountable obstacle between me and a mafia-boss-free future—everything I've been working on for the past few months. And he's still an overbearing, controlling bastard when it suits him to be.

Yet, I'm floored—and maybe even a little disarmed—by his concern for my welfare and safety. Not to mention, the man attempted to provide me with a bit of freedom. His offer to give me back some control over my life caught me completely off guard.

Of course, Nik's rules about how I get to exert that little shred of control are ridiculous. But as bossy as he may be, at least he isn't ordering me around just for the sake of it. Well, not entirely. Nik believes he's protecting me. The idea is absurd, but it's not just an arbitrary whim on his part.

On top of all of it, his generosity shocked me. Nik is rich enough to hang out with the likes of Bezos and Gates, so it's not like he will miss the money or the Mercedes-Benz. Still, the man has enough dirt on me that compensating me financially for my services isn't necessary. The *stronzo* never did.

I don't know what to make of Nik. It doesn't make things any easier that I'm still insanely attracted to him. Nonetheless, all the reasons why he and I shouldn't be romantically or sexually involved are still valid. Regardless of whether we are friendly or not, I must wrap up this job of his as soon as possible—for my own sake, for my own heart's sake, too. A man as controlling as him is the last thing I want—or need—in my life.

"That's Maxim." Nik points at the screen as a dark-haired man enters the frame—his friend who was murdered that night. At last, I can put a face to the name, and it's a very handsome one. Maxim's brown hair falls in waves over his forehead, his eyes flashing blue as he faces the security camera. Even through the low-resolution surveillance footage, his high cheekbones and strong jawline are hard to miss.

As discreetly as possible, I glance at the man next to me. He is clenching his jaw, eyes glued to the screen.

"How long had you two been friends?" I ask, unsure what to say but feeling the need to break the silence between us.

"Pretty much my entire life," he says with a sigh, picking up the remote to skip the footage forward. "Here it is."

Nik pauses the video, and the frame is frozen as the surveillance camera focuses on a tall-looking man. He is lean, seemingly in his early sixties. His salt-and-pepper gray hair is cropped short, and he is dressed in a dark suit with a dark shirt underneath.

"Who's that?" I ask.

"That's Patrick McGuire. That's the man we're up against," Nik replies.

Gasping, I turn to face him on the couch. "Patrick McGuire is the leader of the Irish mafia." For some reason, I feel the need to say that to Nik, the leader of the Russian *bratva,* because I just can't believe my luck. Of course there is a third mafia boss involved in my life. Naturally.

"I'm aware of that."

"You didn't mention I'd be helping you take down the head of the Irish mob."

"I didn't think it mattered. You weren't in a position to refuse me, regardless of who we were up against. Besides, considering my line of work—which you were fully aware of before you agreed to my terms—you can't honestly tell me that it's a huge surprise that our enemy is the leader of a rival family."

Nik presses play on the remote, and I turn a little in my

seat so I can watch the video footage and stare him down at the same time. It doesn't seem to faze him at all.

There's no point in wasting my energy being frustrated that Nik has kept McGuire's identity a secret. He is not going to change his mind. I'll just have to use it as extra motivation to wrap up this job as fast as possible.

This film study will take a while, so I might as well get comfortable. I prop my feet on the coffee table before us, following Nik's lead. With a sigh, I lean back, searching for a comfortable place to rest my neck and head. I end up bumping the bruise on my temple against the couch. I inhale sharply, wincing a little—the spot is still very tender.

Nik's sharp eyes and ears catch the subtle signs of my discomfort. "What's the matter?" he asks, turning to face me and pausing the footage again.

Frustrated, I sigh. If he's going to pause the video every couple of minutes for one reason or another, we will never finish watching it.

"It's nothing," I say, reaching for the remote in his hand. "Just something your man Boris and his buddy gave me to remember them by."

Nik's expression shifts. Still in possession of the remote, he stretches his hand towards my head. I recoil immediately.

"Let me see it," he orders me with a dark look in his eyes.

"I don't think so," I say, still futilely trying to wrangle the remote from him. The sooner we finish watching this, the sooner we can get started, and the sooner I'll be free.

"What are you doing?" he asks exasperatedly.

"You're hogging the remote. I'm trying to take it from you so I can watch the surveillance feeds without you pausing it every thirty seconds. Also, I'm so not in the mood for your color commentary, by the way."

"You're not getting the remote. My home, my remote."

"Seriously? Are you that much of a control freak? Did you never learn to share your toys with the other kids?"

Nik sighs. He closes his eyes before rubbing a hand over his face and pinching the bridge of his nose. "I'll tell you what—because I'm a reasonable man, I'll make you a deal. Let me look at your head, and I'll hand you the remote." He shoves the remote into his back pocket.

I study him with care. I'm fast and capable of stripping the clicker from him, but that would entail tackling him and fondling his ass. God only knows what would happen then. At this point, I'd have to be an idiot to trust my questionable self-restraint to prevail over my lust for him.

"Fine," I say through gritted teeth. "But be careful. It's still tender." I turn so he is facing the side of my head where the two brutes struck me, pushing my hair away from the bruised area.

Nik scoots closer to me. His brow furrows as his fingers brush against my scalp. His touch is light and gentle, but the bump is so sensitive I wince again.

"Forgive me," he says, a remorseful expression flashing over his face. I nod in response. He feels around the bruised area a bit more. "My men did this to you."

"Yep. Boris's buddy struck me when I put up a fight," I say, even though I'm not sure if he was asking a question or just stating a fact.

"I'm sorry, Kat. He'll be punished for hurting you."

Nik's sharp tone takes me aback. He can be so charming and flirty sometimes that it's easy to forget that, by all accounts, Nikolai Stefanovich is a vicious man.

Wordlessly, he stands up.

"Where are you going?" I ask.

"I'll be right back. I'll get you some ice and aspirin and make a call to have someone look at that bump."

"Do you mean like a doctor?"

Nik looks at me funny as if my question is preposterous. "Yeah, a doctor, Kat. Head injuries are no joke. You could have a concussion or something worse."

I scoff. Men are such babies...

"Don't be ridiculous. I'm fine. It's just a bruise. By tomorrow, I won't even feel it. Just sit down so we can finish watching this thing."

"I don't think so, Kat. I'll be right back."

I have no choice but to watch impassively as he leaves the room. True to his word, he's back in a moment, carrying an ice pack and a glass of water.

After handing me the drink, Nik reaches behind his back to pull something from his back pocket—a bottle of aspirin.

"Go on," he says, placing the ice pack on my head.

I play along, shooting him a displeased look. It goes without saying that I don't want my head to hurt or anything, but that doesn't mean I appreciate his high-handed bossiness.

"Thank you," I say before drinking the water he brought me.

Nik nods. "The doctor will be over this afternoon."

I roll my eyes, sighing. "Nik—"

With an outstretched hand, he stops my protests and plops back on the couch beside me. "Save your energy for a battle you can win, Kat. You *will* see a doctor today, and that's the end of it."

Exasperated, I glare at him for a second. Nik is completely unfazed by my reaction, as he gently holds the ice pack to my head. It's cold, wet, and uncomfortable, and it soon becomes more than I can take. Before he has a chance to react, I grab it from his hand, intending to toss it across the room.

I'm not dumb enough to telegraph my movements before making them, but somehow, Nik divines my intentions. He calmly stops me, moving my hand away.

He sighs. "What do you think you're doing?"

"Take this wet thing off of my hair. Now. And give me the remote while you're at it," I snap.

"Just a little more, Kat." While pressing the ice pack against my temple, Nik reaches behind his back to pull the remote out of his pants pocket. He offers it to me. I snatch it away before he changes his mind.

I press play, and the screen comes to life, still focused on Patrick McGuire. The man's face wrinkles as he heartily laughs at something said by one of the men surrounding him.

"Do you know any of the guys talking to him?" I ask Nik, who isn't even watching the video anymore. He's staring at me instead—it's unnerving.

Nik glances at the screen before shifting his focus to me. "Most of them. They're McGuire's soldiers. The one to his right is his enforcer, Connor Daniels."

"What makes you think that Patrick McGuire is behind your friend's death?"

Nik doesn't respond right away. He remains silent for so long that I assume my question will go unanswered. After a long stretch of silence, however, he sighs. "It's a long story. McGuire hated Maxim."

Curious, I wait for him to continue, but he leaves it at that. "That's it? Come on, you have to tell me more than that."

"It's enough for you to know that I have no doubts Patrick McGuire is behind Maxim's murder."

This time, I'm the one who pauses the video. I slap away his hand, still annoyingly holding the ice pack, and I turn to face him. "Ok, that's not going to work for me. At all."

Nik raises his eyebrows before dropping the ice pack on the coffee table. He sighs. "Kat—"

"No, it's your turn to listen, Nik. You can't just keep me in the dark and expect me to follow you blindly. If you truly believe I can help you take down the man who killed your friend, then you have to tell me everything you know. Otherwise, you won't be setting us up for success."

"It's not as simple as you think, Kat. There's a lot you're better off not knowing. You might claim you want to know everything I know, but you don't. Not really. And I don't blame you. You didn't seem too eager to get involved in my business when you learned who I am. And you weren't pleased when you discovered McGuire is our target. So, you can't expect me to believe you really want to know everything. The less you know, the better. Trust me."

"But that's the thing, Nik. It's a little too late for that now. I'm already involved. Do I wish I wasn't? You bet. But I am. So I might as well know everything there is to know about what's going on here. The last thing I need is to walk into this dangerous situation with a handicap. I'm not saying tell me every little sordid detail there is to know about the *bratva*. But you need to tell me everything I need to be aware of as far as Maxim and Patrick McGuire are concerned."

Nik stares me down, not bothering to hide his dissatisfaction with my demands. But two can play this game, so I glare at him, too. After long moments of tense silence, he sighs, and I know I've won.

"If you really must know," Nik mutters through gritted

teeth, "McGuire hated Maxim because Maxim was in love with the man's daughter."

"That's it?" I ask, confused. "That doesn't sound too bad. It certainly doesn't sound like enough reason to murder someone."

"You wouldn't understand."

"Well, explain it to me, then. I thought that was the entire point of this conversation."

Nik shoots me a glance meant to warn me to take it easy with the sassiness, but I ignore it. I have a hard time feeling threatened by the man who, a moment ago, was tenderly holding an ice pack to my bruise and looking out for my health.

"It's complicated," he says. "She's been promised to someone else her entire life. By hooking up with her, Maxim put an arranged alliance in danger and publicly embarrassed McGuire. Suffice it to say, if anyone hated Maxim enough to kill him, it was McGuire."

Before I can respond, he gently brushes his fingers against my temple. "Does it feel any better?" he asks.

I roll my eyes, fully intending to tell him off, but his genuine concern makes me pause. "I'm fine," I say instead. "Don't worry about it. The doctor will confirm I'm as healthy as a horse."

Nik seems unconvinced, but he doesn't reach for the ice pack again. I'm relieved he is willing to drop the subject when his hand touches my neck. It stops there, and my breath hitches in my throat. After a brief hesitation, his fingertips trail down to my shoulders.

"What are you doing?" I ask.

"You're all knotted up, Kat. That can't be comfortable. You're carrying a lot of tension on your neck and shoulders."

To my utter despair, Nik starts rubbing his knuckles

down the column of my neck. Up and down, repeatedly. His movements are gentle but firm, and my eyelids grow heavy.

"Well, that's what being kidnapped does to a person, Nik," I say, clearing my throat. Maybe my tone will push him away. God knows I'm too weak to stop him, otherwise.

Nik sighs, and I'm both satisfied and disappointed that it might have worked. But his hands drop to my waist, and he lifts me, plopping my ass in front of him, between his parted legs. His hands return to my shoulders, and he kneads my tense muscles.

"I'm sorry it came to this, Kat. Abducting you, I mean. I wish there had been another way to bring you to me. For what it's worth, you can rest assured that Boris and Ivan will be punished for harming you."

"And who's going to punish you for having me kidnapped in the first place?"

19

KAT

"I'm sure you will punish me, as you have so far—repeatedly and in so many ways," Nik whispers against my skin.

He laughs softly, and there is a flutter in my stomach as his chest vibrates against my back.

"What's that supposed to mean?" I ask.

"Shh. You're getting tense again. I can feel it on your shoulders. Just relax. Forget I said anything," he whispers in my ear. I shiver in response to the proximity of his mouth.

"Nik—"

"Just relax and watch the footage, Kat. Look, there's Connor sneaking away. See?"

I glance at the screen as the man he pointed out as Patrick McGuire's enforcer leaves the museum's gardens.

"McGuire's whereabouts are conveniently accounted for throughout the entire evening. But Connor comes and goes a handful of times through the night," Nik says. "I don't know where he goes for sure since the museum's internal footage is missing, but I'd put good money he was off doing McGuire's dirty work for him."

I try to focus on the video before me, striving not to let myself get carried away by his touch again. But it's a losing battle. It's just so difficult to resist his allure.

Nik's strong hands firmly knead my knotted shoulders. When his thumbs trace the length of my neck, I feel like I can barely breathe.

It gets even worse once I notice myself in the video footage. More specifically, I spot myself in Nik's arms on the dance floor. I observe our back-and-forth as I try to leave the party, and he convinces me to stay. As I watch us on the screen, Nik's firm hands never stop rubbing my shoulders and neck.

His soft laughter tickles the back of my neck. "Ah, there you are, Kat."

Nik's warm breath grazes the hair at the back of my head as we watch our past selves sneak away to the empty room where we had sex. He laughs before nuzzling my neck. His lips flutter against my skin as he says, "Still can't keep my hands off of you…"

"Nik—" I say, unsure of what might come out of my lips next. Will I ask him to stop? Or will I beg him to go on?

"There's your *friend* Dmitri," Nik says, teasingly emphasizing the word.

It's easy to spot Dmitri on the screen. A blonde with a gorgeous body is excitedly talking to him as he glances around the place, markedly uncomfortable. He pulls his cell phone out of his pocket and excuses himself. He wastes no time bringing it to his ear before hastily stepping out of frame.

"I thought blondes were supposed to have more fun," I joke. It isn't clear in the footage, but it seemed like Dmitri faked the phone call to avoid the poor girl.

"I guess brunettes are more his type if today is any indication," Nik says under his breath.

"Can you blame him?"

I shimmy my hips back so I sit closer to Nik's body.

"Can't say that I do. Dmitri's respect for authority leaves much to be desired, but his taste in women is impeccable."

I can't help but laugh.

"Earlier today at breakfast, he was just messing around to try to get a rise out of you, you know."

"I know. He loves to do that. I'm not concerned about Dmitri, Kat. He knows better than to cross the line."

I peer over my shoulder to look at Nik. "And what line is that?"

"Daring to try to take what's mine," he says without hesitation, not breaking eye contact even for a second.

I scoff, turning back to face the TV. "I'm not yours if that's what you're implying."

"You could've fooled me. From where I'm sitting, it sure looks like you are."

"Once again, you're delusional. Just because I'm working for you, it doesn't mean you own me."

"You keep telling yourself that, *milaya*."

"Is that Russian for babe or something like that? Because I can't stand men calling me babe."

"Maybe it's Russian for *mine*," he says against my ear, nipping at it.

I shoot him an unamused look over my shoulder.

"How you do you say *in your fucking dreams* in Russian?"

Nik laughs.

"You're not entirely wrong. I've dreamed about you being mine. Often. Tell me, Kat. Have you done the same?"

I glare at him. "Nikolai, we're keeping things professional, remember?"

"That wasn't a no."

He smirks, completely incorrigible.

"It wasn't a yes, either."

"Now, who's delusional, Kat? If you want me to stop touching you, just say the word, and I will."

It's a dare. I open my mouth to tell him just that, but his hands feel so amazingly rough on my skin, and I love the comforting heat of his body enveloping mine—from his torso against my back to his thighs around my own.

Nik waits for a long moment. When I say nothing, he smiles in triumph.

"That's what I thought."

He chuckles.

I want to wipe that infuriatingly smug expression off his face.

I'm sick and tired of being at Nik's mercy. Apparently, it's not enough that the man controls my fate. He also gets to bend my body and mind completely to his whims.

As much as I hate it, I can't stop him from forcing me to join his dangerous pursuit of revenge for his friend's death. But I'm not ready to concede defeat and surrender to his control as far as the rest is concerned.

His reactions to me yesterday are undeniable signs that he can't control his body's response to mine any more than I can control mine to his.

I'm not too proud to use my body and his sexual attraction to me to regain some semblance of power over this situation. If seducing him is what it will take to bring this unthinkably powerful man to his knees, then so be it.

As Nik's hands massage my neck and shoulders, I scoot my hips closer to his—slowly but deliberately. I want him to know I'm intentionally making this choice.

I inch backward until I feel the firm pressure of his

erection against me. Nik's hands' movements falter for a split second before he resumes kneading my sore muscles.

Eyes glued to the screen, I slowly rock my hips against him. Suddenly halting his languid massage, he hisses in a breath.

I pause, looking over my shoulder at his face. "Everything okay?"

Nik narrows his eyes at me.

"Can't complain."

With a smirk, he resumes his ministrations to my tense muscles.

I don't bother hiding my sigh of pleasure. I want him to know his touch affects me. Because I know that will affect him.

His guarded eyes study me as I watch the surveillance footage. I lean back against him, molding my back to his chest and abs. As my head rests against his shoulder, I rotate my hips against his erection.

Nik inhales sharply and his hands stop massaging my shoulders.

"Kat..." he says, a warning command resounding in his tone.

"You're sure you're okay?" I ask again, ignoring his feeble attempt to ward me off.

Nik raises an eyebrow, glaring at me. I'm starting to realize it is something he will do whenever he thinks I am being particularly challenging.

"I know what you're doing, Kat."

For a moment, I consider feigning ignorance but ultimately decide against it. "Good," I say, giving him a small smile.

My response catches him off guard.

"Are you toying with me again, Kat? I thought you had learned your lesson."

His expression is forbidding and menacing, but the intended effect is ruined when his member grows harder and larger against my flesh. I reward him by moving my ass up and down against it.

His hands slide down to my upper arms, holding me firmly in place. "Kat..." Nik exhales, utterly failing to sound even slightly put off.

"Hey, if you want me to stop touching you, just say the word, Nik."

He clutches my arms even tighter, narrowing his eyes at me again.

But his lips never voice a protest.

I don't bother hiding my grin, pleased at how the turntables have turned in my favor this time. "That's what I thought," I say with a chuckle, mimicking his words and tone from earlier.

"You're playing a very dangerous game," Nik says as his hands trail down my arms. Slowly, he places them on my hips.

"You're just salty that I'm better at it than you are."

My cockiness gets me a raised eyebrow again.

"Is that what you think?"

I smirk, lazily rubbing myself on his cock.

"It's what I know." The soft fabric of my skirt molds to my body with my movements, and his erection, hot and hard, presses against my soft flesh.

Nik's eyes never leave mine as he slides his hands down my hips—down my thighs—until he reaches the hem of my skirt. Without hesitation, he yanks it up, immediately touching me between my legs.

Still maintaining eye contact, he pulls my panties

aside. I don't dare look away from his mesmerizing gaze, even when his fingers part me. A loud moan escapes my lips as he runs his fingers up and down. His movements aren't brusque, but he's not particularly gentle or tender either.

Nik raises his hand, and my underwear snaps back into place. I groan in frustration at the loss of his touch right where I need him the most. He glances at the fingers that were exploring my center before looking at me. A slow, sexy smirk takes over his face.

"You're so fucking wet, *milaya*," he says in a cocky tone. "It looks like I affect you just as much as you affect me."

"I never said you don't. I just pointed out I'm better at using your attraction to me to my advantage than you are. Give me half a chance, and I'll have you eating out of the palm of my hand."

I place a quick kiss on his neck. Nik barely stifles a groan.

"I don't need to use your attraction to me to have you under my control. I already got you right where I want you, Kat."

"We'll see about that, Nik," I say with a wink before delivering a languid, open-mouthed kiss to his neck.

A raspy breath escapes his lips, and he closes his eyes. Still, Nik resists me. In response, I move my ass up and down the length of his erection in a deliberate rhythm.

His breath catches in his throat, so I increase the urgency of my kiss against the skin of his neck. His scent is so mouthwateringly masculine and inebriating that it's hard to fight the distraction. It takes all my willpower to resist the urge to just mindlessly pleasure him and myself.

But this moment will set the tone for all our future interactions, so I try to stay focused. I must remain in control of myself to gain some control over him—the man who holds my life in his hands.

As I increase the tempo of my movements against him, Nik grows larger and even more rigid. He pants, the warmth of his breath grazing my ear and the skin of my neck. A shiver runs through me. Still, I resist the mindless lust.

I take his physical response—and the fact that he hasn't stopped this madness—as encouragement that I'm on the right path. I'm not sure what victory will look like in this scenario, but something tells me I'll recognize it when I see it.

I take his hand and place it on my breast while rubbing my ass against his length. "Touch me, Nik. Please."

With a pained groan, he does. His calloused hand palms my breast, almost roughly. My nipple hardens in return, and he responds by pinching it. I cry out, and it spurs him on. His other hand grabs the other side of my chest.

Nik's on the verge of succumbing to the passion I'm awakening in him, so I place my hands on my thighs, spreading them wide. I grab the hem of my skirt and pull it up to my waist. Just like he did earlier, I tug my underwear aside to finger myself, spreading my wetness around my center.

While caressing my breasts, Nik groans against my neck. I increase the rhythm of my movements up and down his straining cock, and he rewards me by biting down hard on the spot where my neck meets my shoulder.

He's close to breaking, on the brink of completely succumbing to the haze of his lust. His breaths come out in erratic pants as his fingertips mercilessly tease the tips of my breasts. There isn't much gentleness left in him as his hips begin to move in the same cadence as mine.

All I need to do is give Nik a little push, and he will

tumble down. The hard part is preventing myself from falling before him.

As I finger myself, I reach up with my other arm to pull his mouth down to my neck. Nik doesn't fight me, showering me with forceful, open-mouthed caresses on the tender spot of flesh where he bit me. His maddening tongue touches it. The feeling is almost enough to drive me over the edge, but I don't let myself come.

I cry out his name in pleasure, and that almost does the trick. His caresses grow more urgent as his thrusting becomes more demanding.

Somehow, through the fog brought on by the pressing orgasm building in my center, I figure it out. I realize at last what his little reactions are telling me—the way to drive him over the edge is by letting him do the same for me.

"Nik," I pant. "I want to come for you." The sound of his breath catching in his throat—followed by a pained groan—is all the confirmation I need. "Please, Nik. Make me come."

"*Milaya*," he says with a sigh. "You don't ever have to beg me for what I'd kill to give you."

Nik's hands drop to my hips. He holds me so tightly I'll have a bruise tomorrow. His arm snakes around my waist, and his right hand slides down my stomach until it reaches my sex.

I try to pull my hand away, but he stops me, keeping my wet fingers right there. "No, Kat," he says against my ear, wrapping his big hand around mine. "We'll do this together. I'll make you come for me, but we're doing it my way, on my terms."

Frustrated, I groan. This isn't how it is supposed to go. We're supposed to do it *my* way, which involves him losing control and giving in to the erotic pull between us. Instead, the infuriating man has turned the moment into another display of his power over me.

Nik is truly the most maddening man I've ever met. But it doesn't matter. I always play through the whistle. The game isn't over until I say it's over. So, I reach behind me and fumble around the front of his pants, trying to unbutton them.

He lets go of my hips to grab my roaming hand. Easily restraining my wrist, he holds my arm flush against my back. "It's my way or no way, Kat," he says. "So, what's it going to be?"

As I consider my options, his hand, wrapped around mine between my legs, lazily runs our fingers over my wet sex. I can't help panting and squirming a little. I'm so close to the edge he could make me come with the slightest bit of pressure on my clitoris. Nik's undoubtedly fully aware of it, judging by how carefully he avoids the spot.

He runs his mouth down the column of my neck. "What's it going to be, Kat?" he asks again, lips vibrating against my skin.

I resist answering for as long as possible, but he's got me and he knows it. "Your way," I concede at last.

Nik showers my shoulders with kisses. "Good girl," he says, nipping at my ear. "Now, ask me again. Nicely."

I don't even need to inquire. I know exactly what he means. "Please, Nik," I ask, panting and shamelessly rubbing myself against his hard body. He waits. "Please, make me come."

With a barely restrained groan, he does.

20

NIK

VICTORY HAS NEVER TASTED SO bitter.

During my thirty-four years on this planet, I've learned a thing or two about bittersweet wins. I have had more than my fair share of triumphs that have come at a hefty price.

I'm happy I've beaten Kat in her manipulative game, but I can't say I feel any sense of satisfaction. There's no joy in this achievement—just a deep, unshakable feeling of foreboding. Even though I've won this battle, the war between us is far from over. She will keep trying to control me through my foolish, irresponsible attraction to her. And I'm not so sure I have it in me to win the next round.

To make matters even worse, I can now add sexual frustration to the emotional cocktail brewing inside of me. After all, Kat was the only one who found release. She came so hard she is now as soft as a kitten in my arms, every muscle in her body blissfully relaxed. Deep, content sighs have replaced her erratic panting from earlier, and she's the picture of satisfaction and satiety.

While I can't deny I'm very proud of myself for pleasing

her, Kat's obvious sexual contentment is a poignant reminder of my almost painful state of non-fulfillment.

Unfortunately, this isn't a problem I am likely to fix soon. In the last twenty-four hours, Kat has made it abundantly clear—she fully intends to have me eating out of the palm of her hand by seducing me. And God damn her, she just might succeed.

If our brief history is any indication, resisting her isn't something that comes to me naturally.

If our circumstances were any different, I'd love nothing more than to let her try—her secretive, untrustworthy ways be damned. But as things stand, it would be a development I can't afford right now. So resist her I must. Somehow.

I don't know how to accomplish this still unprecedented feat, but at least I have the common sense to realize that giving in to my insatiable desire for her isn't the answer, which brings me to my current unfortunate—and physically painful—situation.

It's all well and good to turn the tables on her and give her a little taste of her own medicine, as I did a moment ago. Kat wanted me to submit to her, to beg her to satiate the desperate craving her merciless teasing brought on. But I managed to get the upper hand. In the end, the little thief surrendered to me.

For now.

That's why I can't let Kat return the favor even if she were to offer. The woman isn't giving up on this reckless scheme of hers. I have no doubts she'll continue to try to bend me to her will, and I can't afford the risk that she might succeed. I need to keep my wits about me if my plans are to work out.

To obliterate McGuire, I need to be fully in charge of myself and those I have enlisted to help me. That includes

Kat. I can't very well control her or myself if she manages to wrap me around her little finger.

Of course, I'd love to sink deep inside her again or feel her clever little hands—and her maddening mouth—on me, but it just can't happen. I'm not confident about my odds of resisting her. On the contrary, Kat is perfectly capable of succeeding in her devious plan. Unfortunately, I'm not convinced I can get her to stop trying. Threats haven't worked, and retribution hasn't either.

I'm toeing a dangerous line. Kat is only helping me with my plans for McGuire because I have leverage over her. If she realizes how unlikely it is that I would ever cause her pain, my leverage is gone. I may be a fool as far as she's concerned, but I'm not stupid enough to believe she'll stick around and help me unless I have something to hold over her head.

The conclusion is simple, although unfortunate. I have to keep myself in check. I have to deny myself the pleasures I know are to be found in her arms because I'm not strong enough to resist her attempts to control me.

Kat lets out another content sigh, a small smile curving her lips as she stretches out her body. "Mmm. Just what the doctor ordered," she says. "Your turn now."

The little thief wraps her arms around my neck, rubbing her plump ass against my cock. In my current starved state, I barely manage to stifle a groan. Untangling her arms from around my neck, I lift her by the waist and set her down next to me. She's still close enough that I can smell her delicious scent, but at least we aren't touching anymore.

"What's the matter?" she asks, an amused glint in her deep blue eyes.

"We should go back to work," I say, glancing at the surveillance footage on the screen.

Kat blinks twice, her smile faltering slightly. After a brief pause, a calculating look shines in her eyes as her lips curve sensuously. She leans forward and hooks her index finger over the collar of my sweater, pulling me closer until my breath mingles with hers and her nose brushes against mine.

"We can work later. Let me take care of you now," she says. Her soft, lush lips deliciously brush against the corner of my mouth.

Somehow, I find the strength to deny her. "I appreciate the offer, Kat, but there's no need to trouble yourself on my account. I'm good."

Her other hand boldly caresses the uncomfortable bulge straining against my jeans. An erratic breath escapes me, and yet, I curb the urge to moan at her touch. "Liar," Kat says, chuckling against my mouth before running the tip of her tongue along the seam of my lips. "You want me."

Her gaze rushes to connect with mine as if daring me to deny it.

I can't. I don't.

I stare back at her in silence.

"It's okay, Nik," she says, looking into my eyes. "You made me feel so good just now. Let me return the favor. There's no reason to deny us what we want so badly."

Kat slowly rubs me up and down over my jeans, right where I need her the most, while wrapping her other hand around the back of my neck. Her fingernails lightly scratch me there before she tangles her hand in my hair. A shiver runs down my spine. "There are plenty of reasons," I mutter through gritted teeth.

"Well, no good ones," she says.

I laugh at her humorlessly, and she narrows her eyes at me.

"I know you want me, Nik. Will you deny it?"

I sigh.

"No. But that doesn't mean anything. It doesn't mean I've forgotten who you are and what you have done. It certainly doesn't mean I'm going to let you control me through my sexual attraction to you."

Kat smiles prettily. "You can't blame a girl for trying."

"No, but I sure can wish she'd stop."

"I don't think you do. I think you like it when I try to seduce you. Actually, I think you love it."

She winks at me. As fast as a whip, she lurches forward, kissing me.

A delicious sigh leaves her lips. Before it's too late, I grab her shoulders and push her away. Unwilling to give her any other opportunities to test my self-restraint, I get up and sit as far away from her as possible, on the opposite side of the couch. I half expect her to follow me right away. She doesn't. Instead, she laughs.

"Back to the footage," I say in my most disapproving tone.

"All work and no play will make you a very dull boy, Nik," she says with another laugh, leaning back on the couch.

"We have all the time in the world to play later. Once the work is done."

Glancing at the TV, I'm reminded of why I'm in this situation in the first place. Maxim's face flashes in my mind as he looked the last time I saw him. He looked so lifeless, his skin shaded by a faint blue tint, his neck marred by the angry ligature marks. It's a sobering memory.

Kat opens her maddening mouth to speak, a playful, flirty light shining in her ocean-blue eyes.

"Kat—" I say, cutting her off before she can suggest

anything. "I meant what I said earlier. I hope you won't hate working for me too much, but make no mistake—this job comes first before anything else. It's the only thing that matters to me right now. I won't let you or anyone else keep me from seeing it through."

Frustratingly, I feel a pang in my chest as that teasing look leaves her expression.

"I understand, Nik. And I will help you as best as I can. I promise. But there's no need for things to be so black and white. We can work *and* let off some steam whenever needed. I can't imagine how much pressure you must be under right now. Why not let me help you with that as well?"

I dare a glance in her direction. The maddening woman is smiling coyly at me.

I sigh again before sternly saying, "We are not going down this path, Kat. And that's my final word on this subject."

"We'll see about that."

I let her challenging reply slide, hoping it will be the end of this subject. Deep down, however, I have a feeling that's nothing but wishful thinking on my part.

I keep my eyes glued to the screen as past Kat discreetly leaves the room where she gave me the most fantastic fuck I've had in years. Maybe ever. Even then, she was already playing games with me. While I was dying to get another chance to have her in my arms, the little thief's only concern had been to disappear with my most valuable possession.

"I've been curious. What made you get into this line of work in the first place?" I ask.

Kat raises her eyebrows. "I'm surprised you even have to ask," she says. "Surely a big, bad *bratva pakhan* such as yourself would have learned all there is to know about me by now."

I scoff. "I'd never be stupid enough to fool myself into thinking that."

She smiles. "Well, be it as it may, I'm positive you looked me up. I wouldn't be surprised to find a file on me somewhere in this room."

"Maybe. I know you were an orphan for most of your childhood. You were adopted later, during your teen years. And I learned of your stellar reputation as one of the best in your field."

"*The* best," she corrects me sharply.

I smirk, pleased she took the bait. "Perhaps. But none of that tells me why you chose this...lifestyle. Not all orphans become part of the criminal underworld's elite. So why did you?"

She remains silent for a long moment. Eventually, she says, "I knew I'd be good at it. It seemed foolish not to pursue what I knew I would excel at. And truth be told, I was tired of hoping, wishing, and praying for things that were never offered to me. If no one was going to give me anything, then I was going to take it myself. What can I say? I like the finer things in life." She shrugs. "I was so done with feeling helpless—powerless, victimized. So tired of being at the mercy of others and unable to take care of those I care about."

Dumbstruck, I stare at her, long after she is done talking. I thought she'd brush me off, giving me a non-answer. Whatever I expected her to say in response to my question, it wasn't this heartfelt statement. For a moment, I struggle to reconcile this vulnerable, caring side of her with the untrustworthy woman I've learned she can be.

If anyone can understand what it is like to be utterly

alone and have to fend for yourself at a young age, that would be me.

I study her in a way I haven't yet. As always, I see her beautifully wrought face and perfectly sculpted body, but for the first time, I also see her delicate hands and athletic but diminutive build. At fifteen, I probably already outweighed her by at least fifty pounds.

As a child in a similar situation to hers, being alone was always a scary and dangerous experience for me. I can only imagine what it had been like for a creature as fragile as her. I shudder just thinking about it. And to think she somehow found it in herself to worry about others and protect them.

As I unabashedly study her—this confusing, intriguing woman who has turned my orderly life upside down—I can't help but wonder who is taking care of her while she's busy looking out for others. I can't help but wish it could be me.

"That's the guy from last night," she says, interrupting my reverie, blissfully unaware of it.

I glance at the screen and see Vladmir approaching me through the museum gala's guests. It's a much-welcome reminder of why we are here.

Maxim.

The man I failed to protect.

"That's Vladmir Smirnov. He works for me."

"I figured that much."

"He's approaching me to take me to Maxim."

"Oh," she says, straightening. "He came from inside the museum."

"Yes." I clear my throat. "That's where they found the body."

"I see. Where?"

"The room had been closed to the public that evening. It

was in the area where they hold their *Italian Masters* exhibition."

"I know where."

We watch the footage for a few moments longer. Vladmir and I disappear from the frame. Patrick McGuire can be seen the entire time. The Irish bastard is clever like that.

Once the surveillance video ends, Kat turns to me. "I'm sorry." I nod in response.

After a moment, she says, "And you think Patrick McGuire is behind the murder."

"I know he is."

"Sorry, I hate to ask—but how did Maxim die?"

"I believe he was strangled to death. A ligature strangulation. They used a garrote, I'd guess."

Kat nods for a second, a solemn look on her face. Suddenly, she frowns. "What do you mean, you *believe*?"

I sigh. I had a feeling she'd catch that.

"Maxim's body...it's missing."

21

NIK

KAT'S EYES WIDEN. "He's missing? But you saw it. Him, I mean."

"I did. Vlad took me straight to him. I saw his body on the museum's floor. A dozen or so of my men did, too."

"Then how come it's missing? How's that possible?"

I grind my teeth. Good fucking question.

"That's what I'd like to know as well. We delivered his body to the funeral home. I was debating if I should have an autopsy done when they alerted me it was gone."

"Well, where could it be?"

"If I knew that, it wouldn't be fucking missing, Kat."

She blinks at me in silence. After a moment, I feel bad for biting her head off. It's not her fault Maxim's missing. I hope.

With a sigh, I add, "I'm sorry. I didn't mean to take it out on you. It's just...it's been a challenging week. I'm sure that bastard McGuire has something to do with the disappearance of Maxim's remains."

"Why would he take the body?"

"To hide the evidence of his crime? Because he wants to

add insult to injury? Or violate Maxim's remains? To fuck with me? Take your pick."

Kat is silent for a moment, seemingly processing all the information I just dumped on her.

"What makes you believe Maxim was strangled with a garrote?" she asks.

"He had ligature marks around his neck and a blueish discoloration on his skin."

"I see. But you were still considering an autopsy."

"Yes. I wanted to be sure that's how he died. People in my line of business can be a little underhanded about this sort of stuff. Even though I was pretty sure I knew how he was murdered, I was still considering whether it was a good idea to get indisputable confirmation. We sent his body to the funeral home that night, and I asked them to give me until the morning before doing anything. I'd have made my decision by then. But a couple of hours later, he was gone."

"Why did you hesitate with the autopsy? When you put it like that, it just seems like a no-brainer."

"I—Like I said, all signs indicated his cause of death was pretty self-evident. I didn't want to have him violated or delay putting him to rest if I didn't absolutely have to."

Kat's eyes soften. "Sorry. I should have thought of that," she says. I nod. "This whole story is insane. A man with mafia ties is murdered at The Metropolitan Museum during a party where the mayor himself was in attendance. Then, his body goes missing. How come this isn't all over the news?"

"I've kept it quiet. It was the least I could do for Maxim. I don't want his name used as clickbait, and I don't want the police interfering with my business. I'll handle Patrick McGuire myself."

Kat is silent for a long time. I don't blame her. It's a lot to take in.

"So, how do you expect me to help you with this? As you know, this isn't exactly my area of expertise," she says at last.

"I know McGuire did it, and I will make sure he pays for it. But I can't just take him out based solely on his history with Maxim. Not without risking a massive war between his family and my *bratva*. The last time there was a war within the Seven Families…it was bad, let's leave it at that. Suffice it to say, I need to avoid a war at all costs. I can't risk my men's lives so recklessly. Now, If I had unquestionable, undeniable proof of McGuire's involvement and guilt, then I'd be justified in taking action. War could be avoided. Lives would be spared."

"I still fail to see how I can aid you with any of that."

I smile at her. "You're beautiful. You're charming as hell and too clever for your own good. I am the *bratva's pakhan*. I'm one of McGuire's rivals. But you are neutral. You're an esteemed member of our little slice of the criminal underworld. One with curves that go on for miles and with a smart mouth that is dangerously distracting. In more ways than one. You can get into places I can't. There are people who will talk to you but not to me. My men are seen as an extension of me, but you… McGuire will never see you coming."

"We weren't being discreet at the party. He could've spotted us together. He might know of our connection."

"I realize that. I'm not concerned about it."

Kat raises her eyebrows. "Why not?"

"Even if he knows about us, it won't matter. If anything, it'd help our cause."

"That makes no sense. You just gave me a whole speech about how I'm neutral, and blah, blah, blah…"

I lean closer to her. "The temptation to take my latest conquest from me would drive him to seek you out. He wouldn't be able to help himself. You'd play him like a fiddle."

"You seem very sure of that."

"I am. Nothing to worry about."

Kat scoffs. "Speak for yourself. You want me to trick the boss of the Irish mafia into giving you a justifiable reason to off him. I have plenty to worry about."

I stare at Kat until she meets my gaze. "I won't let him lay a hand on you. He won't harm a hair over your head. If he touches you, he's dead."

She sighs. "What about the war you want to avoid?"

"Fuck the war. You're under my protection now. If he even dreams about harming you, I'll destroy him without a second thought."

Kat studies my expression, trying to gauge my sincerity. Fascinated, I watch different emotions flutter over her face as she absorbs my words.

"Do you trust me?" I ask her.

The little thief considers my question. "I believe you are sincere. You'll do your best to protect me. But I've known you for such a short amount of time... And it's been a wild ride so far. You can't expect me to trust you just yet. I know you don't trust me."

"Well, you stole from me."

"You kidnapped me."

"*Because* you stole from me."

Kat has the nerve to roll her eyes at me. "Let's not argue semantics, Nik. My point remains. You can't demand that I trust you when you don't yet trust me yourself."

"Again, you stole from me. You presented yourself as an untrustworthy person from the start."

"Get off your high horse," she says, scoffing. "You didn't very well tell me everything about yourself from the start, either."

"I wasn't dishonest. I just didn't tell you what you didn't need to know then."

Kat raises her eyebrows at me, her gaze unwavering. "I could say the same."

"But it's just not the same, and you know it."

"I know no such thing. What I know is that you're being unfair to me. You're setting these extremely high standards for me when you don't uphold them yourself. For example, you resent my attempts to exert a minuscule degree of influence over you through the sexual attraction between us when you've been taking every chance you get to control me—mind, body, and soul."

I narrow my eyes at her. "So you do admit to trying to control and manipulate me."

Kat's response is to roll her eyes at me. "Are you really going to ignore the point I'm trying to make?"

I sigh. I guess I'll have to point out the obvious. "The problem with your logic is that you believe we should be on equal footing, and that's just not the case. I may not have fully disclosed everything about myself the night we first met, but I didn't steal a priceless diamond from you. I didn't betray you."

"I didn't know it belonged to you."

"It doesn't matter. The point I'm trying to make here is that I get to control you. Because you *owe* me."

"What you're really trying to say is that you *own* me."

I shrug, trying to appear nonchalant when the mere thought of truly owning her—mind, body and soul, as she put it—gives me an insurmountable amount of pleasure.

"Unfortunately for you, Kat, I do have leverage over you,

so I get to impose my will over yours. Unless you have an ace up your sleeve I don't know about, I don't think you can say the same," I say.

As soon as the words leave my mouth, I wish I could take them back. Kat squints her eyes at me, and it's as clear as day that she will take my bold statement as a challenge.

She smiles at me. Slowly. "I think you and I know that's not exactly true, Nik. I'm sure you'll come to see that there are different kinds of leverage. If memory serves, you struggle to resist mine," she says in a sultry tone.

"Well, may the best *man* win, I suppose, Kat."

Her only reply is a smirk.

22

KAT

The rest of the morning flies by in a blur.

Soon after Nik made the fatal mistake of challenging me, the personal shopper he said would be coming over to help me select my new wardrobe arrives.

Her name is Caroline, and she has impeccable taste. She and I get along well, and I have a great time for the first hour of her visit. I sigh and squeal in pleasure as she helps me try on all her luxurious offerings.

But as the hours pass, I begin to feel weary. As I stare at the mirror, I physically feel the stress of the past couple of days catch up with me, even as I drool over my reflection.

"So lovely, right? Well, the dress is Chanel, these shoes are YSL, and the bag is Dior. Your lingerie, of course, is Agent Provocateur," Caroline says, smiling at me while gesturing towards the beautiful strips of lace and silk on the bed in my new bedroom—my jail cell.

"It's all gorgeous. I'll take it. All of it, obviously," I say, returning her smile.

Caroline nods, still grinning, before showing me the other gorgeous pieces she selected for me.

Once I have spent enough money to make even multibillionaire Russian mobsters pause, I'm secretly glad when Caroline says her goodbyes.

My relief is short-lived, however, as the doctor Nik mentioned earlier shows up mere moments after her departure. My distractingly handsome captor watches in silence from a distance as the physician examines my head.

As I predicted, my injury is very mild. The good doctor recommends rest and cold compresses, reassuring Nik that I don't have a concussion and should feel completely normal in a few days. The man leaves after reminding us to contact him if my condition changes. After spearing me with another glowering glance, so does Nik.

Glad to be left alone, I hurry to change into clean clothes. Once I feel the soothing touch of a fresh cotton t-shirt and shorts against my skin, I have to fight to keep my eyes open. I feel more exhausted than I've felt in years.

I waste no time getting under the enormous bed's covers. Their weight is comforting, and a sigh escapes my lips as my muscles relax.

Soon, delicious sleep starts to take over me. I don't fight it, slipping into a sweet, dreamless slumber within minutes.

It feels like hours—maybe days—pass as bone-deep relaxation makes all my worries seem far away. Somewhere deep inside my dark pit of unconsciousness, I'm vaguely aware of a presence. I can't say how much time goes by before I detect the soft pressure of warm lips on my forehead, followed by an impossibly gentle Russian whisper.

Yo postoyanno dumayu o tebe.

Deep within the grasp of my slumber, struggling to maintain my precarious grip on sentience, I will myself to memorize it. I don't want to forget it. I want to find out what it means.

The last thing I feel is a slight, warm touch against my lips. As it slowly traces its shape, I succumb to the darkness again. The irresistible peacefulness it brings me is welcome, as much as part of me yearns to linger and enjoy more of the pleasant touch.

At some point, I find myself in a long, cold hallway. It's dark and humid as water slowly leaks down the dirty, gray walls, and the harsh overhead lights flicker.

Faintly, I hear a woman cry. Her sobs and erratic breathing sound terrifyingly familiar. I can't pinpoint where her voice is coming from or who it belongs to. So, I inch closer to a metal door across the corridor from me. As I approach it, it becomes clear the weeping lady is on the other side of it.

A few feet away from it, I recognize the voice as A.J.'s. Her inconsolable cries echo in the hall as I run towards the door; I yank it open, preparing myself for the worst possible scenarios my mind can conjure. But there's nothing on the other side of it. Nothing but darkness.

My best friend's sobs grow more desperate, and I rush to cross the doorway. My surprised gasp echoes as my feet find no ground beneath them. Before I can react in any other way, I scream in horror as air rushes around me.

I'm falling.

Panicked, I flail my arms and legs in despair, reflexively grabbing a coarse rope that my right hand brushes against. Unseeingly, I grip it as hard as I can and manage to stop my free fall. The rough fibers of the rope bite the palm of my hand as my weight pulls me down towards the abyss. Frantically, as my heartbeats drum loudly in my ears, I use my left hand to secure my hold over the miraculous lifeline.

The muscles in my arms burn as I struggle to pull myself upwards towards the light. I glance up and see the doorway I fell through a few dozen feet above me. It's a luminous beacon in the darkness of the precipice. With a deep breath, I will myself to keep climbing, inch by torturous inch. Sweat makes my palms slippery, and I slide further down instead. It drips down my brows, burning my eyes, but I don't dare let go of the rope with either of my hands to wipe it away.

I look up again, screaming in renewed terror, when I spot the *stronzo* standing in the illuminated doorway. His gold rings reflect the overhead fluorescent light from the hallway. He is dressed in one of his expensive Italian wool suits, black in color. He sneers down his tan, Roman nose at me, contempt and malice burning in his pale blue eyes.

I try to ignore him as hard as possible, pushing forward and climbing towards the evil man blocking the door. My palms feel raw and wet as if the skin has been removed like a glove. But at last, I reach the doorway. With a grunt, I grab the edge, groaning in pain as my arms and shoulders protest while I struggle to pull myself up. My groan turns into a cry of pure agony as fine leather shoes crush my fingers.

My eyes meet the *stronzo*'s when he cruelly smirks at me before delivering the final blow. He kicks me hard in the face, and I can't hold on any longer. With a scream, I plummet to what I know is certain death as his mocking laughter echoes around me.

Suddenly, my breath is knocked out of me as I sink like an anvil into deep, freezing water. The cold is so forbidding that I freeze into place, unable to move my limbs. Yet, I urge myself to kick my feet out and push towards what I hope is the surface. In the pitch-black darkness, it's impossible to tell.

My lungs burn with the need to breathe when I finally break through. With a frantic gasp, I inhale a chestful of air.

But before I know it, the current grabs me, pulling me under again.

Again and again, I fight to keep my head above the water, but the current and the waves are stronger and relentless. My struggle is futile.

This is it. I'm dying. The *stronzo* wins.

Despair grows inside me, and I wail, knowing A.J. is soon to follow. I continue to fight, kicking and flailing my arms.

"Shh, shh, *milaya*." A soothing voice sounds impossibly close. "You're safe. I'm here. It's just a bad dream."

Scalding warmth embraces me. Somehow, I'm sitting up. It feels surreally impossible, but I blink my eyes open to find myself in a bed. As I regain my actual senses, somewhat in the back of my mind, it registers that night has fallen. The room is drenched in darkness and faint, pale moonlight.

Soft lips run over my hair and my forehead. Burning hot strength surrounds me everywhere. The clean scent of fresh linen and warm male envelops me. I can't help rubbing my face on it. My heartbeat calms down.

"*Kiska*," Nik whispers, his voice soothing me. "You're alright. You were having a nightmare, that's all. You're here with me now." His arms tighten around me as he continues to rain soft kisses on my head.

"I was drowning," I say, sobbing against his chest.

"Shh, *kiska*. You're safe now."

"I fell in the dark, and I was going to drown. She was going to die... she needed me, and I couldn't save her," I mumble as my tears soak his sweater.

"No one's going to die, *kiska*. It was just a dream. You're okay."

"You don't understand," I say between sobs.

"I'll always keep you safe. Nothing's going to hurt you ever again. I promise."

Nik's lips brush against my ear lobe, but his words make me cry harder. He shushes me again before rubbing my back and whispering Russian words against my hair. After a few more calming breaths, I realize that he's rocking me back and forth.

Too soon, Nik's Russian mumblings cease. A minute or two later, he says, "You need sleep, *milaya*." He leans back, shifting us into a lying-down position while gently holding me in his arms.

"No," I protest heartily. "I can't. I'll just go back to my nightmare."

"No, you won't. I've got you. You're safe. Sleep now."

I resist it, dreading the bad dream. Nik continues to hold me, tenderly rubbing circles between my shoulder blades. To my surprise, it doesn't take long for my eyelids to grow heavy. My exhaustion wins, and unconsciousness overtakes me again as I fervently hope for some dreamless sleep.

The next thing I know, I am burning hot. Awareness gradually creeps in, but I fight to continue sleeping. It is pointless. As sleep evades me, I grow increasingly uncomfortable and even start to sweat. With a sigh, I blink my eyes open and realize it's daytime. The sun glows through the massive windows in the bed chamber, waking me up with its brightness and heat.

After sitting up, I glance to my left, noticing a chair a couple of feet away next to the bed. It wasn't there when I went to sleep the day before.

Gradually, memories of the past night come to me. I recall the man who comforted me, drying my tears. I remember his gentleness and care.

In the broad daylight, it barely feels real. I'm half sure

I've dreamed it all up. After the horrible nightmare, maybe my brain felt the need to compensate for that abject horror with a dream of blissful tenderness.

It is probably best to convince myself it was a dream. So, I roll to my side to get up from the bed. I desperately need a shower this morning.

With a frown, I spot something on the pillow next to mine. I reach for it and pick up a brightly colored plastic bag. It's a pack of hard candy. Before I can stop myself, I laugh in disbelief.

Life Savers.

To keep me from drowning.

23

KAT

NOTHING TASTES as sweet as victory, but these gourmet chocolate truffles come pretty damn close.

There are a ton of things I could complain about the labor conditions at my current job. The impossibility of quitting it, for starters.

Luckily, the state of the pantry is not one of them. For all his many, many flaws, Nik has impeccable taste. I guess that explains what I confirmed last night.

The man's got it bad for me.

Why else would he tenderly tuck me in and kiss me goodnight before comforting me through that horrid nightmare? It's not like his reputation is that of a kind man.

No, there's no doubt about it. Nik can't get me out of his head.

Of course, I'm hardly one to talk, considering I wholeheartedly share his feelings.

Still, I can't deny it's really convenient for my plans that he can't keep his distance from me. Now, I know how to get this situation under control—I must seduce Nik.

A girl's gotta do what a girl's gotta do, but I won't pretend it will be any hardship to try to have my way with him, especially after last night.

As if it wasn't enough that Nik is the most maddeningly sexy man I've ever met, the sweetness and tenderness he showed last night make me crave him even more.

After finding the bag of *Life Savers* this morning, I took extra care with my appearance. I wanted to look extra irresistible to my elusive bed partner. It was a waste of time—Nik is nowhere to be found. All day, I've waited for him to come and find me. But the man is MIA.

Once I grow bored, I even consider calling or texting Nik —maybe even sexting him—but then I realize I don't even have his number. It's a hilarious realization but also a sobering one. There's so much I don't know about my beau, even though he holds my life in his hands—my best friend's, too.

Maybe I should take Nik's unexplained absence as an opportunity to gather intel on him.

Besides, it's not like it's in my nature to sit around and look pretty. I'm not embarrassed to admit I can sometimes be a little fidgety and restless if left to my own devices.

With that in mind, I retrace my steps from the day before and make my way to his office. I half expect to run into him, Dmitri, or one of his other henchmen on my way there, but there is no one to be found. The penthouse seems deserted, which works just fine for me.

I lightly knock on the closed door. After hearing no response, I enter Nik's private study.

Once again, it surprises me how personal the whole space is. Everything in the room screams *Nik*, from his faint scent to the many photographs scattered throughout the area.

I grab the closest one off the bookshelf for a closer look.

Nik is front-and-center, flanked by two other men, his arms wrapped around their shoulders. A slight smile curves his gorgeous lips, and his dark brown eyes sparkle with humor and affection.

I promptly recognize Dmitri at his right side, mid-laughter. His beautiful, pale, blue eyes squint with unconcealed delight.

I take too long to realize Maxim is the third man. He was even more striking than the low-resolution, grainy surveillance footage displayed. His deep blue eyes were hypnotizing. Even in the photograph, they shine with mocking amusement and undisguised intelligence. I can't help feeling like I'd have liked him a good deal.

Behind me, Nik's office door unexpectedly opens. The sound startles me, and I almost drop the picture frame. I place it back where I found it instead before turning around. My gaze locks with Nik's, and he raises an eyebrow at me.

"Honey, you're home," I say, giving him my most sugary smile. Behind him, Dmitri chuckles under his breath.

"What are you doing out of bed?" Nik asks me. "I sure hope you aren't disregarding medical advice just to snoop around my office."

"What can I say? You're too intriguing and irresistible. I couldn't help myself," I say. Dmitri laughs even louder.

Nik squints his eyes at me, clearly not sharing his *protégé*'s appreciation for my wit. "You should be in bed. Resting. As the doctor ordered."

"I'm more than happy to go back to bed if you agree to join me there. But I can't promise we'll be doing much resting." I wink at him.

Nik's only response is an aggravated sigh as he ruffles through a stack of papers atop his desk, no longer bothering to spare me a glance. His feigned displeasure doesn't bother or concern me in the slightest. After last night, nothing will convince me I can't thaw his Siberian icy heart.

"Hiya, Kat," Dmitri says, smiling at me.

"Hello, Dmitri. You look nice today," I say. He cuts a striking figure in his light gray suit and white dress shirt. His outfit's colors compliment his dark blond hair, beautifully bringing out the light blue color of his eyes. The way the broad expanse of his shoulders fills out the finely tailored jacket doesn't hurt, either.

Dmitri smiles at me, and had I been a couple of years younger, my heart would have skipped a beat.

"Thank you," he says. "And you look nice every day. More than nice, actually."

I laugh in response to his raspy flirtations as Nik forcefully puts his coffee mug on his desk.

Dmitri and I ignore him.

"Don't you have somewhere to be, Dmitri?" Nik asks, irritation dripping from every well-enunciated word.

"Not really, Nik," Dmitri says with a sigh. "I'm done for the day. But it seems like you have a lot going on right now. Here's an idea, Kat—since Nik here is too busy to keep you company, why don't you lead the way to your room? I'll make sure you don't get too lonely while you rest." Somehow, he manages to make his words sound both innocent and full of innuendo.

Nik stands up so abruptly that his chair falls backward. "That's it," he mutters through gritted teeth. "You're done. Get out."

I swivel to face him, petulantly crossing my arms over my chest. "You said I wasn't your prisoner. You said I could have friends over."

Nik's eyes burn with undisguised passion. "Not this insolent fool. And most certainly not in your bedroom."

I study him while mentally weighing my options for my answer. With a sigh, I shrug my shoulders, turning to Dmitri. "Oh, well, Dmitri. You heard the boss-man. We'll have to take a raincheck on that."

"*Kat*," Nik interjects, an unmistakable warning ringing in his tone.

With my back turned to Nik, I wink at Dmitri and he smirks at me.

"I guess I better bounce, Kat," he says with a sigh of his own. "But I'll see you around." He winks at me.

"Yeah, I hope I'll see you soon," I say, fishing around my jeans pocket with my index finger. After pulling out the candy, I offer it to Dmitri. "Life Saver?"

Nik comes around his desk at once and grabs my arm, forcing me to face him. "If you're looking for trouble, you've found it," he says, staring intensely into my eyes as his breath touches my lips.

"Don't worry, Kat," Dmitri says. "He doesn't really mean it. He knows that I'm all bark and no bite as far as you're concerned. You see, my heart's taken."

Intrigued, I give him a curious look, even while my attention remains focused on Nik, mesmerized by the pull his fiery intensity has over me.

Before I can ask Dmitri any questions about his mysterious love life, Nik narrows his eyes at me. "Dmitri, I believe I've told you to get lost. I won't say it again. As for you, Kat, if you're well enough to go looking for trouble, you're well enough to get to work. Get dressed. Put on something nice. We are going out."

With that, he returns to his desk and turns his back to Dmitri and me, thoroughly dismissing the two of us.

With a final wink and a smirk directed at me, Dmitri bids me goodbye, whispering *"good luck"* under his breath.

On my way to my closet to follow Nik's orders, I pause, pointing to the disks on his desk. "Are those copies of the surveillance footage you showed me?"

"Yes, why?"

"Do you mind if I borrow them for a while?"

Nik raises his eyebrows, surprised by my question. After shooting me a considering look, he shrugs and hands the CDs to me. I grab the offering and exit the office before he can change his mind.

After changing into one of my new outfits—a red silk slip dress—I search for Nik. I find him waiting for me by the penthouse's front door. He's changed into a new set of clothes, too. He is so handsome in his black suit and black dress shirt that it hurts me a little. I don't bother hiding my appreciation as I take my time looking at him from head to toe.

Nik rolls his eyes at my enthusiastic reaction to his good looks, and I spin around on my heels to show him my new dress. "Do you like it?" I ask, coming closer to where he stands.

"It's beautiful," he says off-handedly, fussing with his cufflinks.

"Thank you. You bought it."

"I figured. Ready to go?"

"Just lead the way, boss."

With a long-suffering sigh, Nik shoots me an unamused look I'm starting to get too familiar with. Without another word, he holds the front door open for me, motioning me toward the foyer. We enter the elevator, and he presses the garage button before stepping away from me. He doesn't stop moving until he is as far away from me as the enclosure allows, resting one shoulder against the wall.

Charmed, I smile at him before leaning against the opposite wall, my body completely facing his.

"Can I ask you a question?" I ask, trying to catch his eyes as he tries to avoid mine.

With a sigh, Nik answers, "Can I stop you?"

I shrug good-naturedly. "Probably not. Tell me about Dmitri."

He glares at me. "You can't be serious."

"I'm just curious about your relationship with him. I know he works for you, but you obviously have a lot of affection for him. I've been wondering if the two of you are family."

"Not by blood," he says, turning to face me. "His mother used to work for me. She made the greatest *borscht* I've ever had in my life."

"What happened to her?"

"She passed away a couple of years ago. Cancer. Lovely woman," he says. "Dmitri was probably in his early teens when I first hired her. I suppose you could say I watched him grow up. And I guess the lines got blurred somewhere along the way over the years. He's become a little brother of sorts to me."

"What about his dad?"

"He was never in the picture. Elena raised him by herself." Nik shakes his head with unconcealed disgust.

The elevator stops, and its doors slide open before I decide what to say. Nik leads me to a small, black limousine, opening the door for me. I sit on the rich brown leather seats as he sits across from me. The air-conditioned interior is a welcome change from the humid environment in the garage.

"You never told me where we're going," I point out,

adjusting my dress so its slit displays my legs to their best advantage.

Nik does his best to ignore my attempts at teasing him. "My accountant's engagement party is tonight. I was going to skip it, but since you're obviously feeling fine, I thought we might as well go."

"Oh," I say, surprised. "So, it's a date, then. I thought it was a work thing."

The look Nik shoots me is pure exasperation. "It is most definitely a work thing. For your information, as it happens, McGuire and I share the same accountant, so I'd bet good money he'll be in attendance tonight. Which reminds me," he says, pulling a small object out of the inside pocket of his black jacket, "I want you to put this on."

On his outstretched hand is a small recording device. The little voice recorder is barely bigger than my fingertip. After picking it up, I remove the plastic tab on one of its sides to reveal the adhesive patch. I don't bother to argue with Nik about it, wasting no time sticking it to the skin between my breasts.

I bat my eyelashes at him, leaning forward and giving him a great view of my cleavage. "Can you spot it?"

Nik clenches his jaw and shakes his head.

"Are you sure? Maybe you should take a closer look."

"*Kat,*" he mutters in warning through gritted teeth.

"What?" I ask, feigning innocence. "Just want to make sure I do my job well. Speaking of which, I assume you have a plan for how I'm supposed to help you catch McGuire."

Nik nods. "I need you to seduce him. Or better yet, I need you to let him think he's seducing you."

It's my turn to raise my eyebrows at him. "Excuse me?"

With a sigh, he says, "The great thing about McGuire is that I can always count on him to be boringly predictable.

The man is a womanizer and a *bon vivant*. He's hated me for years now. You're simply more temptation than he can handle. He'll be tripping over his own feet to try to steal you from me. So, I'm counting on you to charm him into confessing to putting the hit out that got Maxim killed. Maybe you'll need to hint at secretly despising me and only being interested in me for my money." He shrugs. "I don't know. All that matters is that we get hard proof that he's behind the whole thing. With it, I can rightfully take him out without causing a major war and bloodshed."

I study him as I absorb his words. I can't say I'm pleased about tangling with yet another mobster, but I'm also not surprised this is Nik's plan.

"Will you have my back if things go south?" I ask, thinking back to his earlier promises about protecting me.

"Without a doubt," he says, with no room for questioning in his tone.

I nod once and take a deep breath. "If I'm going to get up close and personal with McGuire, you need to tell me more about his history with you and Maxim."

It's Nik's turn to take a deep breath. After a brief second of hesitation, he says, "It's a long story. A few years back, Maxim was a bodyguard for McGuire's daughter, Erin. One thing led to another, and they got romantically involved. The problem is that Erin had been engaged to someone else. Someone who, just like her dad, wasn't too happy to learn that a mere *bratva* soldier had taken the Irish princess's virginity."

I stare at him for a second, a little shocked at his words to formulate an answer while a million questions rush through my brain.

Before I can ask any of them, he interrupts my racing mind to say, "We're here."

24

KAT

The final traces of the sunset fade away as Nik and I emerge from the car at the front steps of an opulent mansion. I guess being an accountant to two mafia bosses must pay very well.

We walk into the house, and a dark-haired man in his early thirties joyfully greets us. "Nikolai! You've made it."

Nik offers his right hand for the host to shake while his left one rests on the small of my back.

"John," my date says in a somewhat warm tone. "I wouldn't miss it for the world."

John, the accountant, lets out a howl of laughter. "Oh, yes, you would. I know you better than that, pal."

Nik shrugs his broad shoulders, giving the other man a sincere smile. "John, this is Kat Devereaux. Kat, this is John Gates."

John offers me his right hand, and I shake it. "Welcome to my home, Kat." He smiles at me.

"It's a pleasure to meet you, John. You have a beautiful home," I say, glancing around the extravagantly adorned foyer. The place is gorgeous—beautifully built in the Mediterranean style.

"I can't take any credit for it. My beautiful bride, Sheila, has great taste, if I do say so myself." John winks at Nik and me, self-deprecatingly. "But please, make yourself at home. I'll bring Sheila around to meet you once I manage to find her."

I smile at him as Nik leads me away. My heels click on the pale gray marble floors as we make our way to the adjoining room where John and Sheila's guests are gathered. The large room sports glass walls that span its entire perimeter. We stand close to the entrance, people-watching for a moment. Nik glances around the room impatiently. A beautifully tended garden and pool are visible from here under the full moon's glow.

A server walks by, and Nik grabs two champagne flutes. After handing one of them to me, he says, "Stay right here. I'll be back."

Without another word, Nik leaves me, taking long strides toward a gorgeous woman standing by herself near the bar. She straightens up once she spots him making his way to her.

They talk for a moment. The woman fidgets with her wine-colored velvet dress and brown curls as Nik leans forward to speak to her. She doesn't say much until he pulls a small pouch from his jacket pocket and places it in her hands.

The brunette looks at the small bag for a second and then at Nik's face, frowning slightly. Her delicate fingers retrieve a gold ring from inside it. Her mouth widens, and her eyes blink violently as she holds on to it as if it were her very own lifeline.

Nik nods before turning his back to her and walking back to where I stand.

Bemused, I glance between him and the mysterious woman, growing even more concerned as I notice her brush away tears. She is still profoundly entranced by the jewel my handsome Russian just gave her.

Nik reaches me, and I stare at him, stunned, as he slips his arm around my waist again before asking, "Are you hungry? Because I'm starving. God, I hate these ridiculous parties. All the champagne and canapés you could want, but not a single hearty meal in sight..."

He politely waves to someone across the room, but I can't be bothered even to pretend to care at the moment.

"What the hell was that?" I ask, realizing he has no intention of explaining what I just witnessed.

Nik looks at me, confused. "What the hell was what?"

"*That*," I say, pointing toward the unknown brunette as discreetly as possible.

"Oh," he says, a certain smidge of darkness coloring his tone. "Nothing you need to worry about."

"Oh, no. Don't give me that. You have to tell me what the hell I just saw."

"It's nothing. Really, Kat—"

I cut him off. "I'm not going to drop this, Nik, so you might as well save yourself some time and tell me."

He closes his eyes and clutches the bridge of his nose tightly. After a wordless moment, he sighs. "If you *really* must know, that was Erin."

"Erin? As in Erin McGuire? As in Maxim's lover and your arch nemesis's daughter?"

"*Shh*. Will you keep your voice down?" he mutters through gritted teeth, glancing around to ensure no one's heard me. "Yes, that Erin."

"Wow," is all I can think of to say. After a moment, I add, "What did you give her?"

"That's none of your business."

"I mean, I know it was a ring. I saw that much. But why would you give Erin McGuire a gold ring?"

"What part of '*this is none of your business*' do you not understand?"

"What part of '*I'm not going to drop this*' do *you* not understand?"

Nik sighs loudly and grunts out something in Russian.

"What does that mean?"

"It means may God deliver me from nosy women who can't mind their fucking businesses to save their lives."

"Cute," I say, crossing my arms. "Hey, if you won't tell me, maybe I'll just ask her."

Nik grabs my arm very tightly. "I don't think so. Did nobody ever tell you about curiosity killing the cat?"

"Ha-ha," I say, rolling my eyes. "I get it. Because my name's Kat. Like I've never heard that one before. Now, spill the beans, or I will cause a scene."

Through gritted teeth, he says close to my ear, "Once upon a time, Maxim and Erin had this stupid idea of running away together. He proposed to her with that ring you just saw. Just as they were about to make their escape, word of their affair and plan got out. McGuire took her to Ireland, and I was forced to banish Maxim to Russia. Somehow, Erin had the ring returned to Maxim, and he kept it throughout all the years he was in exile. After his death, I found it with his belongings. I figured he'd have wanted her to have it."

Stunned, I stare at him, processing all the information he shared. I remain silent for a long while, thinking of the senseless heartbreak and regrets that will forever remain unfinished business for the pretty girl across the room. Suddenly, Nik's fingers tighten almost painfully around my arm. His whole body goes rigid next to me. A split second later, he noticeably forces himself to relax before his arm snakes around my back until his right hand rests possessively over my stomach.

Nik's abrupt change in behavior astonishes me until I spot a distinguished-looking middle-aged male approaching us. An insincere smile contorts his lips. It doesn't take me long to recognize him as the man Nik identified as Patrick McGuire when we watched the museum gala's surveillance feeds.

"Nikolai," the man says in greeting.

Nik nods in acknowledgment. "Patrick."

"I thought that was you from the other side of the room. I wanted to come over and pay my respects. I was so terribly sorry to hear about Maxim. What a pity." The Irish shakes his head, frowning.

Nik only stares at him in response, but McGuire doesn't notice his reaction. Or at least, he acts that way.

"And the whole situation with his missing remains, too. Truly a disgrace, if you don't mind me saying," Nik's nemesis says.

"I appreciate the sentiment, McGuire," Nik says at last. "May I introduce you to my fiancée, Katherine Devereaux? Kat, this is Patrick McGuire."

McGuire raises his eyebrows so highly they almost reach his hairline. He studies me appraisingly, taking me in from head to toe.

I school my features into a pleasant smile. *Fiancée?* Thanks for the heads-up, Nik.

"Fiancée? Wow." Patrick McGuire smiles at me.

"Enchanted to meet you, Kat." He offers me his tan hand, and I shake it gingerly.

"Likewise," I say, leaning against Nik. He caresses my stomach in response, and McGuire doesn't miss any of it.

"How long have the two of you been dating?"

"Oh, not long," I answer. "It's been a bit of a whirlwind romance, I suppose."

"What can I say?" Nik adds, shrugging one of his broad shoulders. "When you know, you know."

I turn my head to glance at Nik and catch him already gazing at me. His eyes lock with mine and the same fire I saw in them the night we met burns hot. I press my body closer to his as he tightens his hold around my waist.

"I think I'll take your word for it." McGuire says with a chuckle. "But you must tell me a little about yourself, Kat. I simply must know more about the woman who's captured Nikolai's infamously cold heart."

I turn my attention to him and find his eyes sparkling with unconcealed interest, bouncing around Nik's hands possessively placed on me.

Smiling, I ask, "What would you like to know? I'm afraid I'm probably very dull if compared to you gentlemen."

McGuire lets out a sharp and loud laughter. I can't tell if it's sincere or not.

"I seriously doubt that. Are you from around this area?"

"I am," I say.

"Where did you two meet?"

I glance at Nik, implying that the answer is an inside joke McGuire wouldn't get. "I guess you could say we met at work. Well, I was working, at least."

Nik scoffs. McGuire's interest grows even more noticeable.

"Interesting. And what did you say you do for a living?"

"I didn't. But if you must know, I suppose it wouldn't be a lie to say I work in the acquisitions and procurement field." I giggle.

Nik laughs under his breath, kissing my hair. McGuire practically vibrates with the effort to curb his curiosity.

"I can see why Nikolai is so taken with you, Kat. You're a very intriguing woman. Tell me, would you give me the pleasure of a dance? You wouldn't mind it, would you, Nikolai?"

I look at Nik questioningly. He gives McGuire a cold but exquisite smile that doesn't quite reach his gorgeous brown eyes. "Not at all," he says. After making eye contact with me again, he adds, "Kat knows to save the last dance for me."

I smile teasingly at him, raising myself on my toes. "Don't worry, my love. I know who I'm coming home with tonight." I brush a quick kiss against his lips, but he pulls me closer to press a hard, long one against mine.

Nik's caress leaves me a little shaken—and unsure of what is real emotion on his part and what is just for McGuire's benefit—but I make myself smile sweetly at Nik before taking McGuire's hand. He leads me to a small dance floor where a few other couples are gathered, a couple of dozen yards away from where we left Nik. The Irish mobster pulls me into his arms as the song starts. I half expect him to hold me uncomfortably close or place his hands somewhere inappropriate, but he behaves respectfully—a perfect gentleman.

McGuire chuckles lightly. "Your Russian is watching me like a hawk. I can't say it's anything new, but seeing him so bent out of shape over a woman is still amusing. Even one as charming and beautiful as you."

I glance in Nik's direction and confirm he is observing us. I'm not sure how much of his display is for McGuire's benefit and how much is due to genuine feelings of jealousy. After all, even though he isn't half as indifferent to me as he'd like me to believe, there's no doubt that nothing matters to him as much as destroying the man dancing with me.

"He's just protective of me, that's all," I say, hoping he'll take the hint that Nik might make him pay if he harms me.

"I can't blame him. I'd be very protective of someone as captivating as you, too."

I laugh, pretending to be charmed by his attempt at flirting. "I'm sure a man like you has plenty of much more captivating women than me throwing themselves at him."

"I don't know about that, Kat. I'll give Nikolai this—his eye for beauty is unparalleled."

"Oh, stop. You're making me blush." I teasingly shove against his chest, and he pulls me a fraction closer to him. Years of practicing the art of deception are the only thing preventing me from grimacing in response.

"I'm sure this is nothing new to you. Heartbreakingly beautiful women always know of their power and aren't afraid to yield it."

"I'll plead the fifth to that."

McGuire chuckles. "I have to say, I can't shake the feeling there's something familiar about you. Have we met before?"

I shake my head. "I'm sure we haven't. I'm positive I'd remember meeting someone as dashing as you."

His soft laughter has a hint of darkness to it. "Careful, Kat, or I'll think you're encouraging an old man's crush on you."

I shrug. "What can I say? Old habits die hard. But we should probably keep this little back-and-forth of ours between ourselves. I wouldn't want Nik to worry unduly."

"No, of course not. Speaking of him, here's your knight

in shining armor," McGuire whispers close to my ear, glancing over my shoulder.

I turn and practically run into Nik's chest. He wasted no time coming to fetch me after the song ended.

"I believe that was the end of your dance, McGuire," Nik says.

McGuire chuckles again. "Right. Kat, it was a genuine pleasure to meet you. I can only hope I'll see you again soon." He bends over my hand to press a kiss against it. "I guess you'll have your dance now, Nikolai."

Nik shoots him a glance that is nothing but icy fire. "I'll enjoy it at home," he says before wrapping his arm around my waist and leading me away.

After a moment, when we are at a safe distance from the dance floor, I whisper, "You were so right, Nik. He couldn't help himself. The man was bending over backward to entice me away from you. I'll have him eating out of the palm of my hand in no time. Great job with the whole jealous boyfriend act, by the way. He completely bought it."

"Fiancé," Nik practically snarls through gritted teeth.

"What's that?"

"I'm your fiancé. Not your boyfriend," he says with a grunt.

"Right. That's what I meant. Great job. But I wish you hadn't surprised me with that. A little heads-up would've been appreciated, boss."

Nik murmurs something intelligible as he clenches his jaw. He increases his pace, firmly and swiftly leading me away from the guests.

"Where are we going?" I ask, confused. We're almost jogging through the entrance foyer.

"Home." Nik's hold over me tightens as he increases his pace.

"But we just got here!"

"We did what we came here to do. Now we're leaving."

"But I didn't even say hello to Sheila!"

Nik glares at me as if I have lost my mind. "Who the fuck is Sheila?"

"John's fiancée," I say, staring at Nik like he is the one who's lost it.

"Fuck John. Fuck Sheila, too," he says in a scarily calm tone.

Nik yanks the front door open before pushing me through the doorway. His relentless grip on my arm never wavers as he makes us halt in front of the house. A second later, his black limousine pulls over to where we stand.

The driver quickly exits the car, but Nik waves him away impatiently. Without a word, he opens the car's door, motioning for me to get in. I resist him.

"What's your problem?" I ask, making all my frustration clear.

"Kat. Get in the car," he orders in that eerie tone again.

"Not until you tell me what's wrong with you. I did everything you asked of me," I say, struggling against his hold on my arm.

"Oh, I know you did. Trust me. I'm so fucking aware you did everything I asked," Nik says, raising his voice.

"Then I'll ask again. What the hell is your problem? What else do you want from me?"

Nik pulls me flush against his body, leaning forward until his forehead touches mine. In that deadly calm tone of his, he says, eyes ablaze, "I want you not to go within a mile of that vermin ever again. I want to break every finger in his repulsive hands so he knows better than to touch you. I want you to never smile like that again at any other man but me. What I *really* want," he rasps, a mere inch away from my lips, "is to bend you over and fuck you into submission until you accept you belong to me."

I hold his gaze with mine unflinchingly. My heart is racing, and my breath comes out in erratic pants, but I don't shy away from his stare. I raise my chin as I correct him, "No. What you *really* want is *me*."

Nik's deep brown eyes darken at my words, and he opens his mouth, his challenging intent unmistakable in every bit of him. But a heartbeat later, almost miraculously, something different flickers over his expression. He closes his mouth. And then he opens it again.

"God help me, I do," Nik says under his breath. His admission is undeniable. Unshakable.

My eyes never leave his as I say, "Then fucking have me."

Before my mind even registers his movements, Nik yanks the limousine's door open, dragging me inside.

25

NIK

I warned her.

Over and over again, I told Kat it was a bad idea for her to play these foolish mind games with me.

As usual, Kat didn't listen. Even worse, she kept pushing and pressing my buttons, trying to get me to surrender all control in the hopes of having me eating out of the palm of her hand—just like she promised she would do with McGuire.

Fucking have me, Kat dared me.

If only it were that simple.

So I drag her into the back of the car with me, kicking and screaming.

I do what I have to do. I refuse to give her the satisfaction of seeing me completely snap, losing all semblance of discipline and control. After witnessing her with McGuire, I'm dangerously close to it.

I won't let her win this battle of wills. No matter what, I can't afford to let her wrestle the control over our *status quo* from me.

Clearly, Kat won't accept defeat easily. As I toss her on the front-facing car seat and take the one across from her, she gives me a piece of her mind. The bane of my existence goes on and on and on about how she's so freaking done with mobsters, that we will be the death of her, and that I'm the worst of them all. After huffing and puffing, Kat complains that she's damned if she does and damned if she doesn't, as far as I'm concerned.

As I've known for a while, the woman has a flair for the dramatic, which explains why she won't give up on her tirade. As I silently listen, Kat tells me that Mother Theresa herself would've had a hard time putting up with my mood swings and poor communication skills.

"For the love of God, just shut up," I groan, tapping the partition between us and the driver, indicating that he should start driving.

"Why don't you come over here and make me?" she asks me, her flirtatious words in high contrast with her sharp tone.

I lean forward, resting my forearms on my bent knees. "I want you to listen to me, and I want you to listen very carefully," I say as calmly as I can manage. "I strongly advise you to tread very carefully right now. I've been very tolerant with you so far, but you have no idea how on edge I feel right now. My self-control is within an inch of snapping, and you won't like me very much if that happens."

The look Kat shoots in my direction makes my blood boil.

"Try me," she rasps, crossing her legs. "Somehow, I really doubt that."

"You're playing with fire," I warn her.

"Good," she says, brushing her dark hair away from her

face. "It's about time. Because what I've been feeling for you is pretty incendiary. And don't even bother telling me you don't feel the same—not after last night, and definitely not after tonight. I know a jealous man when I see one."

"This isn't going to end how you hope it will," I mutter through gritted teeth since it's not like I can deny what is so apparent.

"I'll take my chances," she says, sliding towards me over the leather seats.

"Katherine," I snap as she rises from her seat, moving in my direction, "I'm only going to say this once. Your silly attempts at seducing me aren't welcome."

Kat drops her plump ass on my lap, smirking. Wordlessly, she wraps her arms around my neck as she turns, sitting astride me. She leans forward and tortures me by licking the seam of my lips before whispering against them, "Liar."

I don't know if I make the first move or if she does, but without another word, I grab fistfuls of her luscious dark hair and pull her mouth closer to mine. Soon, I can no longer tell where her breaths start and mine end. It's pure, unadulterated bliss. I wrap my other arm around her waist, desperate to obliterate any distance between us.

Kat pulls my hair hard, and I groan in both pain and pleasure. "If you don't like my teasing, then why are you moaning?" she asks, a playful glint in her deep blue eyes as she rains kisses down my neck.

"I groaned, not moaned. And I'm already dying to take you right now," I say against her flesh. "Don't push me."

"Then take me," she says against my ear, biting my ear lobe. "I want you. I need you—with me, on me, and in me."

A sound somewhere between a snarl and a tortured

moan escapes me, and I grab her red silk dress, yanking it over her head. I take one look at her undressed body displayed on top of mine, and it almost unmans me.

Kat's gorgeous breasts are fully exposed, her dusky pink nipples taut under my gaze. Her mouthwatering curves are almost entirely bare, except for the tiny sliver of pale silver silk covering her between her legs. The straps of this maddening excuse for underwear she's chosen to wear tonight are tiny, sparkling crystals.

Aware of my appraising glance, Kat doesn't shy away. On the contrary, she leans back, resting her hands on my knees and spreading her legs wide open.

I gaze at her face, and something in my chest tightens at her expression. She's studying me as I watch her, a look of pure lust and satisfaction glittering in her eyes.

"Like what you see?" the minx asks me, bringing her hands to her stomach. Kat slowly trails them all the way to her chest. She cups the breasts I'm dying to touch, slowly rotating her hips over my straining erection.

"You know I do," I say, grabbing her long hair and wrapping it around my right fist. With my left hand, I trace the edges of her silk thong. I cup her firmly over the expanse of the fabric, pulling her face close to mine with my right hand.

"You're mine to touch. No one else's, Kat," I say, practically snarling. The sight of Kat in another man's arms brought home the need to remind her that she belongs to me.

With a smile, Kat agrees. "No one else's, Nik."

"Good girl." I brush a wet kiss against the spot where her neck meets her shoulder.

"Why don't you fuck me hard enough to make me forget all men but you?" Kat's breathy plea is almost more than I can bear. I grab hold of her silk thong, and with one hard yank, I rip it from her skin. She gasps. "Oh, yes, please, Nik..."

I cup her again, slipping my index and middle finger between her lips. She's warm and wet, and I can't help groaning against her neck as I bite it.

"Nik," Kat says, panting again. The sound of my name coming from her lips as I finger her wet pussy almost breaks me. Unable to stop myself, I bend over to suck on her tight nipples, my fingers drawing slow circles around her center. She presses her hips down hard on me. On my hand. On my cock. Even through the thick fabric of my pants, I feel her warmth.

"*Kiska*," I say against her chest. "You're so wet. I need to feel you around me..."

"Do it, Nik. Fuck me. Now," Kat demands.

With my other hand, I slap her ass hard once as I tease her entrance with the tip of my fingers. "Ask me nicely," I whisper against her mouth.

"Nik," she pants against my lips, placing her hands on both sides of my face. "Please fuck me. Hard. Please, Nik. Pretty please, with a cherry on top."

With a sigh, I push her away from me. "Bad girl. You're in trouble now. On your knees."

Kat's eyes widen slightly before a mischievous glint sparkles in them. "Are you going to spank me now?" she breathlessly asks, kneeling in front of me.

"No. There would be no point. You'd enjoy it too much," I say as I unbuckle my belt and unzip my pants.

Her eyes widen more in realization. "Oh," she says with a gasp.

"Quite so," I say, pulling my painfully hard cock out of the restraining confinement of my boxers. I wrap her beautiful, long hair around my wrist again, pulling her closer. "Now, come here and take your punishment like a good girl."

And God help me, looking up at me through her thick eyelashes, she does.

Kat tentatively licks the glistening head of my erection as I watch, mesmerized. Still looking into my eyes, she twirls her tongue down my entire length, and a tortured sound vibrates through my chest.

"Kat," I groan. Or beg. God only knows.

She sinks me inside her warm mouth in one fluid movement. Kat's tongue caresses me as she gently sucks me deeper and deeper inside her. With no hint of hesitation, she works her way down my length. As she gazes up at me, Kat bobs her head up and down in a maddening rhythm, bringing me too close to the edge far too soon.

"Good girl. Good, good girl." I sigh.

Kat's eyes water slightly for a moment as she tries to take me even deeper inside her wet mouth. She picks up the pace in her movements, and her right hand wraps around me as well, flawlessly matching her rhythmic torture.

I take in the erotic sight of her—wholly bare and on her knees—pleasuring me with her mouth. I realize that her other hand is sunken between her legs, mercilessly rubbing back and forth.

"Stop," I order. "The only way you're getting off is on my thigh."

Kat moans around my cock, disregarding my command entirely. Instead, she takes me in deeper and faster inside her mouth, just as her clever little fingers increase the intensity of their movements between her wet folds.

"Kat," I warn her, but I know it's pointless. I'm too far

gone to stop her. As I give in, I tell myself I will punish her for disobeying me later—again and again—all night long.

My eyes slide shut against my will, reluctant as I am to tear my gaze away from the erotic perfection in front of me.

"*Kiska*, I'm so close."

Suddenly, Kat releases me completely. Still on her knees, she straightens up before leaning over my bent legs to blow air on my pulsing erection. Even the movements of the hand she's employing to pleasure herself slow down.

"Nik," she purrs, "I think it's time we renegotiate the terms of our deal."

It can't be.

I freeze in place, struggling to catch my breath. And yet, I know this is really happening. I'm the one to blame for it. After all, she never even bothered hiding her intentions of manipulating me through sex.

I knew better than to let it get to this. I knew better than to let my guard down with her.

I should have been stronger than this. I should have known better than to allow her pretty eyes and meaningless words to fool me.

My blood runs cold.

I always remember my painfully learned lessons. This won't happen again.

I recompose myself, straightening and zipping up my pants before schooling my expression into a display of indifference.

Kat might've won this battle, but I'll be damned if I'll let her get any satisfaction out of it.

"Nik," the little thief has the nerve to say hesitantly.

I can't even bear to look at her—the woman I couldn't tear my eyes from a moment ago.

Reckless idiot. Lovesick fool.

Relieved to notice the car has stopped, I glance at the windows and recognize the familiar sight of my garage.

Without another word to the untrustworthy, bewitching creature at my feet, I exit the car, slamming its door behind me.

I don't look back.

26

KAT

PEOPLE OFTEN SAY that everything looks better in the morning.

Those people are liars.

After Nik stormed away from the car, leaving me behind, completely naked and alone, I took a moment to reassess my approach to our peculiar situation.

I returned to my room in the penthouse after donning my dress. Nik was nowhere to be found.

Hours later, the cold anger and disappointment in his eyes at my poorly calculated move are still fresh in my mind.

After calling A.J. and washing up, I eagerly welcomed the deep numbness that a whole night of sleep promised, hoping the old saying would prove true. Perhaps everything would look better in the morning.

The warm sunlight brushes against my face, forcefully waking me up, and I groan as I sit up.

The events of the night before rush to the forefront of my mind, almost as if they had never left it. They may very well never have, considering how restless and pointless my attempts at sleeping had been.

There's no point in lying to myself, denying what I know is true.

I wish I could take last night back and do everything differently.

If only I possessed the power to go back in time and never mention to Nik anything about renegotiating the terms of our deal. I wish I could go back and not tarnish the moment with calculations and scheming. And not only because, as it turned out, the whole thing was a fiasco that set me back instead of forwarding my goals of rebalancing the power scale between us. But mainly because the moment *had* been extraordinary. Nik has kept me at arm's length since our true identities were revealed, but something snapped within him last night, pushing him to show me his hand. He revealed a vulnerable side I hadn't seen before. Now, I regret ruining his attempt at letting me in—even if just by an inch—with machinations and plotting.

It didn't make things any better that it happened not even twenty-four hours after Nik tenderly soothed and comforted me through my terrible nightmare episode.

If only things did look better this morning...

If only I could spend the rest of the day under these soft and crisp Egyptian cotton sheets, wallowing in my misery... But that would accomplish nothing. It wouldn't make anything better. I made a mess, and now I have to clean it up —simple as that. There's no point in crying over spilled milk. As I've learned long ago, no one will save me. Nobody is going to clean up my messes.

So I get dressed. I put on my makeup. I do my hair. I go through the motions as I think, analyzing my options.

Perhaps not everything looks better in the morning, but I believe there's truth to a different saying—where there's a will, there's a way. And I'm willing to work to fix my mess with Nik.

Serendipitously, my phone pings just then.

I put down my hairbrush and pick up the cell phone once I see it's a text from A.J. When I called her last night looking for a shoulder to cry on, she told me there was still nothing but radio silence from the *stronzo*. I was relieved to hear this since lately, it seems like whenever something goes wrong, then everything else does as well. Plus, this reprieve allows A.J. to pursue Camilla's lead in peace, which she badly needs now that she's working our angle solo, courtesy of my angry Russian.

Despite everything on her plate, A.J. immediately noticed something was off with me. After filling her in and sharing my latest blunder, I asked her for a favor. I told her about the museum gala's surveillance feeds and how our little heist ruined the internal footage. I asked her to try to work her magic on it, and she promised she would try.

Mere hours after our phone call, her message is unexpected but welcome.

> I couldn't sleep last night. You might have a point about my Diet Coke "addiction", as you like to put it. I'm still working on your surveillance videos, but I thought I'd share what I have so far.

A video follows her text. I click on it, and after a moment, I identify it as footage from the metal detectors at the museum's entrance. I pause the video and make sure to reply to her message before I forget to do it.

> You're the best! I owe you one.

A.J.'s response comes right away.

> After this mess with the stronzo, it was the least I could do. Besides, bitch, please. After all these years, who the hell is keeping track of who owes whom what?

With a smile, I send her a heart emoji, promising to catch up with her later.

I grab my phone and search for Nik, hoping he is at his office. But as I pass the kitchen, the scent of freshly baked muffins beckons me. So, I decide to grab a plate and fill it with some of the homemade goods.

Full plate in hand, I walk around the penthouse, hoping to run into Dmitri. I could use his insight into Nik's mood this morning—plus a little advice on correcting my mistake. Unfortunately, he's nowhere to be found, so I head to Nik's office, wondering if he is even there. For all I know, he might not even be home.

The door is closed, so I knock on it, thinking it would probably be a bad idea to barge in unannounced if he's in there working.

Nik's voice reaches me after a moment. "Come in."

Hesitantly, I do. I push the door open and walk into the room. Nik sits behind his desk, bent over a stack of papers with a pen in his left hand. He's wearing a royal blue sweater, and his sleeves are rolled up, exposing his forearms. With his other hand, the Russian props up his head. He doesn't look up when I enter.

"You're left-handed," I remark dumbly.

Finally looking up from his work, Nik shoots me a look that tells me I'm a very unwelcome interruption. "What are you doing here?" he asks, not bothering with pleasantries.

"I bring a peace offering." Even though I feel less confident than usual, I smile at him.

"Muffins. From my own kitchen. Be still, my heart," he says, sarcasm dripping from every word.

"Oh, no, that's not what I meant. I mean, I do believe that food is often the way to a man's heart, but I brought the muffins because I haven't eaten yet, and I figured maybe you haven't, either. But my peace offering is something else." I pull my phone from my pocket and wave it in front of his face.

Nik raises his eyebrows and puts down his pen. "I'm listening."

So I explain to him that last night I asked A.J. to look at the museum's internal security feeds, hoping she could recover some of the footage damaged by the device I used during the Flame of Mir's heist.

"She got back to me this morning," I say. "She hasn't been able to save all of it. Well, not yet, anyway. But she sent me what she's been able to salvage so far. Would you like to see it? I can probably aircast it on your TV."

Nik gets up from his chair to sit on the couch facing the TV, motioning for me to sit beside him. I put A.J.'s video on the screen before sitting down.

"Are those the metal detectors by the front entrance?" Nik asks, growing a little interested. I nod in response.

We watch countless people come and go, walking through the large metal detectors and making small talk with the security guards stationed there. Men empty their pockets into plastic trays that get scanned, and the same happens with women's purses and clutches.

Eventually, I spot myself on the screen, watching as I walk up to the security guard—a young man in his early twenties—and smile at him. I chat him up, playfully slapping his arm, and he turns red like the Flame of Mir. His unconcealed pleasure is clear in his coy smile, and my past self walks past the metal detectors without getting scanned or having her evening bag's contents checked.

Nik scoffs. "I should've known," he says.

I shrug in response. "A.J.'s device would've set off the alarm. We didn't have time to figure out a way to conceal it so I could walk through the metal detectors. I had to make use of the resources available to me."

"Oh, and you did. If I recall correctly," he retorts. I consider challenging his hypocritical words and attitude, but after what happened between us last night, I let it go instead.

Soon, we spot Nik on the screen. He walks through the metal detector. The young guard approaches him, asking him to empty his pockets. Nik merely glances at the man before an older guard comes along. Familiar with Nik, this man waives him on before turning to the younger man and chastising him.

I snort. "Oh, you're one to talk."

"It's different," he says.

"Oh, really? And why's that?"

"For starters, I wasn't there to commit grand larceny," he points out.

"Well, he didn't know that."

"He did, though. The guard knew who I was."

"All the more reason to frisk you thoroughly, then. It's what I would've done if I had known who you were."

"If memory serves me, you did. Very thoroughly," he adds smoothly.

I shoot him a look, surprised. Nik's eyes are still guarded, but they have a definite mischievous glint. They're at least twenty degrees warmer than the arctic ice I saw in them in the limousine.

"You and I have a different recollection of that night, then. I remember your very fine attire being almost completely undisturbed throughout our *rendezvous*. The same couldn't be said about myself, of course," I tease, wondering how he'll react to my attempt at levity.

To my surprise, he chuckles. "And yet," he says, eyes glued to the screen, "you managed to keep my diamond hidden the entire time. Was it in your purse?"

"Oh, come on, that's too obvious. That's the first place anyone would look if they learned it was missing before I got away."

"Where, then?"

I tear my eyes from the TV and find him staring at me. With a smile, I share, "Hidden pocket in my dress. Right here." I tap the spot between my breasts.

"Clever," he says, an amused smile curving his beautiful lips. He's always so breathtaking when he smiles.

"When your attentions started to focus there, I almost panicked, thinking you'd spot it and I'd be caught red-handed. That was when I decided to strip for you so you wouldn't get too close and so I could carefully put my dress away."

Nik laughs loudly. "Impressive improvisation skills." He smirks. I shrug in response, grinning back at him.

We gaze at the screen, but I'm relieved to detect the faint ghost of a smile on his face. A moment later, we watch Dmitri go through the metal detectors without any of our shenanigans. He places his wallet, phone, pack of gum, and car keys in the little plastic tray. After it's scanned, he retrieves his items before leaving the area.

We also spot Vladmir. He empties his pockets into the

tray. Once again, nothing in them is interesting at all. I grow bored watching him pick up his cell phone, lanyard with keys, and a money clip.

I'm disappointed that my peace offering to Nik is so dull when we see McGuire on the screen. Nik immediately straightens up next to me on the couch. We observe with interest as the man empties his pockets. The Irish mobster throws his phone, leather wallet, pack of cigarettes, lighter and fountain pen in the plastic tray. Shortly after him, we see the guy who Nik indicated as McGuire's right-hand man go through the same process. His pockets' contents aren't much more interesting—nothing but a phone, wallet, plastic lighter and wired headphones.

With a sigh, I say, "I'm sorry. This is disappointing. I didn't watch the whole thing before bringing it to you. I honestly thought it was going to be more helpful than this."

Nik shakes his head. "No, this is great. It's another piece of the puzzle."

"You don't have to be nice. It's useless. It didn't tell us anything new."

"I'm not trying to be nice. And it gave us brand-new information. We now know what McGuire and Connor had with them the night Maxim was killed."

"So what? It's not like they were carrying anything unusual."

"True, but we could have something on the murder weapon. Connor might've used his headphones wires to strangle Maxim."

"Or he might've been killed with a weapon of opportunity," I point out, shrugging. "We haven't learned anything conclusive."

Nik shakes his head again. "No, I know McGuire well. There's just no way he'd leave it to chance. He wouldn't come to the party intending to kill Maxim without the means to carry out the act at hand. He wouldn't count on just finding something lying around."

"You might be right," I concede.

After thinking for a moment, I want to add that maybe we need to approach this whole mystery in a better way. I'm not so sure we should be solely focusing on McGuire. Perhaps it'd be wise to consider other options. But after last night, I can't bring myself to say it now that Nik's mood has improved. He's much more excited than I thought this video would make him. I don't want to make this feeling disappear just yet, not when I angered him last night after he showed me kindness the day before.

Instead, I hesitantly place my hand over his as it lies stretched out over the couch's leather. "Nik, I'm so sorry about last night. I wish I could go back and do it differently. I don't know how much this means to you, but please know that I deeply regret it."

I half expect Nik to ask if my apology means I'll be giving up on my plan to try to wrestle control from him through sex. I dread the prospect since I am unprepared to answer that question. To my relief, he doesn't ask it. He just looks at me, his eyes carefully studying my face.

Nik remains quiet for so long that I start to worry he won't even acknowledge my apology. Eventually, though, he nods. Surprising me, he asks, "Do you want to get out of here? There's something I'd like to show you."

27

KAT

SHOCKED, I glare at Nik for a long, silent moment.

He must take my confusion as uncertainty because he says, "It has nothing to do with Maxim or McGuire, I promise. Just something fun. Something I used to do a lot."

After this intriguing and mysterious statement, I tell him yes, of course I'd like to "get out of here" with him. What else could I say? I need to find out more about whatever it is that Nikolai Stefanovich does for fun.

Nik excuses himself, ordering me to meet him at the door in five minutes. I almost pace back and forth in front of the door as I wait for him, dying of curiosity.

"Ready?" he asks, giving me a smile that warms his eyes even more. He's wearing a black leather jacket, zipped all the way up. I study him as he drops his phone and keys in his jeans pockets. He looks so good I could eat him with a spoon—the whole container in one sitting.

"You have no idea," I say. His only response is a soft laugh.

We ride in the elevator down to the garage in silence. It

disturbs me how at ease he is. I don't think I've ever seen him this content—and almost even relaxed.

I'm bursting at the seams with a million questions, but last night's events still linger in my mind. I don't want to ruin this moment or his mood. I don't want to burst this happy, comfortable bubble we're in right now.

Nik and I finally get to the garage and he leads me to a white Mercedes G-Class car. I'm surprised when he opens the passenger side door for me with a small smile.

"Where's your driver?" I ask.

"I'm driving today. I think I'd like it better if it's just the two of us for this," he says enigmatically.

I get in the car and buckle up as he walks around the vehicle to reach the driver's side. After turning the car on, he shifts into reverse and pulls out of the parking spot.

"Are you going to tell me where we're going?" I ask.

"Nah, I don't think I will. I think it'll be more fun if it's a surprise." With a smirk, he slips his sunglasses on as we exit the garage and merge into traffic.

The sight of him with his black Wayfarers on is, of course, devastating. It takes an excessive amount of self-restraint to stop myself from asking him to pull over so I can jump his bones immediately. Somehow, I manage it. Instead, I tell him, "Maybe you haven't noticed this, but I'm not exactly great with surprises. I'm not a go-with-the-flow kind of girl."

"I don't know about that, Kat. I think you've been going with the flow just fine. I can't say that learning that you're a bit of a control freak would surprise me, though."

I scoff, outraged at his hypocrisy. "Me? A control freak? You're one to talk, mister."

Nik laughs again. The lovely sound doesn't make my life

any easier. The urge to throw myself at him is almost unbearable.

"You are literally trying to control me through sex, Kat." He smirks at me.

"I'm just doing what I can with the hand I've been dealt. I can't just ignore the resources at my disposal."

Over the rim of his sunglasses, Nik practically undresses me with his eyes. He takes his time looking at me from head to toe before sighing. "I know just how you feel. I have a hard time ignoring your *resources* myself. No pun intended."

Once again, the man is just more than I've bargained for. I could deal with grumpy Nik. But smirking, flirty Nik is way more than I can handle.

"Listen, it's your fault, too," I say with an unladylike snort. "If you weren't so freaking bossy, I wouldn't feel the need to wrestle some of the control of this situation from you."

"I'm not bossy, Kat. I'm the boss. Of you, at least." He smiles again and my heart does a somersault. I roll my eyes at him, and he laughs. I could really get used to the sound of it...

After a moment of comfortable silence, I start getting restless. Fidgety, even. Nik hasn't said anything else. He seems perfectly content to just sit there and drive, looking gorgeous.

"Hey, shotgun picks the music, right?" I ask, needing some distraction.

"Sure, why not?"

I connect my phone to the car's sound system and spend the rest of the drive occupying myself with the soundtrack to our little impromptu drive—nothing too romantic, nothing too sexy.

At last, Nik pulls into a graveled side road. Shortly after, he slows down as we approach an open field. From my car seat, I glance around the area. There isn't much around us. I spot an asphalted road and a massive expanse of grass, but nothing else.

Nik comes over to my side. After opening my door, he offers his hand to help me out of the car.

"Where are we?" I ask. The words are barely out of my mouth when I realize the asphalted road is a landing strip. A tarmac. "Is this an airfield?"

"Of sorts. I used to come here a lot," he says, pulling me away from the car.

As Nik leads me toward a small airplane, I'm so distracted by its bright red and white colors that I don't notice the man approaching us.

"Nikolai," he says in greeting. "It's good to see you, man. It's been a while."

"Yuri." Nik shakes the man's hand. "This is Kat. Kat, Yuri here is our pilot today."

"Our pilot?" I ask, turning to face him. "As in, we are going into that thing?"

"Yeah. It'll be fun, you'll see." He smiles at me again before turning to Yuri. "Ready?"

"I'm ready when you are," the man joyfully replies.

"I'm not going into that thing," I tell Nik, digging my heels in.

"Oh, come on, it'll be fun, Kat. You'll enjoy yourself, I promise." He laughs, amused by my hesitation.

"No, I won't. I won't enjoy plummeting to my certain and horrific death when that paper plane crumples up in the air."

As he drags me closer to the plane, Nik chuckles. "It's completely safe, I promise."

"It's so tiny, Nik," I protest.

Nik climbs into the plane and turns to me, stretching out his hand to help me climb into the death machine. "You don't have to come if you don't want to, but I think you should give it a shot. It's completely safe. I've done this a dozen times."

"Nik," I cry, ready to tell him why I think this is a bad idea, but he interrupts me.

"Do you trust me?" he asks, his hand still outstretched.

I look at him. His eyes are warm, searching my face. The wind ruffles his shiny dark hair, and he looks so gorgeous that my heart aches a little. Wordlessly, I take his hand. His answering smile is like a fine glass of whiskey, warming me up down my neck, through my chest, and down to my belly.

Nik effortlessly pulls me into the plane. After leading me to my seat, he helps me buckle up before sitting down in front of me. We both put our headsets on, and the plane's engine roars to life.

Yuri says something over the intercom system, but I can't discern his words over the deafening sound of my thundering heart.

I could have mentally prepared myself if Nik had warned me we would be doing this. I would've had time to get ready for this moment. As it is, I feel entirely out of sorts, like I'm already free-falling from a mile up in the sky.

Nik clasps my hand, holding it tightly. I look at him, and his expression takes my breath away. His eyes are like molten ore, and there is a carefreeness in them I haven't seen before.

Without much preamble, the plane takes off, and it's my turn to squeeze the Russian's hand. Mid-laugh, Nik grabs my other hand, squeezing both my hands tightly in his.

We rise higher and higher. I shut my eyes as my stomach drops and my ears pop.

A minute or an hour passes—I couldn't say. Nik squeezes my hand again.

"Kat," he rasps. "Open your eyes, *milaya*."

Reluctantly, I do.

"Eyes up here," he says. "Just look into my eyes."

I do as he says. After a moment, it helps calm down my nerves. Maybe because staring into this man's eyes is my kryptonite.

"There you go," he says in a soothing voice. "You're doing great. Now, take a deep breath and try to relax your muscles. Just try it."

Still looking into his eyes, I do, to a small degree of success. "This isn't so bad," I say tentatively.

"It really isn't," he says with an encouraging smile. "We're almost ready for Yuri to start the maneuvers."

"*Maneuvers?*! You didn't say anything about maneuvers."

Nik laughs. "It's an aerobatic flight, Kat."

"Oh, god, I'm going to puke."

"No, no, just look into my eyes. You'll be fine. You're safe, and you're going to have fun."

"Nik..." I gasp, unsure of what else to say. He clutches my hands tightly, his eyes never wavering from mine.

He's right, I realize. I'm going to be okay.

Here's this gorgeous man who drives me wild and who wants to share this moment with me, even after I broke his trust the night before. I can either dread the entire experience or let go, taking it as it comes.

"Just let go," he says, his brown eyes ablaze.

With a deep breath, I do. And just in time—as Yuri takes us through a complete loop. I scream in surprise, my stomach dropping to my feet. Somehow, I manage to glance at Nik, and the pure joy in his face takes my breath away.

Yuri rights the plane, and Nik asks me breathlessly, "Not

so bad, right?" I shake my head, and the enthusiasm on his face starts to get to me. "Ready? Here we go again." He laughs, not letting go of my hands.

This time, as Yuri wills the plane into a spiral of turns, my attention is focused on Nik. A laugh bubbles up inside my chest until it bursts its way up as the plane flips us up and down. His laughter joins mine, and I get lost in the moment.

As we float through the blue sky, I feel the same carefree joy I saw on Nik's face earlier. Our gazes never disconnect, our hands never let go, and soon, I can no longer tell where my delight ends and his starts. I feel completely at ease and weightless—not a worry about anything clouding this beautiful moment.

Once the plane starts to come down to prepare for landing, I catch my breath, stealing glances at the man in front of me. He's still smiling, and his hair is a mess. No one's ever been this handsome. And to think that I could've missed the opportunity to witness him like this if I hadn't trusted him, if I hadn't let go of the need to control the uncontrollable. I file that thought for later.

When we get out of the plane, my legs feel like Jell-O, and I almost stumble over. Nik catches me right away before I hit the ground, and we laugh.

"You okay?" he asks, mirth still glinting in his eyes.

I nod, smiling when I realize he still hasn't let me go. I stay in his arms, gazing at his face, not daring to break the spell of this moment.

"Maxim and I used to do this all the time," he says. "It was one of his favorite things to do."

Surprised that he would share that tidbit with me, I wordlessly stare at him, unsure of what to say.

"Thank you," I tell him, finally. For sharing it with me. For letting go of the previous night.

Nik nods.

"This was fun, right?" he asks.

"It was so much fun. I can't remember the last time I had such a blast." I laugh.

He smiles, and it's unlike any of the other smiles he's ever shown me before. This is a gigawatt smile—a take-no-prisoners smile. He's never been this happy and carefree near me, and he's never shown me so much of himself before. Unable to stop myself any longer, I rise on my toes and, wrapping my arms around his neck, I plant a fast, hard kiss on his lips.

It only lasts a second, and when I break it, I grin at his surprised expression.

"What was that for?" he asks me curiously but not angrily.

Still smiling, I shrug. After untangling myself from him, I take his hand, and we walk back towards the car.

Nik and I drive back mostly in silence, the only conversation being his good-humored complaints and comments about my music choice. Shockingly, pop bops are not his thing.

When we return to the penthouse, I feel almost sad to part from him. But I also don't want to ruin a perfect moment. And the day we spent together was as perfect as it gets.

Hoping for the best, I carefully ask, "So, what's the plan moving forward, boss?"

With his swoon-worthy smile still in place, Nik sighs and closes his eyes for a moment. "How about we worry about that tomorrow?"

"Sounds like a plan to me." I smile back at him.

"I'll see you tomorrow, then, *kiska,*" he says as he departs.

28

NIK

THE FOLLOWING MORNING, the unexpected invitation catches me by surprise.

In hindsight, however, I should've expected it. After all, I know better than anyone that Kat makes a great first impression.

At first, I'm content to wait for her in the kitchen, where my maddening house guest seems to stop invariably first thing in the morning. I figure we can have breakfast together, and I can tell her all about the invite as we eat.

After an hour with no sign of her, I grow restless. I decide that I might as well get some work done while I wait for her to wake up. So I head to my office. Soon, I'm forced to admit it's a pointless waste of time. I'm useless this morning. After rereading the same paragraph four times—only to realize I'm still unable to recall a single word from it—I give up.

Frustrated, I rub a hand over my eyes. I'm dangerously unfocused, and it doesn't take any genius to guess why.

I can't stop thinking about her and the hours we spent

together yesterday. About that side of her I hadn't seen before.

I give up, getting up from my chair and exit my office.

Exasperated with my foolishness, I make my way to where she is, unable to resist her gravitational pull over me, while the sound of her breathless laugh in the plane yesterday echoes in my mind.

As quietly as possible, I slowly inch the bedroom door open, peeking through the gap like a hormone-crazed teenager.

I don't immediately spot Kat—just a giant, fluffy, white mass of blankets on the large bed. After entering the chamber, I silently approach the linen cloud. Finally, I see her. She's stretched out under the covers, her lush lips are slightly open as her glossy dark hair fans around her face, over the pillows, like a halo.

My beautiful, dark angel.

I take the chair next to the bed, where I sat a few nights ago when she had that nightmare.

I can't help but feel like a bit of a creep, watching her from a darkened corner of the room as she sleeps, blissfully unaware of my presence. But this embarrassing feeling isn't enough to keep me away. Kat is just too addictive, and her pull over me is too irresistible. As it is, I can barely stop myself from joining her under the soft sheets.

I lose track of time as I unhurriedly take inventory of every visible inch of her. The sunlight filtering through the large windows caresses her hair, granting it a coppery glow. I'm so mesmerized by the sight that I almost don't notice it when she starts to wake up.

Kat groans lightly, eyes still closed, languidly stretching her lush body. I grow uncomfortably hard, but somehow I find the herculean strength to stay on my damned chair.

After lazily blinking her big, blue eyes, Kat sighs, and I want to groan. I don't—but I must've made some type of noise because she turns to face me.

"Do you always watch over all your enslaved women as they sleep, or am I just that special?" she asks me in a raspy voice that has me grasping the chair's arms to keep myself in my place.

I feel appropriately chastised until her face breaks into a deliciously mischievous grin, her eyes glittering with amusement.

No one should be this beautiful.

"I was just making sure you were still alive. I was a little concerned, considering you've been asleep for the past twelve hours," I say, making a big show of checking my watch.

Kat rolls her eyes, still smiling.

"I'd never dream of inconveniencing my demanding overlord with my sudden demise. I wouldn't want you to go out of your way to find another minion to boss around." She brushes her hair over her shoulder.

"I appreciate that. Really. It's so hard to find good help these days."

"And don't you forget it. I expect a very large bonus once I deliver my end of the bargain," she says without missing a beat, her voice dropping an octave.

"I believe that could be arranged," I assure her in the same tone. Kat smiles at me again while holding my gaze. A private, sultry smile this time.

"So," she says, clearing her throat. "What brings you here this morning?"

"We've received an invitation. Patrick McGuire would be honored to welcome us to his newly renovated summer home for his birthday celebration. You must've made a lasting impression on the man." Even to my own ears, I sound bitterly jealous.

"A win is a win, right?"

I nod. "It could mean an overnight stay, so you should pack a bag."

"This is a great opportunity for us," she says, almost vibrating with excitement. "He'll be comfortable on his home turf, so we should be able to make some progress with him."

A homicidal rage threatens to overtake me as I think about Kat "*making progress*" with McGuire.

"I agree," I say instead. "I bet he wants to get a closer look at you and taunt me while he's at it. He hasn't invited me to his birthday bash in years, not since Maxim and Erin's indiscretion. It delights him to make a big production out of inviting the heads of all Seven Families but me. As if I give a shit about his fucking party."

Kat's face falls. It's such a stark change from her smiling expression that I lose my train of thought. "What's wrong?" I ask.

"Oh, it's nothing," she says, too fast. It's a blatant lie, if for no other reason than the horrified look in her eyes.

"Kat. What's the matter? What did I say?"

She sighs. "It's nothing, really."

"Yeah, I don't buy that for a second. It's obviously something. I can see it all over your face. Don't waste your breath denying it. Was it something I said?"

"No. It's a long story. It's... complicated, to put it mildly."

"I've got time," I say unwaveringly. Whatever upset her this much, I need to know all about it so I can fix it. I won't have anything keeping me from seeing her smile at me like that again—not if it can be helped.

"Nik, I—It's a really, really long story. One that isn't just mine to tell."

This woman and her endless secrets will be the death of me. Just when I think we're getting somewhere, the little thief reminds me of all I don't know about her.

"I see," I say, even though I don't. At all.

Kat's painfully beautiful eyes study my face. Whatever she sees there makes her sigh. She opens and closes her mouth several times, seemingly searching for the right thing to say. Eventually, eyes brimming with some powerful emotion I can't quite identify, she says, "Nik, I need you to understand that you and I met during a very convoluted period of my life. I need you to be patient and understanding. There are certain things I have to do to keep my friends —and myself—safe."

Her heartfelt statement gives me pause. "Kat, if you are in any type of danger, I need to know."

"It's not that simple—"

"It's nonnegotiable," I cut her off.

She sighs again. "Look, like I said, it's complicated. I can't tell you all about it right now."

My first instinct is to argue with her or browbeat her into telling me everything. But I quickly realize that would be an unwise approach. If Kat is in trouble, I need her to trust me enough to tell me what I must know to keep her safe. If I intimidate or annoy her too much, I would achieve the opposite effect.

"Well," I say hesitantly, unsure about how to urge her to tell me everything without aggravating her. "What are you comfortable telling me, then?"

Kat blinks. I want to groan in frustration—somehow, I must've messed up again—but she surprises me by shockingly sharing some information.

"I guess I could tell you it's related to the Flame of Mir. It's the reason I took it, I mean. I had to steal it to protect A.J. and myself. She became involved with someone dangerous. Someone who realized he could use his leverage over my best friend to get me to do his bidding."

I'm not sure what I thought she'd say. But it most definitely wasn't that. I end up staring at her for a moment, processing her words and the repercussions of what she just told me. My mind races a mile per minute—then it suddenly stops with a screeching halt once the terrified expression in her eyes registers with me.

"Kat—" I say, unsure of how exactly to put everything I'm feeling into words. How can I convey that I'll never let anyone hurt or scare her again? How can I assure her I'll crush the living shit out of the imbecile who hurt her?

Kat interrupts me before I get a chance to figure out how to voice all these new and alarming feelings. "A.J. and I are still dealing with him, you know. He could still hurt us. That's why I'm not exactly thrilled about this party. I have a feeling he might be invited, too."

So I probably know the bastard. "Tell me his name."

"I can't. I told you, he could still hurt us. I can't take the chance."

"Kat," I say through gritted teeth. "You're going to tell me everything about this man right now. And then I'm going to take care of him."

"Absolutely not."

"Why the hell not?" I yell, unable to control my anger, even though I know that's never the best approach with her.

"You're not listening. I've already told you why. It's too dangerous."

"Not if I handle him for you. You have nothing to worry about."

"Nik, I understand you're dying to recover your diamond. I really do. I'd be livid to lose it, too. Trust me, parting with that beauty was one of the hardest things I've ever done. But I'm not telling you anything else. I have promises to keep and people to protect. I've told you all I can—at least for now—and you're just going to have to respect my boundaries." She has the nerve to shrug.

"Respect your boundaries?" I hear myself roaring. "You've lost your mind if you think this brain-dead idea of yours is going to fly with me."

Kat rolls her eyes at me, utterly unconcerned about my outburst.

"Once you're able to think rationally, we can talk about it more. As long as you understand there are things I won't tell you—for my sake and A.J.'s. I'm sorry about your diamond. I really am. But it is what it is."

"Fuck the diamond," I say with a grunt to the absurd woman as I get up from the chair to pace in front of the windows, trying to divine what's the right thing to say to get her to see things my way. "Can't you see that I can keep you safe?"

Kat shrugs again, maddeningly. "Perhaps. But perhaps not. I just can't take the risk. I know you're used to getting your way, but you're just going to have to accept you can't make me change my mind, regardless of how much you yell or try to bully me."

Her calm, rational tone and choice of words break through the fiery red haze of my anger to find me. She's right. I am acting like a bully, blundering my way through this situation. Stupidly, I am demanding her blind trust when I know that's not how trust works.

Properly chastised, I make my way to the bed, sitting on the edge. "Kat, I—Fuck." I sigh. "I'm an idiot, Kat."

After a brief pause, I laugh humorlessly as I struggle to find the right words to tell her what's on my mind.

"Are you waiting for me to disagree? Because you'll be waiting for a long time," she says. I smile, feeling more than a little relieved. If she's joking around—even if at my expense—then I haven't completely fucked up everything.

As I sit so close to her, on a bed of all places, I can't help but stare at Kat—her face, her hair, her everything. Our gazes connect, and her posture softens a little. Unable to help myself, I lean closer.

"Kat, I shouldn't have tried to push you to tell me more than you're ready to share. I can't stand bullies. I don't want you to think of me as one. Believe me when I say that I know better than most that trust isn't something one can demand from someone. It has to be freely given and fully earned. That's a lesson I learned the hard way long ago."

"What do you mean?"

I hesitate in answering. It's such a painful story, and I couldn't bear it if she looked at me with pity in her deep blue eyes. At the same time, how can I ask her to trust me with her most precious secrets if I'm not willing to share a small piece of my own?

"It's a long story, like you said." I chuckle. "One not worth reliving."

"I doubt that," she softly replies. Kat looks at me expectantly. Unlike me, she doesn't push for more than I am able to give her at the moment. Maybe that's why I decide to share some of it with her.

"Trust isn't something that comes easily to me. Truth be told, I'm not sure I've ever fully trusted someone. Besides Maxim, that is. And even with him, I paid a steep price for that trust. He was my closest friend, my right-hand man. He was supposed to be a bridge between me and McGuire, helping me expand the *bratva*. You know how that turned out." I laugh under my breath humorlessly. "Maxim betrayed me, even though we were the closest thing each other ever had to a family."

"How's that?"

Once again, it goes against my every instinct to answer her question. But if I want to protect her from her mysterious threat, then I need her to trust me enough to tell me all about it. She'll never do that if I'm not willing to do the same.

"We found each other when we were so young. We practically grew up together." I sigh. "His parents and mine weren't in the picture at all. Mine kicked me out before I was old enough to shave, and Maxim was even younger when he was abandoned. We kept each other alive for years. He was my brother. Not by blood, but something else altogether—something much more powerful."

"Oh, Nik." Kat says, her eyes warm and full of compassion. She throws her arms around my neck before pressing her face against it.

"I don't want your pity," I say roughly, even as the feel of her body against mine warms me to the core of my being.

Kat shakes her head. "No, no. I don't pity you at all. I could never pity you. No one should pity you. You survived horrors most people will never truly comprehend. You faced every adversity, rising to heights most only dream about. Pity is the last thing anyone should feel about you."

I groan against her hair. "Kat..."

This woman...

If I don't watch myself around her, she's going to be the end of me.

"Listen to me now," I say before she completely ruins me for good, "I've said all this to say that I know I'm not entitled to your trust and your secrets, even if it sometimes doesn't seem like it. If I ever earn your trust and you decide to share them with me, I'll help you with your problem, and I will make your bully pay for all the worry he's caused you. You *are* under my protection, so use it."

Kat nods against my neck, squeezing me tighter. "I'll keep that in mind," she says after a moment of silence.

"Promise me," I insist.

"I promise. And I'll go to McGuire's party with you."

"You don't have to if you don't want to go. We'll find another way to get closer to him."

Kat shakes her head, pushing me away to look into my eyes. "No, I have to go. I'm tired of letting that horrid man dictate my life. And I'll do what it takes to help you take down the person who took your brother from you." Her bottom lip quivers with emotion.

Like a broken record, I groan again. "Kat—" She'll unman me if I let her.

She shrugs. "Besides, I know you'll keep me safe."

"With my life," I promise her solemnly, meaning it with every cell in my body.

29

KAT

THE FEEL of Nik's hands on my skin is exactly what I need tonight.

His callused palm rubs against mine as he helps me out of the black Bentley that brought us to McGuire's party. The sensation is exhilarating, and as our eyes connect and his hand caresses mine, I feel electrified.

It's a very welcome distraction. For a moment, I almost completely forget about the possibility of running into the *stronzo* during the festivities.

Almost.

As the boss of the Italian mafia and the patriarch of the Salvatore family, Giuseppe Salvatore—the villain I unaffectionately think of as the *stronzo*—could very well be in attendance tonight. I shiver in horror just thinking of facing him while Nik is around.

"Are you cold? You should've worn something that covered more of your skin, *milaya*," my handsome Russian rasps against my ear as he shrugs out of his black suit jacket.

Nik has a point. My backless pink silk dress is gorgeous

but not the most practical attire for this breezy coastal environment.

"I'm fine. Beauty is pain," I say with a smile, stopping him from removing his coat. After all, I need to keep my wits about me tonight, and seeing him undress—even slightly—would make that impossible.

"You must be in constant agony then," he whispers, playfully nipping my earlobe.

I laugh as my nerves subside a little. "You silver-tongued devil. Do you shamelessly flirt with all the women in your employ, or am I just that lucky?"

"Oh, you're lucky. You have no idea how lucky you are. Let me show you." He draws me into his arms, pulling my hips tightly against his. I can't help gasping. Shimmying against him, I try to come up with the most risqué comeback I can get away with right here and now, but our host approaches us then, interrupting our back-and-forth.

"Nikolai! Kat!" Patrick McGuire excitedly greets us, briskly walking down the front steps of his house to meet us. "It's good to see you again. I'm so glad you could join us."

"McGuire," Nik impassively acknowledges the man, shaking his hand.

The Irish mafia boss disengages from Nik after a moment, extravagantly kissing the back of my hand. Next to me, Nik tenses up.

"Kat," McGuire practically purrs with a smile. "Welcome to my home."

"Thank you, Patrick," I respond, biting my bottom lip for his benefit. "What a gorgeous place you have here."

"I'm glad it pleases you. I'd love to give you the tour later. But first, Nikolai, I must show you my new yacht. You haven't seen it yet, have you?"

"I don't believe I've had the pleasure," Nik says, and I almost miss the hint of sarcasm in his tone.

"Well, come with me. Kat, would you care to join us?"

"With these shoes?" I scoff, pointing to my four-inch high stilettos. "You two go on without me. I'll find something to drink instead."

"Are you sure, dear?" McGuire asks me, a slight frown of polite concern creasing his features.

"I'm positive. As a matter of fact, I insist." I wave them off and start to make my way towards the house.

"Very well. We'll catch up with you later," McGuire says over his shoulder, walking away from me.

Nik bends down to whisper into my ear again. "I'll be right back. Vladmir is inside. If anything happens, I'm only one call away." His tone brims with urgency and intensity.

"I don't have your number."

He presses a farewell kiss to my forehead. "Yes, you do. Check your phone. I saved it in it before handing it back to you."

Bemused, I shake my head, as I watch him walk away, quickly catching up to his nemesis with his long strides. I waste no time pulling out my cell phone from my bag. I search through my contacts list, but my confusion grows once I don't find any new entries under the letter "N" or "S." I swipe up on the screen, curiously glancing at the various names. An unfamiliar entry catches my eye—*your boss,* it says. I laugh as I roll my eyes before entering the large house and searching for the bar area.

It wasn't a lie that I didn't want to try to balance my way onto a boat while wearing my nude heels. But the real reason I avoided following the two men has nothing to do with my shoes. If I am to have the displeasure of running into the *stronzo*, then I'd like to face him by myself, as far away as possible from Nik's watchful eyes.

However, as I walk through the finely decorated house—politely nodding and smiling at the numerous guests who make eye contact with me—I don't spot him or any of the men from his inner circle.

Not allowing myself to feel completely relaxed and relieved just yet, I finally locate the bar area.

"A martini, please," I ask the redheaded girl working behind the bar. "Extra dirty."

The bartender nods at me, and I sit on a bar stool, waiting for my drink. As discreetly as possible, I scan my surroundings for any sign of the Italians. That's when Vladmir takes a sit next to me.

"There you are," he grunts, like he usually does, as I have come to learn during my employment with Nik.

"Here I am," I say. "Didn't know you were looking for me."

"Nikolai told me to keep an eye on you until he returns."

"Oh. I see. Sorry about that." I don't want to inconvenience him.

"What are you sorry for?" he grunts again. This time, seemingly in confusion.

I shrug. "Well, I've learned Nik can be a little over-the-top sometimes. Very overprotective. I'm sorry you were handed babysitting duty because of me."

Vladmir glares at me, seeming even more confused. Maybe even a little repulsed by me. "He's the boss. It's not up to me—or you—to criticize his orders. The orders are the orders."

It's my turn to stare at him. This might be the longest sentence I've ever seen him utter. Still, it's obvious the man doesn't like me. That's fine by me. The feeling is mutual.

"Right. Sorry about that, I guess," I say at last, smiling at the bartender in thanks as she hands me my drink. Vladmir has his own glass of clear liquor. Vodka, I'm sure.

I wait for Nik's henchman to say something, but he doesn't. It's clear he's not interested in making conversation with me.

"So," I say, sipping my beverage, "I assume you've been working for Nik for a long time."

"Yes," he says. I expect him to elaborate on his answer, but he doesn't, of course.

"That's nice. You must know him pretty well."

This time, he doesn't even acknowledge me with a verbal response, simply raising an eyebrow and staring blankly ahead.

I sigh.

"I'll take that as a yes. Did you know Maxim well, too?"

This question gets a reaction out of him. "I'm not here to make small talk with you," he chides me.

"Aw, come on, Vlad. It's just an innocent question. I'm just trying to kill time with you while we wait for the boss-man to return from his little field trip. No need to get upset about it."

"Nikolai ordered me to keep you safe—not indulge your idle gossip."

"Gossip? Who said anything about gossip? Like I mentioned, it's just an innocent question. You can't blame me for being curious about Maxim. He's the reason I'm in this situation, after all."

"No, you're in this situation because you're a shameless thief." He takes a healthy swig of his drink.

"Boy, you don't like me much, do you?"

"My opinion of you is irrelevant. Like I said, I'm here to

keep you out of trouble, not to like you or chitchat with you."

"It's okay, Vlad. You can say it. You won't hurt my feelings. I'm not crazy about you either." I wink at him.

"Do not call me Vlad."

"No problem." I sigh again.

We sit in silence for a while. The man is stonewalling me, but I'm not ready to give up yet. After all, I'm still not entirely convinced that Nik should be solely focusing on McGuire as the only suspect in Maxim's murder. I need all the information I can get. Vladmir was there that night and has likely been a part of their circle for a long time. He has to know something of value.

Besides, I'm interested in hearing someone else's opinion of Maxim. Nik is definitely not the most unbiased source regarding the deceased man.

After a long moment of uncomfortable silence, I realize Vladmir is far too stoic and straightforward to fall for my usual bullshit. With his type, a direct approach is usually much more fruitful.

"Okay, very well. I'll cut the crap," I say. "You see, whether you care to admit it or not, you and I have much in common."

Vladmir looks at me as if I'm completely out of my mind. I don't let it annoy me too much.

"No, it's true. Really. For starters, we share the same demanding boss," I add. "You know why I'm here. Nik believes I can help him catch McGuire. He's completely certain McGuire is behind Maxim's murder. Surely you have some thoughts on that."

Vladmir shrugs noncommittally. He sips his drink. "It's not my place to question Nikolai's decisions."

Like a dog with a bone, I'm not so easily dissuaded.

"Right. You're just here to follow orders. I get it. But there's no way you don't have an opinion of your own on this whole thing. Do you think McGuire did it?"

Grinding his teeth, he says, "Even you have to realize this is not the time or the place for this conversation."

"Oh, come on. Don't give me that. No one can hear us over this commotion." I scoff, gesturing to the rowdy guests nearby.

Vladmir must realize I won't leave him alone until he gives me an answer. He surely knows he can't escape me without disobeying his direct orders.

"It's good enough for me that Nikolai thinks McGuire did it," he mutters, looking back over his shoulders.

"Well, you're very loyal to him, I'll give you that."

As I sip on my martini, I realize this is likely all he will give me on the subject. But just because he won't openly say anything that shows he disagrees with Nik's judgment, it doesn't mean he won't share other things.

"What about Maxim?" I ask, no pretense of subtlety.

Annoyance oozes out of him. "What about him?"

"You knew him well, right? I obviously didn't. I just want to hear someone else's opinion of the man. Understandably, Nik speaks of Maxim as if he were a martyred saint. I'm sure he had many qualities, but I'd be interested in hearing a more nuanced perspective on who he really was."

Once again, Vladmir remains silent for a long while. This man takes brooding to a whole new level. Eventually, though, he quietly says, "I want to make something clear. I won't speak ill of the dead."

Interesting. "Of course not," I say.

"I'll tell you this much. Maxim was many things. A saint wasn't one of them."

"Are you referring to the incident with McGuire's daughter?" I ask, glancing over my shoulders this time to ensure no one's heard me.

"Watch your mouth," he says. "Just let the son of a bitch rest in peace, will you? And leave me the fuck alone while you're at it."

"Son of a bitch, huh? I'm guessing there wasn't any love lost between the two of you. What's the story? I'm sure it's a good one."

"Just mind your fucking business and leave me the fuck alone."

"What's the matter, Vlad? I'm not getting too close to some touchy subject, am I? Boy, I'd hate to be you. I can't imagine what it must be like to be so loyal to a man willing to put your life on the line to avenge someone you hated."

I'm not too scared to provoke him a little. My hope is that his reaction will be telling enough, revealing whether I'm close to the truth or not. And maybe even some juicy details of what's behind the bad blood between him and Maxim.

I don't foresee the extent of his anger, though. In fact, when he forcefully grabs me by the shoulders, lifting me off the stool until my feet are dangling in the air, I'm shocked. I didn't expect the stoic Vladmir to snap like this.

"What the hell is wrong with you?" he asks an inch away from my face, shaking me hard until my teeth clatter. His fingertips press deeply on the flesh of my arms, and I know I'll have bruises tomorrow. "Why are you so fucking nosy? You sure ask a fuck ton of questions. Especially for a thief."

"Put me down," I say.

"Do you want to know how I felt about Maxim? I'll tell you all about the bastard. He was nothing but a lucky asshole. All his life, he was always in the right place at the right time. That's how he got everything he ever had. He didn't deserve to be the *pakhan*'s second-in-command. He didn't earn that—or anything else in his miserable life. And whatever wasn't easily handed to him on a silver platter, he took it anyway. Like he did with Erin McGuire. Maxim cuckolded Lorenzo and didn't think anything of it. As if he was fucking entitled to my friend's fiancée. That's the kind of man Maxim was. And if you don't watch your fucking mouth, I won't be surprised if you get a chance to get to know him yourself very soon." Vladmir's green eyes burn with pure, unconcealed hatred.

Nik's angry voice reverberates from somewhere behind me. "What the fuck do you think you're doing? If you don't get your hands off of her immediately, I'll kill you."

30

KAT

Vladmir sets me down so quickly that I lose my balance and stumble backward.

A black-clad arm wraps around my waist, steadying me and pulling me against a muscular chest. A chest that is practically vibrating with uncontrolled anger.

I glance up and find Nik's face. I see it for the first time—this isn't the passionate lover who held me in his arms, whispering sweet nothings in Russian to me. *This* is Nikolai Stefanovich, the Russian *bratva*'s *pakhan*. The coldhearted man whose name and fearsome reputation are enough to make even his mafia counterparts tremble with fear and respect.

I've never seen this crazed wildfire in his eyes before.

In front of me, the fierce Vladmir turns almost as white as the napkins on the bar.

"*Prosti duraka, pakhan. Ya ne khotel tebya obidet. Ya bol'she tak ne budu,*" he says to Nik, his voice shaking.

Behind me, Nik shakes his head slowly. "You knew better than to lay hands on her," he says, almost in a menacing growl. "I ought to kill you just for touching what's mine.

You're well aware of the punishment for putting your hands on your *pakhan*'s woman."

"I understand, *pakhan*. Again, if I may, forgive me for being such an idiot. I didn't want to offend you. I won't do it again. But I understand if you can't let it go." Vladmir's eyes remain downcast.

"Get the fuck out of my sight. You've already caused a scene," Nik says through gritted teeth. I look around and notice half a dozen of McGuire's guests staring at us, whispering. "I'll summon you later once I've decided your fate."

With a slight nod, Vladmir quickly and quietly exits the room.

Nik flips me around in his arms until I'm facing him. The savage fire I saw in his gaze still burns. His eyes roam over my face, searchingly, clearly trying to gauge my emotions. "Forgive me, Kat," he says, kissing the top of my head.

"For what?" I ask in confusion.

Nik looks at me as if my question is ridiculous. "For Vladmir's actions, of course." He wraps his arms around me, gently holding me against his chest and nuzzling my hair. "He should never have even thought of touching you. I'm so sorry. Are you okay? Did he hurt you at all?"

I scoff. "Nik, I appreciate your concern, but I'm completely fine."

Unconvinced, he pulls away a little to look at me, not even bothering to hide his attempt at assessing me for any undisclosed damage.

"I'm serious," I say. "Don't worry. You got here just in time, Prince Charming. Not that I needed your help, mind you. I had everything under control."

It's his turn to scoff. After pulling me back against his

chest, he bends to speak against my ear. "Prince Charming, huh?"

"More like Prince Terrifying." I teasingly shove against his chest, burying my face against it. "I didn't know that side of you, *miliy*."

Nik wastes no time gently pushing me so he can look at my face. There's a delighted glint in his eyes when he asks, "What did you just say?"

With a laugh, I ask, "Did I say it right?"

"Did you mean to say *miliy*?" His pronunciation is utterly different from my butchered attempt.

"Yes, *miliy*," I repeat, sounding better than my first attempt but not nearly as clear as he did.

"Where did you learn that?" Pure, undisguised joy glitters in Nik's beautiful brown eyes. He bites his bottom lip mid-smile, and it's all I can do to stop myself from pulling that tempting mouth down to mine.

"Well, you wouldn't tell me what *milaya* meant, even though you kept calling me that repeatedly. So I looked it up, of course, and learned the male equivalent." I shrug, winking at him.

"Do you know what it means?"

I roll my eyes. "Yes, *honey*. Of course I do, *my darling*."

Nik chuckles again. "You're just the gift that keeps on giving, did you know that?" he asks, tilting my chin up until his mouth is less than an inch away from my lips. His breath mingles with mine as he leans his forehead against mine.

"You're one to talk," I say, and he smiles.

Our eyes connect again as we gaze at each other for a timeless moment. My heart races, and it's no longer a product of the lasting effects of the surge of adrenaline from my altercation with Vladmir.

Will Nik kiss me? Maybe I'll kiss him.

Unfortunately, Vladmir is still on my mind. With a sigh, I feel obligated to ask, even though I know it will break the moment's spell. "What are you going to do with Vladmir, Nik?"

"Don't worry about it, *milaya*," he rasps against my cheek. The goosebumps almost distract me.

"Nik..."

He sighs. The man knows me well enough by now to realize I won't drop the subject until he answers me. He leans back so we can see each other better. "I'm well within my rights to kill him, Kat. He knows that. It certainly doesn't please me that he dared to touch you and almost hurt you."

I gasp, horrified. "Oh, my gosh, Nik. You can't do that. Don't get me wrong. I don't like the man at all, but that doesn't mean I want his death hanging over my head for the rest of my life."

"I shouldn't have said anything," he says, almost to himself. "Just forget about it, Kat. I don't want you to spend another second of your time worrying about him."

I pull at his jacket. "But, Nik—"

He squeezes my hand. "I'll take your wishes and concerns under consideration. I won't do anything that'll cause you grief."

"I think I'd feel better if you promised me you won't do anything drastic. No maiming or murdering. Come on, you can give me that."

With a soft laugh, Nik pulls me by the neck until we are face-to-face once again. His sudden nearness overwhelms my senses, but he rubs his nose against mine, amusement still curving his lips and glimmering in his eyes.

The duality of man—a ruthless mobster who gives me nose-to-nose kisses...

Unable to hold myself back any longer, I rise on my toes

until my lips rub against his. Nik sighs softly, but neither of us deepens the kiss just yet. I slowly turn my head sideways, amazed by the incredible softness of his lips. I part mine slightly and run them along his bottom lip. His eyes shutter closed, and the tip of my tongue caresses the center of his lip. Nik's quiet gasp is followed by his hand tenderly grasping the strands of my hair, clutching me closer.

Just then, something vibrates between our chests.

It's enough to dispel the magic between us, and I move away from him, straightening. With a curse, Nik lets me go and reaches inside his jacket, pulling out his vibrating cell phone.

His eyes never leave me as he answers the call. "This better be fucking life or death, Dmitri."

I smile, taking my turn to be amused. Nik raises an eyebrow.

"I'm sorry, Kat. I have to take this. I'll be right back. Stay right here," he says, squeezing my hand once before exiting the room, animatedly speaking to Dmitri in Russian.

With a sigh, I sit back down on the stool I occupied before Vladmir lost his cool with me. Bored, I glance around the room, daydreaming about Nik's kisses.

My eyes fall on McGuire.

The man is standing by the doorway with an interested look. His intrigued expression leaves no doubt—he witnessed the entire scene between me, Nik, and Vladmir. With a smirk, the mobster raises his glass, winking at me.

Unable to shake an ominous feeling of unease, I return the gesture, a smile that doesn't reach my eyes plastered on my face.

TO BE CONTINUED...

Nik and Kat's story concludes in Book 2 of the Diamond Duet, Diamond Dream. Scan the QR code below to keep reading:

MAILING LIST

Sign up to my newsletter for exclusive bonus content and updates on upcoming releases! **New subscribers get an exclusive epilogue.**

Scan the QR code to subscribe:

THANK YOU!

Thank you so much for reading *Diamond Don*!

I would be incredibly grateful if you would take a minute to share your thoughts about Nik and Kat's story by leaving a quick review on Amazon, Goodreads, BookBub, or wherever else you prefer. Your review could help other readers discover this book.

Thank you!

COMING UP NEXT...

Emerald Duet

Sapphire Duet

Ruby Duet

ABOUT THE AUTHOR

Anna Cole writes thrilling, steamy romance stories about fierce, unapologetic heroines and the larger-than-life, possessive antiheroes who are crazy about them. She spends her time on the East Coast, plotting out all the delicious pain and suffering she will put her characters through on their quest for true love and a happily ever after.

When she's not writing, Anna enjoys sunsets, long walks on the beach, and spending time with her favorite book boyfriends—and her husband and dog, too.